# DIRTY LITTLE MIDLIFE CRISIS

HEART'S COVE HOTTIES
BOOK 1

LILIAN MONROE

2nd Edition Published 2023



Cover design: Laura at Spellbinding Designs
Editing: Shavonne Clarke
Proofreading: Jane Beyer

Published by Method and Madness Publishing PTY LTD
PO Box 168 Subiaco, WA, Australia 6008

Print ISBN: 978-1-922986-41-2

WANT THREE BOOKS DELIVERED STRAIGHT TO YOUR INBOX?

HOW ABOUT THREE ROCK STAR ROMANCES THAT WERE *WAY* TOO HOT TO SELL?

GET THE COMPLETE *ROCK HARD* SERIES:
(WWW.LILIANMONROE.COM/ROCKHARD)

# ONE
# FIONA

A TIRED GROAN shudders out of my best friend's rusty old Toyota. That...doesn't sound good.

On the bright side, Simone's hooptie has successfully gotten us three hundred miles north of Los Angeles and into our destination vacation town. Unfortunately, it doesn't look like it's going to make it much farther.

I grip the worn plastic door handle as if it'll help keep the car together. If Simone's worried about her car breaking down, she doesn't show it. With wild red hair tied back in a messy bun on top of her head and thick, black-rimmed glasses framing her pale blue eyes, Simone looks far younger than her forty-four years—a fact that has often needled at my own insecurities. Time hasn't been so kind to me.

Another screechy noise escapes the hood of the car as we turn onto the main drag of Heart's Cove, and I start hunting the signs on the street for a mechanic. Even if Simone isn't worried about this hunk of junk, I need a way to get out of here at the end of our two-week stay.

We make it about fifty more feet before the engine sputters, the car rattles, and the whole things dies right there on the street. Simone expertly navigates the coasting car to the curb as smoke curls out of the hood in thick black puffs. Parked in a semi-appropriate spot and acting like nothing at all is the matter, she pulls the handbrake and tucks a strand of flame-red hair behind her ear.

I throw my best friend a glance. "We should have taken my car."

"We couldn't take your car. It reminds you of Voldemort."

"Voldemort?"

"He Who Shall Not Be Named. That shiny white Mercedes is the only thing that asshole left you in the divorce and looking at it reminds you of his cheating ass. I see it in your eyes every time you turn the key in the ignition. There was *no way* we were taking your car. Big Bertha did just fine." She taps the dashboard fondly, as if there isn't a plume of dark smoke coming from Bertha's hood. My best friend gives me a meaningful stare. "This vacation is about us, about pampering, about being the women we were always meant to be. Besides, we made it, didn't we?"

"Barely," I grumble, fighting the grin trying to curl my lips.

"I'll find a mechanic this afternoon. We won't need the car for the next two weeks, anyway—everything in Heart's Cove is within walking distance from the Heart's Cove Hotel. It's in the brochure."

Through the windshield, past the smoke, I spy a faded

green-and-white awning above the hotel door. A screen door hangs slightly crooked and lace curtains frame the interior of every window. Paint is peeling on the old siding, but neatly trimmed grass lines the front of the hotel and baskets bursting with colorful flowers hang from every post. A low hedge lines the sidewalk leading to a small parking lot, the other side of which is a well-maintained path to the front door.

This accommodation is quaint, though a bit worse for wear. It isn't exactly what I'd put as my first pick.

Or maybe it's not what John, my ex-husband, would have liked. Do I *actually* mind this place? It's kind of cute, in a lost-kitten-with-patchy-fur-and-three-legs kind of way. If Simone's to be believed, it's got great reviews and a killer continental breakfast.

John would've taken one look at this place and complained nonstop until we found someplace else, maybe even canned the whole vacation—but he's not here. He's in his swanky office in L.A. with whatever hot, young assistant he's decided to stick his junk into. Or maybe a paralegal. Or a junior partner. Or an intern. Or all of the above.

*Deep breaths.*

Simone must see my pursed lips, because she punches me in the arm. "Quit sucking lemons, Fi. Come on. We have art to create."

"How many times do I have to tell you I'm not an artist? Why did you have to choose an art retreat for our big self-actualization getaway? I'm a precision gal. Organizing. Planning. Why can't we have a vacation job hunting or something? At least it would be useful."

Simone lets out a snort and exits the car, casting a quick glance at the smoke still escaping her hood. She kicks a tire for good measure, then slings her purse over her shoulder and waves me forward. "Come on! The sign on the door says to check in inside."

Pushing thoughts of my ex aside, I follow Simone out of the car. The air tastes fresh here, if you can ignore the smell of Bertha's dying engine. Full of floral scents and a hint of salt from the sea, the smell unwinds a knot of tension between my shoulders. Simone's right. I need a vacation—and why not do something that I never would have done before? Why not try something new?

It's not like there's anything for me back in Los Angeles. Now that the fancy penthouse was transferred to John's name last week and my half of its worth has finally hit my bank account, I'm officially homeless. The divorce is settled, so I'm officially single, too. My dream of moving to the hills and getting my picket fence and perfect little family are gone with the penthouse, but I'm trying not to think about it too hard. Starting over at forty-five isn't something I'd planned on.

Simone decided I needed some time to figure myself out, so I'm here. About to do two weeks of art, yoga, and meditation classes in the hope of *finding myself*, even though I'm terrified of what I might discover. I find myself in the mirror every morning, and I'm not sure I like what I see. I'm on the other side of forty-five, with new wrinkles appearing every day. Things are sagging where they never used to, and soft where they were once taut.

Compared to John's younger, prettier, more docile playthings, I feel positively dumpy. I'm not sure a week of painting and *ohm*-ing will help any of that.

Simone's already halfway to the door by the time I take a step. She turns around and plants her fists on her hips, arching her brows at me. "Um, earth to Fiona! Get a wriggle on, girl. Our first class starts in half an hour."

I pause, tilting my head. "I thought you said tomorrow was day one."

"I lied. Deal with it." She pushes a stray piece of red hair off her forehead, looking zero percent remorseful. Her eyes sweep down the street then back to me, shoulders dropping slightly. Speaking more gently, she says, "I knew you'd never get in the car if you knew you had to try drawing something today. Your comfort zone is doing its best to keep you hostage, so you know, desperate times and all that."

"Who are you calling desperate?" I pop a brow.

Simone grins, but before she can open her mouth to answer, a rumble sounds from the asphalt separating us. My best friend's eyes widen as she looks at the ground where a crack is splitting the pavement apart. I take a step back, a hand on my chest.

Then the parking lot of the Heart's Cove Hotel explodes.

No, really. It explodes.

Asphalt everywhere. A geyser of water shooting fifty feet into the air, cascading down on top of us. I scream, putting my purse over my head while I crouch down. Rocks and bits of asphalt rain down around me, biting my skin as they land. I put a hand on the back of my neck, pull it back, and see blood.

What the...?

Water's still raining down on me as shouts erupt. Doors open, and a siren sounds in the distance. I'm still crouched on the sidewalk, staring at the blood on my fingers.

What in the name of self-actualization is wrong with this town? Where the heck did Simone bring me? Maybe I should hightail it out of here, but how would I even do that? Our car is out of commission.

I'm stuck, stuck, stuck. Just like I was stuck in my marriage. Stuck in a penthouse I didn't like. Stuck in a city I never wanted to be in. Stuck around sycophants and snobby housewives preening and gossiping while I felt like I was dying a slow and painful death as life passed me by.

Water seeps into my dress, soaking my back. I curl myself into a ball, worried another stray chunk of asphalt is coming for my skull. My thoughts rush around me, and my comfort zone constricts inside my head.

I should have stayed at home. What if John needs me for something? I should be apartment hunting and trying to find a job. A vacation is the last thing I need. Why would I even deserve a vacation? I need to get my butt in gear and start figuring out how to start my life over.

Emotion chokes my throat, and I feel silly. I'm not the kind of person who falls apart. I'm the rock. I'm the one who keeps the family together.

*That didn't go so well, did it?*

Tears threaten to spill onto my cheeks and I fight my rioting emotions to hold myself together. It's just a burst water main. I have a shallow cut on the back of my neck, but I'm fine. Just wet and weirdly emotional.

Then, a shadow. The water stops, and I hear the pitter-patter of a geyser hitting an open umbrella. The lack of water raining down on me allows me to take a full breath. I lift my head to see the owner of the umbrella currently helping me maintain a shaky hold on my own sanity.

Holy *ohm.*

Heart's Cove might not be so bad, judging by this vision in a wet t-shirt.

Tall, dark, and handsome doesn't even cover it. This guy looks like he belongs in every forty-something woman's wet dream, not in a sleepy town called Heart's Cove. He's broad, and by the way his wet shirt clings to his chest, I can tell he's packing serious muscle. My eyes sweep over the curves of his pecs and shoulders, down his arms and over his trim waist. Snapping my eyes back up before they reach dangerous territory, I see a hint of a smile on his full lips.

"Um, hi," I stammer, standing up as I brush my hands down my navy wrap dress. The back of it is soaked. My dress clings to me as much as his shirt hugs him, and I catch my mystery man's eyes heating as they take me in. A strange kind of warmth knots in the pit of my stomach as I tuck a strand of black-brown hair behind my ear. I gulp, still staring at my savior.

He has dark hair and rich, tan skin with two patches of grey hair above his temples. The rest of his hair is piled to one side in short, loose curls, one of which slides down across his forehead.

I watch in fascination as he lifts a broad hand to sweep the stray piece of hair back, his grey-blue eyes still studying me. Is he even real? I'm not sure people this good-looking exist in real life. Maybe I finally snapped after the last horrendous fifteen months. The geyser was the last straw. Something in Bertha's engine fumes has turned my brain to mush. I've finally lost my marbles.

"I'm Grant." His rich, deep voice sends a tremor shivering down my spine. It sounds real enough.

I barely manage to croak out a response. "Fiona."

His lips curl into a smile, as if the sound of my name pleases him. A curl of heat beads in the pit of my stomach and I place a hand over the offending spot. I feel... I'm not...

I haven't felt this in a *long* time.

Grant lifts a hand toward me, and I suck a breath through my teeth as he reaches around the back of my neck. As I close my eyes, I imagine him pulling me close, crushing me against that glorious chest of his, and taking my lips in his.

A man like him would take control. I can sense it in the electricity zinging between us. He'd pin me to a wall and show me what I've been missing for the past twenty years. He'd light up every nerve ending in my body and be as rough, as commanding, as demanding as he'd need to be.

And I would melt like freaking butter on his tongue. God, his tongue—I wish I could melt on it. Preferably when his hands grip me tight and I feel the raw power coiling in his huge body. *Wet and weirdly emotional*, huh. Yup, still accurate.

But Grant's touch is feather-light when the pads of his fingers brush across the back of my neck. They're calloused, rough. Not at all like John's doughy, soft hands were when he palmed my skin back in the days when we actually touched each other.

Grant's skin may be rough, but his touch is soft. A silent

gasp escapes my lips before I can stop myself, heat flooding between my legs, spreading through my core, and all the way up to the tips of my ears.

This is... Oh, no. Is this menopause? Did I just have my first hot flash under a geyser in the middle of a parking lot?

But when I open my eyes, Grant's expression is soft. "You're bleeding," he says, almost to himself. Before I can stop him, he hands me the umbrella, then grabs the edge of his shirt and rips off a strip.

The man *rips his freaking shirt apart* and uses it to dab at my admittedly very minor wound.

I might faint.

This is a fever dream. This isn't real life. It can't be.

I stare at the strip of skin now exposed by the rip, just above the waistband of Grant's pants. His stomach is hard, and the unholy desire to run my tongue over that bit of flesh bubbles through me without warning.

"Fiona!" Simone's voice cuts through the lust fogging my mind. My best friend runs over, shielding her face with her hands as she laughs. "Can you believe it? I think it's a sign."

"Of what? Poor municipal plumbing?"

Grant lets out a chuckle at my words, and the desire to make him laugh again overwhelms me. I steal a glance at him as Simone walks up to me, her eyes widening as she takes in the specimen standing next to me.

"Well, hello there, handsome. I'm Simone." She wiggles her eyebrows at me, then drops into a curtsy in front of Grant.

A freaking curtsy, as if the man is the King of England.

My best friend is a maniac.

"Grant," he replies with a smile, not at all bothered by the fact that Simone is insane. "I'd better go check on the twins. They've been having trouble with the hotel maintenance lately, and I'm sure they could use a hand." I make to give him the umbrella, but he shakes his head. "Keep it. I don't mind getting wet." A flash crosses his eyes as his gaze drops to my lips then away, so quickly I wonder if I imagined it.

Call me the Wicked Witch of the West, because I'm about to melt right where I stand.

Simone squeals as she hooks her arm through mine, and we watch Grant stride around the geyser, his white shirt soaking through and clinging to every muscle in his back. "He is *delicious*. It's definitely a sign."

"A sign of what?"

"That this vacation is *exactly* what you needed."

"He's just a friendly local."

"I *hope* he's friendly," Simone answers, the word sounding *very* different when she says it.

I shake my head, laughing, and nod to the hotel. "Should we go find out what's going on?"

"Yeah, but first let me grab some tissues. I don't want to drool all over the hotel floor if I'm going to be in the same room as that *friendly local*."

Rolling my eyes, I fight the smile off my face and jerk my head toward the green-and-white awning, setting off in the same direction as Grant went as if there's a tether pulling me toward him.

Maybe Simone's right. Maybe this vacation was a good idea, after all.

# TWO
# FIONA

CARNAGE GREETS us on the other side of the lobby door. In one glance, I see why Grant wasn't bothered by Simone's wackadoodle greeting. Or the geyser, for that matter.

To our left, a tiny, round old lady winds up and hurls her shoe across the room. "You two-bit hussy!" Her nostrils flare as she stomps a bare foot down. Anger rolls off her in black waves, and I instinctively take a step back. Her cropped white hair is curled and set in place like a helmet, wrinkled skin flushing red.

But it's the eyes that get me. Beady, black, and so full of hatred they make my gut clench uncomfortably.

On the other side of a room, a woman dodges the thrown shoe and takes a step forward. "I'm going to have to sage the entire block now that you've sullied our hotel with your presence, Agnes. She-devil."

"Take your sage and shove it up your—"

"Ladies," Grant says, extending his arms between the two women.

Agnes, still vibrating with rage beside us, crouches down and sets herself up to run at the other woman. How fast a woman her age can run, I'm not sure—but I wouldn't want to end up on the wrong side of her attack.

The target of Agnes's rage is a woman in her seventies wearing a leopard-print muumuu. She has chunky turquoise jewelry adorning her neck and earlobes, and long silver hair that frizzes around her head like a halo. Spreading her arms as if to cast a spell, she points a finger at the tiny ball of rage beside me. "Get. *Out!* This is your fault." She waves a finger outside at the unofficial fountain in the parking lot. "I don't know how, but I sure as heck know why. Because you're a damn *cow*, that's why! You've got the brain of a fruit bat!"

"Dorothy, if you could just take a step back, please." Grant lowers his eyes to stare into Dorothy's. I swoon a little at the warmth in his voice. Not only was he a gentleman with the umbrella outside, but he's obviously the peacekeeper of this little standoff.

I lean toward Simone. "Was *this* in the brochure?"

"Shh," she says. "It's better than the movies."

Behind Dorothy, on the other side of the reception desk, another woman about the same age stands in a pale pink pantsuit, her fingers curled around a string of pearls. Her features are similar to Dorothy's. Are they the twins Grant was referring to outside? The lady behind the desk is the put-together, classy version of Dorothy's boho-chic style. "Come on, Agnes. We don't stomp around your bookstore like a—"

"Like a *what?*" Agnes spits, whirling on the woman behind the desk. She doesn't wait for an answer, choosing to hurtle across the room and crash into Grant's broad frame. He catches her in one swift movement, lifting her high up until her feet dangle off the floor. A hellcat in motion, she screams and scratches, trying to get to Dorothy behind him. Her arms flail, legs kick, and inhuman sounds escape her throat.

My eyes snag on Grant's biceps. They're as big as Agnes's head, and he's obviously not struggling to keep her up. Struggling to avoid her sharp nails and well-placed kicks, sure. But not having any issues holding her three feet above the ground.

I take a step forward to help, but Simone puts a hand on my arm. "Not our fight, Fi."

"But—"

She jerks her head to the scene before us. Agnes lets out another scream, fisting her hand into Grant's dark-brown hair and tugging so hard he yelps.

I'm...a little jealous.

Dorothy's not helping the situation. She climbs on Grant's back, reaching over his big shoulders to try to grab some of Agnes's cropped hair.

Agnes, in response, snaps her teeth toward the arm. Vicious. Definitely not getting on her enemies list.

Grant struggles, still wrapping his arms around Agnes's squirming body, as Dorothy scrambles farther up his back. She twists her hand into his shirt, screaming obscenities at the ball of hatred dangling from Grant's arms. Almost in slow motion, I watch Dorothy climb higher on Grant's body, clinging onto him like a monkey on his back, curling her fingers into his wet and torn t-shirt.

When she jerks herself up higher to reach Agnes, a loud rip sounds in the small room. From neck to hem, Grant's shirt tears in one swift line, revealing a drool-worthy chest.

I might need some of Simone's tissues.

For a moment, I forget about the fight. I forget that shoes might be thrown at my head in the crossfire, and I don't even wonder what kind of relaxing retreat I'm supposed to expect in this town after today.

Every single scrap of my attention is occupied by the glistening, bulging, muscular torso that's just been exposed. I...*whoa.*

In a swirl of leopard-print and turquoise, Dorothy falls to the ground with the remnants of Grant's shirt still grasped between her hands. She lands with a thump, sprawled out at the big man's feet, a wet scrap of fabric clutched to her chest.

Stillness falls over the room.

"Yummy," Simone says out the corner of her lips. "Wouldn't mind licking that man clean."

Grant's glistening body looks ungodly. A sprinkling of salt-and-pepper hair covers his strong chest, and his muscles bulge and contract as he slowly lowers Agnes to the ground.

The old lady's mouth hangs open as he straightens, her face just about level with his belly-button. I watch her lips open and close before she gulps, letting her gaze linger on Grant's chest.

I can't blame her. I'd have that reaction to being so close to a perfect torso, too.

"I don't think I've ever been jealous of anyone as much as I'm jealous of Agnes right now," Simone whispers.

I stifle a giggle. I've been fighting a grin all morning, and it's more than I've wanted to smile in weeks. Months. The desire to laugh is so foreign to me, it feels wrong.

Well, I mean, laughing right now *would* be wrong. I have no doubt Agnes's second shoe would be aimed at my head.

Dorothy groans, rolling onto her side. "Get out of here, Agnes. Unless you can turn the water main off, you should go back to the cesspit from whence you came."

Grant makes a warning noise in the back of his throat, and Dorothy shuts her mouth with a snap. She glares through his legs at the ball of rage named Agnes, who turns around and startles when she sees Simone and me. Her fury hits me in the chest like a dagger and I wince, clutching my purse to my body as if it'll help stop the force of her gaze.

Agnes barks.

I jump and shuffle aside, then turn my wide eyes to Simone. "Did she just bark at us?"

"Like a gosh diggety darn *dog*!" Dorothy calls out at the top of her lungs, the words clearly aimed at Agnes's retreating back.

I chance a glance out the door, watching the little old woman hobble toward the parking lot, still wearing one shoe. The geyser is at full blast in the parking lot, a ring of spectators watching a maintenance vehicle pull up a manhole cover in the street.

I swing my gaze to the room, really seeing the lobby for the first time.

We're in a smallish room paneled entirely in painted white

timber. Flowers dot every side table, with comfortable-looking chairs arranged in small conversation nooks. Sunlight dapples through the lace curtains, and a sense of ease fills the space now that Agnes the Hellcat is gone.

I let out a sigh, raking my fingers through my hair. "Hi," I say with a smile as all eyes turn to Simone and me. "We're here for the art retreat. We signed up for the two-week stay."

"Lesson number one," Dorothy huffs from the floor, extending both arms and wiggling her fingers toward Grant so he helps her to her feet, "stay away from that horrible woman."

Grant scoops her up and sets her down on her feet with a gentleness that surprises me.

Dorothy brushes her muumuu off and adjusts her chunky jewelry before nodding to Grant. "Sorry about your shirt."

"He won't need it," the woman behind the counter says with a smile. "But oh! You're bleeding." She sweeps her way around the reception desk and reaches for his shoulder, where a small line of red grows brighter by the second.

"The harpy scratched him," Dorothy mumbles, running her fingers over his broad chest. "She should be thrown in jail and the key should be tossed into the Pacific, I say. That witch is a menace."

Simone shifts beside me, biting her knuckle as the two ladies fawn over Grant.

He stands there, fighting a grin, glancing across the room to meet my eye. Shrugging as if to say, *What are you gonna do?*, Grant lets Dorothy run her fingers all over his chest as the other woman hobbles back around the desk to grab a first aid kit.

"I'm fine, Margaret, really."

"You're bleeding," she says in a no-nonsense tone. "Sit." She points to a chair upholstered in floral fabric, and Grant dutifully takes a seat.

Dorothy dabs at his chest with a piece of gauze, running the wad of white fabric between his pecs and over his neck. "Poor dear," she says, splaying her hands over his shoulder. "You poor thing, Grant. Getting in the middle of all that ugliness."

"You'll be patched up in no time," Margaret murmurs, dabbing at the scratches on his other shoulder with an alcohol-soaked pad.

"I should feel uncomfortable," Simone says, a broad smile on her face. Her eyes twinkle as she glances at me. "But all I can think is that I want to be them when I grow up."

If the alcohol burns on his cuts, Grant doesn't show it. He just grins and rolls his eyes before nodding his chin at me. "Fiona's injured, too."

Margaret turns to us. "Oh?" she says. "Which one of you is Fiona?"

I lift my hand and spin around, tucking my hair out of the way to reveal the nape of my neck. Did I just hear Grant inhale through his teeth? "Just my neck," I say. "The asphalt got me outside."

"That's Agnes's doing," Dorothy growls, still dabbing at uninjured portions of Grant's chest. "I don't know how, but she made that water main explode."

"We don't know that," Margaret says, tucking her used supplies to the side. Every movement is clipped, tidy, and efficient. She's the polar opposite of Dorothy, who moves in graceful sweeps and seems to be really, *really* enjoying mopping up Grant's chest.

Can't say I blame her.

"Sit." Margaret points to a chair next to Grant's, and once I'm there she gets to work patching up the back of my neck. It only takes a minute or so for her to clean the wound and bandage it up, and I force myself to stare at the worn timber floor.

All I want to do is let my gaze climb up to Grant's. I want to see those grey-blue irises twinkling as he lets an elderly lady fondle his chest. I want to watch his lips quirk as I sit here, wondering what the heck I've gotten myself into.

"There." Margaret's gaze shifts to my friend. "And are you Simone McMaster? You booked the luxury honeymoon cabana?" Almost imperceptibly, her brow arches, eyes darting from me to Simone and back.

"It was cheaper than two rooms," Simone replies, grinning. "We're divorcées on a strict budget." Her eyes flick to Grant, then to me. The meaning is clear. *Single*, she's saying, *and open for business*.

"Simone," I hiss, cheeks burning.

My best friend's eyes gleam as she takes a step to the side and wiggles her eyebrows behind Grant's back.

"Oh, I don't ask questions." Margaret throws the used medical supplies away and straightens her silk blouse. "Love is love, you know."

"Quite right." Dorothy gives Grant's chest one last swipe before tearing herself away from him. "Not that Agnes would know anything about that. I don't think that woman would know love if it smacked her upside the head."

"She *is* quite horrible," Margaret answers. "Sad, really." She glances at Simone. "I'll get your paperwork ready, then you can head on through to the art studio. We'll have to check how the cabanas have held up after the geyser, but you should be able to check in after your class."

I lift my gaze outdoors, where the geyser has been subdued, with only a gaping hole in the pavement and a massive wet patch as evidence of the chaos we just witnessed. Four men wearing fluorescent vests and hard hats stand with their arms crossed, staring at the damaged pavement, while another crouches near the manhole in the street.

The two women move to the desk, and I let my gaze drift to Grant. His lips are curled into a sinful smile, and that bead of heat grows in the pit of my stomach.

If it only takes a smile for me to want to climb him like a tree, well, I'm in trouble.

"Welcome to Heart's Cove, ladies," he says in a low growl. "Pleasure meeting you, but if you'll excuse me, I have to prepare for class."

As soon as he walks away, Simone slips into the chair he just vacated. She grabs a magazine from the small round table separating us and starts fanning her face, falling back in the chair with a sigh. "Fiona, girl, if you don't ride that man till he makes you forget your own name, I think I might need to disown you."

"I don't know what you're talking about."

"Uh, bedroom eyes, much? I nearly came in my pants just watching you two."

"Don't be disgusting."

"Nothing disgusting about two single, consensual adults engaging in hot, dirty intercourse."

I shake my head. "We don't know if he's single."

"He's single!" Dorothy calls out from behind the counter, her eyes on the paperwork in front of her. "Although the man is more of a one-and-done kind of guy. Never seen him actually date anyone. No commitment. Been that way since he got to town, just lives in that big house by the ocean all by himself." She doesn't look up from her papers.

Margaret heads for the door, presumably to talk to the convention of construction workers standing around the damage.

My cheeks flame. I shake my head. "I'm not ready for that. It's only been..." I frown, not wanting to say it out loud.

"Voldemort served you with divorce papers fifteen months ago, Fi. And how long before that since you've actually had an orgasm? How long since you've enjoyed sex? You don't need to give that jackhole another minute of your life."

I stare at the door where Grant disappeared and let out a breath. Everything inside me screams that I'm not ready. Insecurities rear up, and the thought of being naked with another man...

*Oof.*

I'm not sure I can bare myself like that. Open myself to scrutiny. Show someone every part of me, especially when he looks like that, and I look like me. There's no way a man like Grant would even want me. He probably has all kinds of young women throwing themselves at him.

John has hot young women all over him, and he looks like a sack of potatoes with arms and legs. A guy like Grant? Please.

Still...what if Fiona were right? What if I could just...move on?

John did, didn't he? Why not me?

And there's the fact that there's something rolling in my blood, simmering just under the surface of my skin. I don't know if it's latent rage or frustration or recklessness, but for the first time in months—years—I want to...

I don't even know what I want to do, but I feel like I'm about to blow. Like there's something inside me that wants *out.* Maybe scratching that itch would help. Dorothy said he's a no-commitments guy, which could actually work out in my favor. I just got out of a long marriage and I'm not ready for anything—

What the heck is wrong with me? I met the guy half an hour ago and I'm negotiating the terms of our fictional hookup? This energy building inside me needs an outlet, or else I'm going to make a bunch of *very* bad decisions. I purse my lips and slump in my chair, then stiffen. "Did Grant say he had to prepare for class?" I slap my hands over my face. "He's the teacher, isn't he? Not only does he look like *that*, he's also artistic and creative?" I groan. "He's going to see how terrible I am at art."

"No such thing as terrible at art. The point of art is just to do it, not to be good at it." Simone stands up. "Remember, Fi. Today is the first day—"

"—of the rest of my life," I finish. "Spare me the clichés, please."

"I was actually going to say that today is the first day of a hot and dirty affair between you and the fine piece of ass that hasn't taken his eyes off you all morning, but sure. We'll go with your line." She grins at me, then pulls me up to my feet and slings her arm around my shoulders. "Look, if you're not ready, you're not ready. But let's just try to draw some pretty pictures, stretch our bodies and minds, and actually enjoy ourselves for a couple of weeks, okay? Then you can go back to your number-loving, organization-freak, managerial-brained, event-planning self."

My eyes brighten. "You think I could get a job event planning?"

"I think you could do anything you put your mind to, girl."

My shoulders relax, and I give my best friend a nod. "I love you, Simone."

"I know," she grins. "Now come on. Let's go draw some naked people."

Sighing, I take a step to follow her, then freeze. "Wait. What?"

# THREE
# FIONA

SIMONE ONLY GRINS at me when I pepper her with questions. Maybe she was joking about the whole naked people thing.

While Margaret meets with the maintenance workers outside about the geyser, Dorothy hands me a towel to help me dry off and leads us through a door at the back of the lobby into a courtyard bursting with color and greenery. I immediately slow down and take a deep breath, closing my eyes for just a moment.

I need this. Time to myself. Time *off*.

Ever since John came home one evening, dumped his briefcase in the foyer I cleaned, ate the food I cooked him, and unceremoniously told me he wanted a divorce, I've felt untethered, floating, aimless. It was three days before Christmas, and it shocked me to my core. My life has been shaken up and turned upside down, and I'm supposed to just...go on. I'm supposed to keep on living like my entire plan hasn't been shattered. Like every safety net I've spent decades building hasn't been shredded by the man I thought I could trust. Like I haven't been lying to myself about the state of my marriage for years.

I've been in survival mode, just moving from one divorce mediation hearing to the next, from movers to real estate agents to job applications and *please explain the ten-year gap in your resumé* questions to rolling myself up into a ball and crying on the bathroom floor.

I haven't taken a deep breath of fresh air in...I don't even know. Too long.

Simone pauses, glancing over her shoulder at me. Her eyes soften, and she dips her chin as if to say, *I get it*. And she does—she went through a divorce eight years ago, too. She knows exactly what kind of grief and heartbreak are coursing through me. I wouldn't be here without her. I'd probably be on some bathroom floor right about now, wondering why I feel like I want to peel my skin off and try on someone else's body, someone else's life.

I take another breath, pausing at a flowering tree to brush my fingers over the petals. Soft, delicate, beautiful. How long has it been since I've thought something was beautiful? How long since I've seen life in full color?

Hurrying to catch up to the two women, I follow Dorothy's swaying leopard-print muumuu through a doorway and into a brightly lit studio. About a dozen chairs and easels have been set up in a semi-circle, with a chair positioned in the center. Uh-oh. That looks suspiciously like a chair meant for a model. A naked model, if Simone is to be believed.

Most of the seats are filled, and Dorothy sweeps her arm toward two empty stools.

Simone grins at me and takes the rightmost seat. She drops her purse on the floor, then mumbles something about finding a bathroom.

I nod and slip into the other stool, glancing at the woman next to me. She's got curly brown hair, brown eyes, and a furrowed brow. I glance at her easel, where she's clipped a single sheet of paper to a board, and the woman is nudging her charcoal and pencils into exactly the right spot.

Dorothy plonks a box of supplies between Simone and me. "Take what you need," she says with a smile. "And *enjoy*." She wiggles her eyebrows as if I'm supposed to understand what that means.

A pleasant silence settles over the room as the artists get comfortable. I sit on my stool, trying to subtly glance at what everyone else is doing. A few people have their own satchels full of supplies, and a few low murmurs float through the room. The people on the other side of the semi-circle seem to know each other.

The woman next to me huffs. She's wearing jeans and a fitted shirt, and her back is straight, shoulders back. Every movement is precise, with only a spot of red high on her cheekbones to betray any kind of frustration.

"Everything okay?" I ask.

She looks at me, wide-eyed, as if only just realizing I'm there. "Oh, hi. Yes, everything's fine. I just... No matter how much I practice, I never seem to be able to get this right. It's not like baking pastries, you know? You can't measure the ingredients and follow the directions and be confident it'll end up like it did last time. Art is so..." She snorts, shaking her head. "So *unpredictable.*" She nudges her charcoal over a fraction of an inch, then takes a rag and wipes her fingers.

"Here." I pull over another stool and put it between us. "Use this for your supplies."

Her lips curl into a smile and she nods gratefully. "Good thinking. I'm Jen, by the way."

"Fiona." I clear my throat, then lean closer. "So, this class... What exactly are we drawing?"

"It's a life drawing class."

"Right." I nod, remembering Simone's words from the lobby. "And that means the models are..."

"Naked." Jen shifts in her seat, lining up her pencils on the stool I brought over for her supplies. She lets out a breath, nodding. "This is so much better. I should have done this last week. Maybe that's what's been missing. A bit more organization to help me get in the zone."

I barely hear her, because my brain is still focused on the first word she said. *Naked.* My eyes drift from one seat to the next, noting that every one of them is full.

Simone slips back into her stool, giving me a sly grin.

If Grant said he was preparing for this class, and every seat is already filled... I crane my neck, looking for an extra easel. He'll need one if he's going to—

The door opens, and Grant strides in wearing a navy blue bathrobe. It's tied loosely at the waist, revealing a triangle of gloriously muscular chest.

I squeak as my eyes bulge and my face grows heated.

Turning to look at Simone, I duck below my easel and give her a pointed stare. "Is he..."

Her lips are fighting to grin, and she lets out a giggle. "I had no idea. I swear." She pokes her eyes above the easel and I do the same, watching as Grant adjusts the chair. Feeling my gaze, he flicks his eyes to mine.

Heat gushes through my core. I squeeze my thighs together and duck back down below the easel, sucking in a deep breath.

Grant isn't the teacher. He's not a student. He's the *model.*

For a life drawing class.

Where we draw naked people.

Oh. My. Goodness.

My face is on fire. I put my hands to my cheeks to make sure I haven't accidentally burst into flames.

Jen shifts beside me, still fiddling with the position of her pencils and bits of charcoal. She doesn't seem to realize what's about to happen. What we're about to see.

"This retreat is *definitely* getting five stars from me," Simone whispers, plucking a piece of charcoal from the supplies Dorothy left for us.

I clip a thick piece of paper to the board on my easel, choosing charcoal as well. I've never done this. I've never drawn *anything*, except maybe when I was a kid. I'm not an artist.

And now I'm supposed to try to draw *Grant*?

My breaths come fast, and I squeeze my eyes shut for just a moment.

Dorothy's voice sounds from the far end of the room. "Okay, people. We're going to start with some quick poses, thirty seconds each. Then we'll move on to one-minute poses, five two-minute poses, and we'll finish up with one twenty-minute pose. Any questions?"

I poke my hand up, and Dorothy nods to me. "Yes?"

"I, uh..." I trail off. What am I trying to say?

*I don't know what I'm doing.*

*My face is so hot I'm afraid I'll end up with permanent brain damage.*

*I haven't seen a naked man other than my ex-husband in twenty years and I'm not sure I can handle the sight of this one without drinking an unhealthy amount of wine to prepare myself.*

Gulping down my flurry of inappropriate questions, I clear my throat. "Where are the extra papers?" My voice is a squeak.

"Over here, dear." Dorothy points to the shelf of supplies lining the wall nearest to me. "Help yourself."

I nod, trying to smile but knowing I must look unhinged.

Grant meets my gaze, his face impassive. Neutral. Like there's nothing at all embarrassing about the fact that he's about to drop trou in front of a dozen amateur artists. In front of *me*.

Simone reaches over and puts her hand on my thigh. "You okay?"

I glance at my best friend. "If I faint, I'm blaming you."

She rolls her eyes, giving my thigh a tap. "It's only a cock, Fiona. Get a grip." She giggles. "If only you were that lucky."

"Have you *seen* who that cock is attached to?"

Her grin is positively evil. I'm not sure I believe her when she says she had no idea this was going to happen.

Then, without preamble, Grant unties the robe and lays it over the chair, presumably so his balls don't touch the bare metal of the seat. I squeeze my eyes shut for a moment at the thought of his balls touching anything with me there to witness it.

Simone draws in a sharp breath, and Jen shifts in her seat.

I look at Jen first, seeing the intent gaze with which she watches Grant take his first pose. Her fingers hover over her supplies, and when Grant grows still, she starts drawing. And she's good. Damn it, she's *really* good. Precise, with a grid drawn through her sketch, it looks like she's calculating every inch of her drawing.

I look at Simone's easel, and she's started sketching, too.

My hands are still clasped in my lap, charcoal untouched, blank page clipped to my board, eyes still not daring to look at the perfect male model in front of me.

A bell dings, and Grant moves. The only sound in the room is the rough scrape of pencil and charcoal over paper, the smudging of fingers over the drawings, the delicate clink of soft movements on metal stools.

With one last breath, I chance a look.

He. Is. Breathtaking.

Pure power in a human body. He has his back to this side of the room, arms cocked as if he's about to launch a baseball, muscular legs flexing. And his butt. Oh, his butt.

It's freaking glorious. I want to bite it. My mouth starts to water as I watch him, eyes sweeping over every curve and bunch of muscles.

The bell dings, and he moves. He crouches down, back rounded, kneeling on one leg as he places his head on his fist.

My hands tremble, clutching a piece of charcoal, and I

manage to make a few rough sweeps. The pure beauty of the man makes my throat tight, but the absolute focus of the room takes away the discomfort. It's not sexual, it's almost...studious.

He's not Grant, the man made of pure sex and power who saved me from the geyser outside. He's not the mediator in elderly women's bitter feuds.

He's just...gorgeous.

For the next three poses, all I do is sketch. I don't even have time to think about whether my drawings are good or not, because things move quickly. He shifts from pose to pose with the grace of a dancer, but his body is lethal.

Then he turns around. His eyes find mine, and my gaze immediately drops to the space between his legs. Oops.

My charcoal stays suspended over my paper as I swallow two or three times, just looking at him. The way he stands, proud, unashamed. The way it...hangs.

I close my eyes for a moment just to compose myself. I haven't seen a dick other than John's in over two decades. I haven't *liked* the look of one in about as long. But this one...

He's not human. He can't be.

It's too hot in here. I should get my hormones checked. This isn't right.

I chance another peek at his face again, but his eyes have taken on a faraway look. I let my own gaze drift over his shoulders, flexed and powerful, his chest, his chiseled abs, and again down to the thing I've never thought of as beautiful until right this moment.

Knots form in my stomach as I squeeze my thighs together. I can't think straight. My head is full of cotton. Every time I sweep my charcoal over the paper and try to capture his form, it's never as beautiful as what's in front of me. It's never as strong, as proportional, as absolutely perfect as the real thing.

And I can't draw *that*. You know what I'm talking about.

Even though I want to. I want to do a lot more than draw it.

My head is a mess and I worry at my bottom lip, wondering why I suddenly feel like a different person. I'm usually in control, organized. Like Jen. I've never felt off-balance like this. Not even when I first met John.

When Grant moves into the longer poses, his side to me with his leg bent so my view of his cock is shielded, I feel like I can finally breathe again.

Simone leans over, whispering, "If you don't ride that cowboy till the cows come home, I'll never speak to you again."

I shoot her a glare, my cheeks heating again. What can I say? I can't deny that I want to. I can't pretend that I want to continue living like a nun, forgetting what it feels like to be a woman.

John and I had sex half a dozen times in the last five years of our marriage. I thought it was because we were getting older, because things get stale, because maybe my body had changed and he just wasn't attracted to me anymore. Goodness knows *his* body sure changed.

I thought I was broken. I thought that part of my life had just...faded away.

Well, it's not faded now. High-definition, fully saturated, 4K resolution. That energy bubbling just under my skin heats up, and my whole body fills with pure electricity.

I am a *woman*, and I am not broken. I'm not dried up and

finished. I'm not ready to tuck my desires in a box and throw away the key.

With a kind of fervor, I start sketching again. For once, I don't listen to my insecurities. I don't care if my drawings suck and if I'm not doing Grant's body justice. It doesn't matter. I'm here for *me*. I'm here to fix the part of me I thought was irreparable. I'm here to stitch together the pieces John tried to break.

This heat in my core is like a flare in the dark of the night. Bright. A beacon.

My life is not over just because I got a divorce. It's not over because I turned forty-five this year. It's not over because I need to start over. Far from it.

Grant moves into a seated position for the longest pose of the class, and his eyes find mine once again. This time, I don't look away. I don't shy away from the heat building in my core, from the lust burning in his eyes. I don't turn my head away and duck down behind my easel.

Once the spell on this room is broken and the focus is shattered, I might regret it. Latent embarrassment might catch up to me if I see Grant in the street, fully clothed, remembering what he looked like in this room.

But I don't care. There's danger in his eyes. Darkness. Desire.

And it's aimed at me.

A siren sounds in the distance, and everyone jumps. A few seconds later, the alarm for the poses dings, and Grant stands up, draping his robe over his body. His eyes climb up to mine as he ties off the robe, and warmth unfolds in the pit of my stomach.

It's not until he turns his back to me that I let out a breath.

Simone leans over, pointing at the drawings on my many sheets of paper. "You missed a spot." Her finger circles over all the blank spaces I left between my drawings of Grant's legs, and my face turns hot all the way up to the tips of my ears. Her grin is unapologetic, and I swat her away without speaking. I still don't trust my voice after all that.

"How'd your first class go?" a deep voice says over my shoulder.

I freeze, turning to see Grant standing on my other side. Jen has already packed up and headed for the door, and he sits down on her vacated stool. My eyes drift over his robe, knowing exactly what lies beneath.

He opens his mouth, but I hold up a hand. I can't do this right now. I can't let him break the spell that was just cast over me, and I'm not ready to move anything forward with him. Whether or not I *ride that cowboy till the cows come home* doesn't matter, because right now, I feel *good*. I feel alive. I don't want him to ruin it by saying something that makes me think he's just like every other man. Just like John.

I want this illusion to last.

So, I say the first thing that comes to mind. "Before you say anything, Grant, consider this. You are at peak hotness right now. A-plus. Mount Everest height. You just acted like a gentleman outside, then prevented a fight in the lobby, and now spent twenty minutes looking like a dancer or a warrior or... I don't even know."

"A model?" Simone supplies.

I nod. "Yes, a model."

"And that means I can't speak now?" Grant's brows draw together, his eyes glimmering with humor.

I shake my head. "Anything you say will inevitably diminish the hotness."

"Is that right?"

I nod. "It's the truth. Hot guys open their mouths and immediately become less hot."

"Fact." Simone nods.

He moves to speak, but I hold up my hand. "Just trust me on this one, Grant. It's for the best."

With eyes glittering, he lifts his fingers to his mouth and zips his lips shut, throwing away the key.

I nod. "Good. And good day." I turn away, packing up my art supplies as a soft chuckle resonates behind me. I listen to the soft scuff of his feet on the ground, and finally lift my heated face to Simone.

She just laughs. "You're in trouble, girl."

# FOUR
# GRANT

STANDING in the change room adjoining the studio, I scrub my hands over my face. I've never had a figure drawing class like that before. Never so...intense.

I kept wanting to look over at Fiona, to see the redness in her cheeks and the way her gaze darted all over my body. When she glanced down between my legs...

Let's just say I had to turn away for the next pose.

I inhale the scent of cleaning supplies and dampness. The changing room doubles as a storage closet, and I take a seat on a creaky wooden bench beside the wire shelves. Leaning my back against the concrete block wall, I close my eyes for a moment.

I came to Heart's Cove fourteen years ago to start over. To forget my old life. To move on.

It's worked so far.

I've started a life here, spent time doing carpentry and drawing and getting to know the townspeople. I *am* one of the townspeople now. Up until today, I thought I was happy—or at least content. Satisfied.

Then I saw Fiona crouched on the street, shielding herself from the geyser in the parking lot, and something snapped inside me. That familiar need that I thought I'd beaten down inside me—to protect, to look after, to shield. Those exact feelings are what got me in trouble all those years ago, and I thought I'd moved past them. I thought I'd killed the part of me that cares about women in that way.

I was wrong.

Squeezing my eyes tighter, I try to shove away the image of Fiona turning to look at me, the heat in her eyes when she met mine, the little whimper that came out of her mouth when I touched the nape of her neck.

This is ridiculous. I don't even know the woman, and I'm already wrapped around her little finger. It'll pass. It has to. Plus, she'll leave. They always leave, especially in a tourist town. She doesn't need me to take care of her.

Why does that make me sad?

When everything happened fifteen, no, almost sixteen years ago now, something broke inside me. Snapped like a twig, and I knew it would never be mended. I accepted it. I knew I'd live the rest of my life alone. Knew I'd die alone. That's why I moved here afterwards, why I tried to start over.

Today...

I sigh, peeling my eyes open and staring at the dark room, my eyes catching on jugs of cleaning products and the old mop in the corner.

Let's just say today, something woke up inside me. I haven't felt this kind of attraction toward a woman in over a decade. Haven't felt that tugging in my gut that tells me I care. Haven't *wanted* to care.

It's ridiculous, really. I barely know the woman. It's dumb lust, and I should probably do my best to stay away from her. I should follow her advice and keep my mouth shut.

My body has other ideas, though.

Maybe I should listen to it. Sleep with her, get it out of my system, go back to my life as it was.

I tug my underwear and jeans over my legs and reach for my shirt, only to remember it was destroyed. Which means I'll be walking out there, feeling the heat of Fiona's gaze on my chest again, and my body will probably react in ways that get very uncomfortable in a tight pair of jeans.

Resigned to my fate, I open the door.

Dorothy's grinning face waits on the other side. She looks at me with an arched eyebrow, letting her eyes drop to my chest for a moment.

I should probably care about the twins flirting with me and fondling me. I should probably pull away and tell them to stop when they reach for my chest, but the truth is, I've never really minded. It's not sexual, but it's... Well, I'll just be honest. It's the only physical touch I feel from another human most of the time. Dorothy's inappropriately long hugs are the only time I get to feel like a person and not some invisible man.

Sure, I occasionally sleep with women, and I get physical touch there, but it's not the same as a hug. Sex with someone usually ends in me slipping out of bed and heading home alone.

Dorothy lifts her eyes up to mine and shoves a piece of

clothing toward me. "Marge said to give you this." She waves a hand, shrugging. "I told her it should be a crime to cover up a body like yours, but does she listen to me? No. She's more worried about what's *proper*."

I take the shirt from her and unfold it, already knowing it's too small. It's pink and clearly cut for a woman's body. Emblazoned on the front of it in glittery silver writing are the words, *Heart's Cove Hottie*. "This is going to make me look proper?"

"What?" Dorothy arches a brow, studying my expression. "It was the most appropriate shirt we had at the gift store for you."

A laugh tumbles out of me, and Dorothy takes a step back. She frowns, tilting her head. "You laughed."

I shrug. "Yeah, so?"

"You don't laugh, Grant. I've known you fourteen years and I've seen you laugh twice."

"Have you been keeping track?"

She lifts a hand to count off on her fingers. "Once was when Agnes fell into that old pond in Memorial Park and came up with a lily pad on her head—don't blame you, it *was* hilarious—and the other time was your fortieth birthday when Mr. Cheswick told that stupid joke."

"What's a pirate say when he turns eighty?" I fight a grin. "Aye matey!"

"Like I said," Dorothy replies, "idiotic joke. You weren't even turning eighty!"

"I appreciated the sentiment."

"I think you were drunk."

"That too."

"What are you waiting for?" She jerks her chin at the shirt crumpled in my hand. "Put it on. We can't have you walking around topless."

"You didn't seem to mind earlier."

Dorothy puts her hands on her hips, her leopard-print dress swirling around her legs. "Grant Greene. Do not give me that kind of attitude. Put on the damn shirt."

The authority in Dorothy's eyes is familiar, and I dip my chin, knowing I won't win this battle. I unfurl the shirt and pull it on over my shoulders, tugging the skin-tight pink fabric down just below my belly button. I hear the fabric strain, the seams crackling as if to rip as I pull it down, and look at Dorothy with an arched brow. "Happy?"

She takes a step back, bringing her finger to her chin. Her eyes sweep over the sparkly lettering, the fabric plastered over my body, the strip of skin exposed around my waist between the too-small shirt and my pants. "Looks lovely. Come through." She waves me out of the change room-cum-supply closet and into the studio.

I follow her out into the lobby, where Fiona is standing, running her fingers through her shoulder-length dark hair over and over again.

"What do you mean, the cabana is uninhabitable?" She glances at her friend Simone and turns back to Margaret. "We have nowhere else to stay."

Margaret's shoulders round, her lips bracketed by deep lines. "I'm so sorry, ladies. When the water main exploded, it caused additional damage to the cabana section of the hotel. We can, of course, refund you the cost of your stay, but we're unfortunately fully booked otherwise. The peak season has already started for us in Heart's Cove."

"This is the only hotel in town," Fiona says, the pitch of her voice rising. "And Simone's car broke down. We're stranded. There's nowhere else for us to stay."

The panic in Fiona's voice tugs at my chest. For the second time today, the urge to take care of her overwhelms me. It's more than just that. I want to wrap my arms around her and shield her from everything bad in the world.

So, the words come out of my mouth before I can even think about them. "You can stay at my place."

All three women turn to look at me, and even Dorothy swivels her head beside me. Four sets of eyebrows climb up high.

Fiona's eyes—deep, forest green, and full of worry—drop to my torso. Her brows draw together, a line appearing between them. "'Heart's Cove Hottie?'"

"Dorothy!" Margaret exclaims. "I told you to give him an appropriate shirt from the gift shop."

"What do you call this?" She jerks her thumb at me. "He's a hottie, isn't he? And this is Heart's Cove, is it not?"

Margaret rolls her eyes, pinching the bridge of her nose.

"Answer me honestly, ladies." Dorothy sweeps her arms toward me like she's Vanna White. "Is this inappropriate to you?"

"It's perfect," Simone answers, her lips twitching. "I agree with Dorothy."

"You would," Fiona answers, the lines in her face relaxing. She flicks her emerald eyes up to mine and shakes her head, huffing out a laugh. Then she glances at her friend, speaking softly. "What are we going to do?"

"You'll stay at my place," I answer, striding toward them. "It's on the edge of town, there's lots of room, and like you said—you're stranded. I've been wanting to start a bed and breakfast, anyway."

Dorothy snorts. "Right."

I shoot her a glare, but ignore her. "I insist."

"First of all"—Fiona lifts a hand—"don't waltz in here acting like you can order us around. *If* we stay at your place, *we* will decide."

My lips twitch. Bull-headed, stubborn, beautiful woman.

She lets out a breath, eyebrows arching as if she's surprised by the strength of her own words. Then her brows relax and she exchanges a glance with Simone. My gut tightens when she says, "We'll pay you."

I hold up a hand, shaking my head. "Please. Let me help you."

Simone arches her brows at Fiona, who shrugs. I watch Fiona suck her lip between her teeth and nibble on it as she shifts her weight from foot to foot, and I stifle a groan. My body's reaction to this woman is visceral and inappropriate and almost overwhelming.

Then, Fiona's shoulders drop and she dips her chin. "Okay. Thank you. That's twice you've saved us today."

"Three times if you count your brush with Agnes the She-Devil," Dorothy pipes up, shuffling behind the counter next to her twin.

"What's the deal with Agnes and you guys, anyway?"

Simone glances at the two ladies, then at me. "Why the violence? What happened today?"

Dorothy's eyes glimmer. "I may or may not have bought every almond croissant within a ten-mile radius, and they may or may not be Agnes's favorite. Allegedly."

Margaret snorts. "For the eighth day in a row." She glances at her twin. "And you're allergic to nuts."

"Agnes started it! She—"

"Let's go," I say to my two new guests, not wanting to go down that road with the twins. "I'll carry your bags to my car." I herd the women out the door and across the parking lot, where orange barricades have been set up around the damaged pavement. A few men are working on fixing the leak, and I have no doubt the water will be back on within a few hours.

WALKING into my old house on the edge of town with Fiona by my side makes my gut clench in a way I'm not used to. I haven't had anyone stay with me since I moved into this house ten years ago, after I finished my carpentry apprenticeship and felt like I needed a bigger project. I've spent the past decade fixing the place up, telling myself I'm going to start a B&B, but never actually taking the final steps.

Maybe this is a sign.

Working on the house has been a kind of therapy for me, and hearing Fiona's intake of breath as she walks in is the final healing balm. She turns to me, eyes shining, and squeezes my forearm. Electricity zings through me at her touch, and she drops her eyes to stare at her hand.

She felt it, too.

Clearing my throat, I nod to the stairs to our left. "Guest rooms are upstairs."

"This place is incredible. It's homey but masculine, luxurious yet simple."

"You like it?" I ask, my throat tight.

Her eyes roam over the chair rail that was a pain to install, the furniture Mr. Cheswick helped me create, and a strange sort of awe creeps into her eyes. Fiona opens her mouth to answer, emotion weighing heavy on her expression.

A noise makes us turn toward the front door, where Simone hauls her bag across the threshold.

She blows out a breath, shaking her head. Eyebrows inch up. "Is this all yours?"

I nod. "Bought it before this town became a tourist destination. The property extends to the ocean. You're welcome to wander."

"You have to let us pay you for the stay," Fiona says.

"Does this mean you'll allow me to speak?" I arch a brow as my lips curl. "Even if it diminishes my hotness?"

Fiona sweeps her eyes around the foyer, the wide staircase, the front living room full of furniture I've built over the past ten years. She nods. "I'll allow it, but only if you let us pay you for the stay."

Simone grunts. "Don't bite the hand that feeds, Fi. Just accept that something good has happened, for once." She levels her friend with a stare, arching a brow.

"Do you have trouble accepting good things?" I ask, taking both suitcases and heading for the stairs.

"Does she ever! Fiona is basically Mrs. Doomsday Preparation, and if something good happens, all she can think about is how it won't last."

"That's not true," Fiona answers from behind me. I feel her gaze on my back, and I wonder how the pink shirt looks from back there. Probably as ridiculous as it looks from the front. She sighs. "Maybe that's what makes me good at planning and project management."

Simone grumbles a response I don't catch.

"We all have our demons," I answer, turning to the two doors on the right side of the hallway. "These are yours. I'll grab some sheets."

Simone thanks me and chooses the closest door, mumbling something about a shower and change of clothes.

As soon as her door closes, Fiona turns to face me. "Thank you, Grant."

My name coming from her mouth sounds sweeter, somehow.

Throat tight, all I can do is nod. "It's no problem, really. Marge and Dorothy helped me get settled when I first moved here. I probably owe them a thousand favors by now."

"I think they take payment in ogling and touching your chest," she grins.

"You noticed that, did you?"

"Hard not to, *hottie*." She brushes her fingers over the lettering on my chest, and a dagger of heat pierces the pit of my stomach.

I take a step back, and Fiona drops her hand.

"Sorry," she mumbles, redness sweeping over her cheeks.

"Let me know if you need anything." My voice is thick and I take a step to the side, already heading for the stairs.

Why did I say they could stay with me? What possessed me to invite Fiona and her friend into my life?

I've survived the past decade and a half because I've kept to myself. I've busied myself fixing this house up and doing odd jobs around the town. I took an early retirement and resigned myself to a simple, quiet life by myself. On my own.

Alone.

Isn't that how I should be? After what happened all those years ago, I knew I'd end up alone. It's the only way to make sure I never have to go through that kind of pain again.

Now Fiona walks in, all curves and luminous eyes and a bright smile, and I want to let her in? I want to crack my chest open and show her all the blackened parts of my heart?

I don't know the woman. I feel...something...for her, but it's physical. It's a reaction to the way her eyes heat when they look at me, how her body makes flames lick the pit of my stomach.

Nothing more.

Maybe I *should* sleep with her, because then this feeling is sure to pass. I can just scratch the itch, then let her be on her way at the end of her two-week vacation. Then she'll leave. They all do.

# FIVE
# FIONA

A COLD SHOWER washes the embers off my skin, and I emerge clean, fresh, and more in control of my body.

We shouldn't have accepted Grant's offer—but what choice do we have? Our room at the Heart's Cove Hotel is destroyed, and nothing else is available. We don't even have a car to drive to the next town over.

It was a generous offer and I appreciate it, but I saw how uncomfortable Grant was when he showed me to my room. He doesn't want me here. As soon as we can find something else, Simone and I should move to different accommodations.

When I exit my room, Simone's door is open. She's lying in bed, a stack of clean sheets on the chair next to the door, her head propped against the headboard with a book open in her lap. She smiles at me. "Ready to head into town for a meditation session and dinner?"

I force my lips to curl. "Sure."

We head out the front door, where two bicycles have been propped against the front porch. A note is on one of the seats: *Use these whenever you like.* There's no signature, but the broad, neat handwriting reminds me of Grant. Powerful, in control.

I show Simone the note and shrug. "You down for a bike ride?"

She grins, grabbing one of the bikes and slinging her leg over. "Heck yes! I feel like a kid again."

With one last glance toward the house I already love, I head back down the long driveway and toward Heart's Cove.

AS IT TURNS OUT, meditation and dinner are exactly what I need, even though meditation turns into an hour-long session of getting a numb butt as I sit on the floor while my mind wanders. But when I stand up—and massage my sore behind—I'm oddly relaxed. I don't remember the last time I just let myself sit and be still. My first day in Heart's Cove has me already unknotting muscles I hadn't even realized were tense. I've barely thought of my ex-husband, and haven't worried about what I'm going to do next.

For the first time in years, I've just...enjoyed myself.

Two weeks in this town is starting to sound far too short. We just need to get our accommodations figured out, because there's no way I'm going to impose on Grant for any longer than necessary.

But as we ride the rusty old bikes back down his long driveway onto the four-acre property, a sense of calm settles over my bones. The truth is, I don't want to leave. His home is gorgeous and comfortable.

We park the bikes on the side of the house and Simone makes her way upstairs. Instead of following her, I head down to the back of the house where Grant told me the kitchen was. The sun is going down and I'm starting to feel sleepy, but I just need a cup of tea to help me relax.

When I reach the back of the house, the hallway opens up onto a huge farmhouse kitchen. Finely crafted white shaker cabinets line three walls, with a big island in the middle covered with a timber butcher's block worktop. The sink is deep and white, and the whole thing feels like home. I run my fingers over the worktop, letting out a sigh.

"You like it?"

I jump, yelping, and turn to see Grant near the French doors on the other side of the kitchen.

With a hand to my heart, I nod. "You scared me. And yes, I love it. This is basically my dream kitchen. My place in L.A. was..." I wrinkle my nose. "Really modern. Not to my taste."

"Why'd you choose it, then?"

"I didn't." I snort, shaking my head. "My ex-husband picked everything out, saying if he ever had clients or partners coming to the apartment, he wanted it to be appropriate. Translation—he wanted to impress a bunch of people he didn't even like. Never mind the fact that I was the one who spent most of the time in there." I glance at Grant, who moves to the sink to wash his hands. I cringe at myself. "Sorry. I shouldn't talk about him."

"Don't apologize. We all have scars. Tea?"

A smile tugs at my lips. "That's what I came looking for."

"I was hoping you were looking for me." He says the words with his back to me as he fills the kettle, so low I almost miss them. But my heart flips and my stomach clenches, and I lean back against the far counter to regain my balance.

This man is... He's something else. I watch his big body move gracefully around the kitchen, setting the electric kettle on its base and flicking it on. He's changed out of that ridiculous pink tee and into a loose-fitting linen button-down shirt, tan trousers hanging low on his hips. When he turns around, my eyes drift down to the triangle of skin exposed on his chest.

"Did you design it?" I ask. "The kitchen."

"I built it." He shrugs, speaking casually, as if everyone builds their own kitchens. As if everyone can reach into my mind and create a real-life Pinterest board of my dream house and let me stay in it for free. My heart thumps as I look around the room, feeling a deep kind of attraction to this man.

I'm not even sure he could say *anything* to make that attraction fade. The man could have the personality of a wet sock and his home would make up for it.

I wonder what brought him to this town. Why he chose it, what he was running from. I wonder what makes him tick and how he takes his tea. I wonder how often he laughs, and if I'll get to hear it before I go to bed tonight.

I wonder if I'll ever see his naked body again, if I'll ever get to touch it.

My fingers curl around the countertop behind me as I inhale through my teeth, trying to regain control over my rioting body. I feel warm, comfortable, yet on edge. Every time Grant moves around the kitchen—grabbing mugs, taking out a tea bag, reaching for the sugar—it's like every sense of mine is tuned into him. I can *feel* him moving, as if I'm right beside him.

When he hands me a mug after asking how I like my tea (with lots of sugar), he jerks his head to the open French doors and I follow him onto the porch, where two Adirondack chairs are positioned to look out on the ocean. I take a seat, blowing on my tea to help it cool.

"So, your ex-husband," Grant starts, clearing his throat. "What happened?"

I take a sip, immediately regretting it as the too-hot liquid burns my tongue. Exhaling sharply, I set the mug down on the arm of the chair, then shrug. "We grew apart, I guess. He worked a lot, and expected me to stay at home. I kept myself busy with local fundraisers and events, being a part of the community—*his* community—but when the dust settled, I couldn't really look back and be proud of anything I'd done. We didn't put the time into our relationship, and then twenty years passed, and I guess we realized we didn't really know each other anymore. It was a slow death."

Grant makes a soft noise, his eyes faraway as he stares at the ocean. Tangerine and dusty pink streak across the sky as the sun dips lower, the chill in the air not quite unbearable. Being here with him is comfortable. There's no pressure to talk or explain, but I...want to. I want to talk about this to him, and for the first time in months, there's no sharp pain associated with the words.

I suck in a breath, needing to say it out loud. Needing to make the truth heard. "He also cheated on me repeatedly over the past five years, so there's that," I say, reaching for the mug again.

Grant's head snaps toward me, his eyes dark. "Asshole." The word reverberates in the space between us, a harsh edge to his voice. Like he wants to hurt my ex-husband for causing me pain.

"Yes." I let out a dry huff, shaking my head. "But I wonder if I could have tried harder before it got to the point that he was looking for something elsewhere. If I could have prevented it somehow."

"The only person to blame for your ex-husband cheating is your ex-husband, Fiona." His eyes are dark when he speaks, as if he wants me to understand him. Wants me to internalize what he's saying.

I pinch a smile and nod. "Yeah. That's what Simone says."

"You should listen to her."

"What about you?" I ask, trying another sip of my tea. It's warm but not hot now, and I let out a soft noise as I sip it again. "When did you move to Heart's Cove?"

"Fourteen years ago," he says. "A year and a half earlier, when I was thirty-five, I had a heart attack, took some time off work, and decided I needed to change my life. Otherwise I'd be dead by forty. Eighteen months later I picked up and moved across the country, from New York City to here."

"Oh." My eyebrows jump up.

"I was...under a lot of stress." His eyes drift out toward the ocean again, and I feel like he's wrestling with what he wants to say. Like there are layers of pain and secrets in his past that he doesn't want to tell me.

Not wanting to pry, I just nod. The soft music of the ocean is soothing, and we listen to the sounds of the night for a few minutes. Crickets, distant waves, the rustling of the wind through the trees. It's peaceful, as if the whole world is accepting me in a quiet embrace.

Then, Grant speaks. "I was working at a corporate law firm, doing hundred-hour weeks."

I stiffen, gripping my mug. He was a lawyer? Like John?

What the *actual* hell is wrong with me? The first man I'm attracted to after my divorce is basically a hot version of my ex-husband? Am I farking *insane*?

Red flags flap all around me, and I almost miss Grant's next words. "It...happened," he chokes out, and I wonder what exactly *it* means. The heart attack? Or something else? He gulps, shaking his head. "I struggled through for another year, then quit and came here to find peace. I needed to be alone. Thought I...I deserved to be alone."

"That makes two of us," I say, forcing a smile. Unease churns in my gut as I steal a glance at Grant. "Simone keeps saying we're on a journey to find ourselves, and I'm here wondering if it'll be worth the trip." I huff out a laugh, trying to quell the panic rising inside me.

He's a lawyer. A freaking dirty law jockey. He probably screwed his assistants, too. That's probably what *it* was. Some drama with all the women he was sleeping with. Just like John. Life caught up to him.

But Grant doesn't look anything like John. His house is the polar opposite of our swanky, soulless modern penthouse. He offered up his home to us without hesitation, which speaks to his generosity. He has the body of a Greek god. He *quit*. Didn't want the life that John so craves.

As he reclines in his chair, my eyes drift over the white linen fabric of his shirt, fingers itching to unbutton it. I want to run my tongue over his chest, kiss his neck, taste his lips.

Desire winds through my core, but there's something else, too. I feel calm here. I can *think*. My mind is clear, and I know it's more than this town. It's Grant's presence, it's this beautiful house, it's the sound of the crickets and the sea in the distance. It's the aura of calm and control and bridled power that exudes from the man sitting beside me.

But he's a lawyer. He's one of *them*.

Am I really so stupid as to make the exact same mistakes all over again? For the first time in years, I've had a day where I feel like my old self again. I've felt attracted to a man. I've laughed. I've thought about *myself*, for once. When was the last time I put myself first? Has it ever happened?

Even the thing I wanted most—to be a mother—I set aside when John refused. I gave up...*everything*. In time, I accepted it. I no longer want a baby, and I know my childbearing years are pretty much over. Instead of clinging onto my resentment for John, I let it go.

And now, I feel a sliver of hope. I have a tiny, tenuous grasp on myself, on a future that looks brighter than my past. A future where I can stand on my own.

I can't let go of that feeling. Not for anything. Definitely not for an ex-lawyer—even if he is gorgeous and generous and all I want to do is wrap my arms around him and wipe that scowl off his face. Grant may be beautiful, but I'm not ready to give anything up for another man. I've sacrificed too much of myself already.

"I should go to bed," I say in a tight voice, standing up. "Do you mind if I drink my tea in my room?"

"Drink your tea wherever you like," he says, lips relaxing into a half-smile. "Goodnight, Fiona."

I ignore the shiver of desire that teases through my insides as he says my name. Standing up, I nod to him and hurry through the beautiful house and up to my room. I lock the door and lean against it, putting my tea down on the top of the dresser behind me and dropping my face into my hands.

He's hot, I'll give him that. The art class today woke something up inside me that I thought died long ago. He's nice to look at.

But he was a lawyer. He's just like John.

No matter how my body reacts to him, I can't make the same mistakes I made before. I can't fall for the same old charm, the same kind of man.

Simone says I need to hook up with someone. She wants me to enjoy myself, to feel like a woman. But what if I can't separate sex from emotion? Am I really ready to get involved with someone like Grant?

The energy churning in my body makes my movements jerky, nearly uncontrollable. I take a deep breath, knowing I need some kind of release, but unsure where to get it. The last thing I should do is let myself get tangled up in a man—any man, lawyer or not—before I'm sure of who I am and what I want.

I need to resist this attraction to Grant, otherwise I'll end up right where I started. Heartbroken, overwhelmed, and insecure.

# SIX
# SIMONE

DUSK AND DAWN are my favorite times of day. Leaving Fiona to find her nightly cup of tea, I find my feet taking me outside, to the fresh air and soft grass and waving trees. I wander down a beaten dirt path on the side of the house, letting my hands drift through leaves and tall grasses, inhaling deeply.

Fiona and I have been friends since college, and she's been by my side during some of my toughest years. That's why I suggested this trip, why I organized it—but I need some time to myself, too. To figure out the mess I'm in.

Big Bertha dying on me isn't good. I brushed it off and laughed when Fiona got worried, because I know that's what she needed—for me to be a rock when she's struggling—but if I'm honest with myself, I'm worried. My freelance copywriting work has dried up, and my savings are dwindling. I've cut into my emergency fund and might actually need to start drawing from my retirement savings.

And there's that pesky text message waiting for me on my phone. El Bastardo texted me this morning, and I haven't had the courage to answer. Eight years after our divorce, all of a sudden he wants to *catch up*.

Ugh.

Somehow, he knew—he just *knew*—that I'm going through a rocky time. There's some wavelength my ex-husband can sense when I'm feeling unsteady—a bat signal shining in the night sky that screams, *Strike now! She's vulnerable!*—and that's when he chooses to text me. When I'm most likely to respond.

My feet take me deeper into the trees as my mind whirls. Money stress is the worst kind of stress. I've been through a divorce, a miscarriage, I've mourned the deaths of my parents... but there's something about knowing I might not be able to make my mortgage payment next month that just makes me want to lie down and give up. Like I've failed at being an adult, somehow. There's a kind of shame in it I don't want to address.

I won't fall apart, though. Not for these two weeks. Not while Fiona needs me.

Wandering through the trees, I let the sound of the ocean soothe my tumultuous thoughts. The geyser was a bit of a blessing—we won't have to pay for accommodation now. That money should be enough to cover the car repairs so at least I can get home at the end of this trip.

Maybe we should have taken Voldemort's car.

I run through calculations in my head, hoping Fiona won't continue to insist we need to pay Grant. It's only when I realize darkness has fallen that I look around the woods and realize I've wandered off the path.

Shit.

I take a few steps through the underbrush, listening for the ocean. If I can listen for the waves, I can orient myself and find my way back to Grant's place. It's so quiet now—have I walked inland far enough that I can't hear it?

Another noise—faint, faraway—reaches my ears. *Thwack. Thwack. Thwack.*

Walking toward it, I try to note what I can. Which direction does moss grow on trees? South? Doesn't really help me when I don't know what direction Grant's house is in. My heartbeat speeds up, but I wrestle it down. No sense panicking. I wrap my thin sweater tighter around my body and walk toward the noise, hoping it's someone friendly. Hoping they can help me get home, or at least point me in the right direction.

After a few minutes, the trees start to thin and I spy a building through the trunks. I loose a long breath, finally admitting to myself that I was scared. Being lost in the woods at night in a town I don't know is...well, it's bad, even for me. I'm not a shining model of responsibility, but I'm not usually *this* bad. Hurrying, I walk through the trees toward that house. As I get closer, I note the long wooden logs forming the walls of the cabin, the mossy roof, the sprawling clearing with a few outbuildings.

And in front of it all, a muscled, shirtless man.

Of course he's shirtless.

What is it about this town? Is there something in the water, and can I have some?

He raises an axe above his head and brings it down in a powerful stroke. A log cleaves in two, both pieces falling to the ground. I watch as the man bends over, his corded, lean muscles writhing under his skin as he picks up a log as big as my thigh, setting it on his chopping block. A huge tattoo curls down his side, from his shoulder blade around to his front.

"Uh, excuse me—"

The man whirls, holding his axe like a weapon, raising it as if to throw.

Well, alrighty then. Not as friendly as Grant Greene and little old Dorothy. Maybe he's related to Agnes.

"Who are you?" he grunts, eyes darkening as he looks me up and down.

"Simone," I squeak. I clear my throat. "I'm Simone. I'm staying at Grant Greene's place and I went for a walk, but I seem to have gotten lost. Can you please point me in the right direction?" My voice, mercifully, doesn't tremble. I take a step closer to him as he lowers the axe, propping it against the stack of logs.

He takes a rag out of his back pocket and dabs at his brow, watching me. My eyes dart to his bicep, then his chest, then his cut abdominal muscles. Yum.

*Focus, Simone. Focus.*

The man arches a brow. "You walked all the way here from Grant's place?"

"I have a lot on my mind."

He grunts, and I'm not sure if it's an angry noise. I don't speak Antisocial Lumberjack. Turning his back on me, he gives me a view of the gleaming muscle and tattoo that my fingers itch to explore. "I'll drive you."

"That's okay, if you just point me in the right direction—"

He whirls, eyes flashing. "It's late. I'll drive you." Every word clipped, emphasized.

I nod. "How do I know you won't drive me off into the middle of the woods and murder me?"

Shrug. "You don't."

Well, that's comforting. I watch him walk toward the house, where an old pickup truck is parked. Should I, or shouldn't I? Glancing over my shoulder to see nothing but dark woods, I let out a long breath and scamper after him. Don't have much choice. Or maybe I'm a silly woman who can't resist a shirtless piece of man-meat.

"So, what's your name?" I ask as I slide into the passenger seat. He's still not wearing a shirt, and I let my eyes drift over the trim waist, the bead of sweat rolling down between his pecs.

"Wesley." He turns the key in the ignition, putting his hand on the back of my seat to start reversing down the driveway. A man of few words, then.

"Have you been in Heart's Cove for long?"

"Came back six months ago."

"Oh." I nod, folding my hands in my lap. "You grew up here?"

"Is there a reason you're asking all these questions?" He stops the car, leveling his pine-green eyes on me.

"It's called a conversation, Wesley." I roll my eyes. "I say something, then you respond with something related, then we do it again a few times. It's actually considered quite normal among humans."

His nostrils flare, a muscle feathering in his jaw. "I came back six months ago to bury my parents. Now I'm living in the house my grandfather built, trying to sort through their affairs and figure out what to do from here. Happy?"

I'd feel sorry for him if he wasn't such a freaking asshole. Instead of answering, I turn my head and look out the window. We drive in silence until we get to a driveway I recognize. I must have walked for miles without realizing it.

Wesley pulls the car around so my door is in line with the driveway, then stops. Guess it's not door-to-door service, but if it means I don't have to spend another minute in the car with this brute of a man, then fine.

"Thanks for not murdering me in the woods," I call out before slamming the door, then stomp back to Grant's house. It's quiet, and when I get upstairs, Fiona's door is closed. I let out a breath, easing my way into my own room.

Another man who loves to be a jerk, especially when he comes across a woman in need. Wonderful. I must send out a beacon that attracts these assholes.

I need a shower. I'm hot and uncomfortable, and I need to get the sight of Wesley the Shirtless Lumberjack out of my head. Preferably forever.

# SEVEN
# FIONA

"SO FIRST, we have a yoga session, then a late breakfast, then a few hours to ourselves, then a pottery class at two o'clock." Simone pedals her bicycle, taking her hands off the handlebars to brush her orange-red hair from her face. "Sound good?"

I huff, grunting. "Yeah." My legs feel like lead and my butt is so sore it feels like it might fall off. I haven't ridden a bike in far too long, and this is only the second day in a row a bicycle has been our only mode of transportation. "How are you riding so easily?" I ask, gearing down too far so my feet pedal into nothing. I gear the bike back up—oops, too far—and finally settle on a speed so I can ride beside Simone.

She leans on the handlebars again, smiling. "Spin class three times a week. My ass has gotten used to the pain."

"Remind me never to do spin," I grumble as we clear the last line of trees and make it to the main drag through Heart's Cove.

Simone leads us toward the hotel, but stops off half a block away. "This is it." She jerks her chin to a dark building with a narrow door to the side. The whole bottom level is dark, but there's a handmade sign directing us to go up the stairs to the studio above.

I arch a brow. "Is this place legit?"

"Fi, darling, relax." Simone parks her bike on a nearby stand and waves me forward so she can lock them together. "I told you we were going to spend two weeks together doing things that will hopefully get you out of your comfort zone. You used to love yoga."

"That was before my life imploded."

"All the more reason to start again." She beams at me, tying her hair up as we walk toward the door. It creaks when Simone pushes it open, and I follow my best friend's yoga-pants-clad butt up a narrow, steep stairwell. We emerge into a bright, friendly space with cubby holes lining the wall to the left and a half-dozen people in various states of undress.

A young woman in her twenties folds her body in half and stands up again, her taut stomach carved with muscles I didn't even know existed. I tug my shirt down, glancing at Simone. She's already at reception, signing us in and accepting two loaner yoga mats from the woman behind the desk. We're led through to a larger room, dimly lit, with an entire wall of mirrors.

Because that's what I want right now. To be able to see myself in all my soon-to-be-sweaty glory. It's only my second day of self-actualization and I'm not ready to find myself that intimately. Mercifully, Simone leads me to the back corner, a grin on her face. "We can start back here today. You look like you might murder me if I put us up front."

"And chop you up into little pieces, too. Just like the shirtless axe murderer from the last night."

Simone giggles, handing me a mat to unfurl. I was worried when she told me about her traipse through the woods, but she just shrugged and told me to relax. So I'm trying to do just that —with mixed results. We line our mats up and lie down like the two other people in the room, waiting for the class to start.

I've only been here a day, but already I've had more time to sit and think than I've had in the past twenty years. Time to reflect on the fact that I got married at twenty-four years old and thought it would be forever.

Time to wonder how it all fell apart.

Time to replay the past day in high definition, especially the part where Grant dropped his robe and reminded me that my lady-bits are still very much alive and functional.

Taking a deep breath, I try to unceremoniously shove those thoughts down a deep, dark hole. He's hot, but I'm not going to pursue anything. It's for the best, anyway. This vacation is about me, and I don't need some big, burly man distracting me.

Movement to my left makes me crack an eyelid, and I notice Jen from the life drawing class setting up beside me. I whisper her name and wiggle my fingers.

She gives me a small smile and returns to her mat, lining it up exactly perpendicular to the front mirrors and folding her towel into perfect thirds before setting it down beside her mat. Every movement precise, as if she needs millimeter accuracy in everything she does.

Before I can ask her about it, the rest of the people from the lobby enter, and a short, lithe woman walks to the front of the class. She has long hair that's somewhere between brown and blond tied up in a topknot. Her eyes are kind, and her wide mouth curves into an easy smile. She looks about my age, albeit quite a bit fitter. Her steps are sure as she walks barefoot across the polished wood floor. She starts some gentle music and lights a couple of candles before welcoming us. When my heartbeat starts to increase, I take a deep breath and try to calm myself down.

This is a vacation. Me time. I should just enjoy it.

So, for the next sixty sweaty minutes, I try. I stare at the half-naked twenty-somethings in sports bras and tiny spandex shorts contorting their bodies, and I do my best not to fall flat on my face. Simone lets out a few choice grunts, and I grin at her right before a fart falls out of my behind. Oops.

Not so easy doing yoga after a two-year hiatus, apparently.

She scowls in response, and I fight a giggle. Then, the teacher says my favorite word: savasana. Dead man's pose. Also known as my favorite yoga pose, because I get to just lie on my back and fall asleep.

When the teacher ends the class, I open my eyes and let out a sigh. The creaks and stiffness plaguing my bike ride into town have melted away, and I have to hand it to Simone—I do feel better. Doing yoga after so many months off feels like meeting an old friend.

Jen already has her mat rolled up by the time I heave myself to my feet. The teacher appears near my yoga mat, smiling. "You're new."

It's not a question, but I answer anyway. "Yeah. We just got here yesterday."

"Victims of the geyser, I heard."

"Word gets around." I glance at Simone, who smiles.

"Heart's Cove is a small town," the teacher says as she extends a hand. "I'm Candice." She glances at Jen, who has her towel and mat tucked under her arm. "You're leaving already?"

"Work. Got to get to the restaurant to prep, but I'll be back to go over the café menu for the festival."

"Thanks, Jen." Candice smiles, then turns to me and Simone. "Jen works at the Michelin-starred restaurant in the next town over. She's a pastry chef." She turns back to Jen. "Will you come by tonight to help with the painting?"

"Only if you promise to let me tape off the edges. I've seen what you consider a straight line." Jen arches a brow, waves to Simone and me, then walks toward the exit.

Candice grins after the woman, shaking her head. "She's been my friend since we were six years old, but I still think she's a huge weirdo. But I guess her precision is what makes her good at baking."

Jen pauses at the door, turning around to stick her tongue out at Candice.

The yoga teacher just laughs.

Another knot of tension unwinds between my shoulder blades as a smile works itself over my lips. I exchange a glance with Simone, and I feel...comfortable. It's impossible not to, when everyone is this friendly. I've almost forgotten about my conversation with Grant from last night. He's a lawyer, sure, but he's not like other lawyers I've met. He's not like John. No one here is.

As if I summoned him myself, I walk out into the lobby and see him leaning against the reception desk. A squeak escapes my lips as my already-red face turns even brighter.

Why does the man always have to look so good? He's wearing paint-splattered jeans that cling to his strong thighs and a navy button-down shirt with the sleeves rolled up. Thick, corded muscle wraps around his forearms. Yum.

Grant doesn't seem to notice my partial breakdown at seeing him. His face cracks into a smile and my middle goes gooey. That's not good. I'm supposed to feel nothing for him. He's supposed to be a distraction I don't need.

"Fiona," he says, as if he's been waiting to see me all day. With sunlight streaming in, his eyes look more blue than grey today. "How was your yoga class?"

"Great," I croak, then clear my throat. "It was really good." I glance over my shoulder at Simone, who's all of a sudden very, very interested in the wall of cubby holes. "Do you do yoga?" I arch my brows, wondering what other interests Grant is into besides nude modeling. Clearly, he's a renaissance man. Definitely nothing like John.

He shakes his head. "Nah, just here for a job."

Candice walks up beside me and wraps her arms around Grant. "You're here! Thank you for coming."

I freeze, eyes widening, a stab of something piercing my gut. It feels a lot like jealousy, which makes me feel silly. I've known the man twenty-four hours and I can claim nothing over him. I have no right to feel jealous.

Plus, I knew he was too good to be true. He's probably the town player as well as being a certified Heart's Cove Hottie. Didn't Dorothy say something about one-night stands? Probably has a thing with all the women in town between twenty and fifty years old. I'd be another notch in his bedpost, no doubt. Better off staying away from him.

If I keep reminding myself of it, I'll follow my own advice, right?

I avert my gaze, not missing the glance Grant throws my way. I don't understand what I see in his eyes. Regret? Worry?

He gives Candice a quick hug and extricates himself from her arms, combing his hand through his thick, dark hair.

My eyes crawl back to him and linger on his chest, on the slabs of muscle straining against the fabric of his shirt. I shouldn't be attracted to him. I'm staying at his house, and doing anything with him would be...messy. Not to mention it's too soon. Sure, it's been fifteen months since the divorce started, and three months since the ink on the papers dried, but still. I'm not ready.

Right?

"Is there anywhere to get a good cappuccino around here?" I ask, finally lifting my eyes back to Grant's. He's taken a step to the side to put some space between him and Candice, but she hasn't seemed to notice. Another student has come up to her, and she's in the middle of giving them a hug, too.

Maybe she's just a hugger. My shoulders drop a bit at the thought and I release a breath.

Grant rubs the back of his neck. "Not really. Candice is going to set up a coffee shop in the old restaurant on the first floor this summer, but the permanent café in town closed down about six months ago."

"What happened?"

"The owners died. First Mrs. Byron of cancer, then Mr. Byron a month later. I think he just couldn't face life without his wife," Candice finishes, shaking her head sadly.

"That's so sad."

Candice lets out a sigh, shrugging. "We've been trying to get Wesley to open the café back up, but he's struggled since his parents passed. Just stays in that log cabin near your place"—her eyes flick to Grant—"and comes into town for groceries and beer."

"Did you say Wesley?" Simone pipes up from behind me.

"Yeah. Lives a few miles from me. Grumpy bastard," Grant replies.

"Oh hush," Candice says. "The man is mourning. Give him a break."

"He was grumpy before his parents died, too."

Candice grins, and I glance at my best friend. Simone's cheeks flush, and I give her a questioning glance. She waves it away.

"Tell you what," Candice says with a smile climbing across her face. "We're about to give the studio a mini-renovation before the Fringe Festival. If you and Simone stick around to help, I could whip some coffees up downstairs and make everyone some breakfast? There's a George Foreman grill, and I make a mean breakfast sandwich."

Grant looks at me, eyebrows arched. "I could use the help.

Need to install new cubbies and give the whole place a fresh coat of paint. Then do the same downstairs."

"We'd love to," Simone says, hooking her arm around my shoulders. There's a gleam in her eye I don't like, and she smiles from ear to ear. "We're free until two o'clock this afternoon," she adds, swiveling her head to wiggle her eyebrows at me. She looks at Grant again. "You wouldn't happen to be modeling again today, would you?"

He laughs, shaking his head. "Nope. Just once every couple of months."

"Guess we were just lucky on our first day," I say without thinking, then my face turns hot and red again.

Candice appears with a stack of pink fabric, dropping it on the reception desk. Glittery writing adorns a stack of shirts. *Heart's Cove Hottie.* She jerks her thumb at the clothing, smiling. "You can wear those to save your clothes from getting wrecked. I'll go make coffees and food."

I walk up to the shirts, unfolding one of them and glancing at Grant. Standing close, I can smell his rich, manly scent, the same scent that lingers in his home. Citrus and sawdust. My head spins. I tear my gaze away from his eyes and look at the shirt in my hands. "What's the deal with these shirts, anyway?"

"Dorothy meant to order a hundred of them, but she accidentally ordered a hundred boxes." Grant's lips curl into a grin that makes my knees weak. This would be a lot easier if he wasn't so gorgeous.

"Don't tell Marge," Candice calls from the stairwell. "She doesn't know."

"They're hidden in the yoga studio attic." Grant chuckles. "So, help yourself. Call it a souvenir."

I pull on one of the shirts and watch as Simone does the same, then let my gaze drift back to Grant. He's leaning over a toolbox, a strip of skin exposed at the small of his back. My fingers itch to run across it, and I ball my hands into fists to stop myself. My nails bite into my palms, and I close my eyes to regain control over myself.

It's too hot in here. Too stuffy. There's altogether too much sexy male skin for me to think straight.

When I open my eyes, Grant is looking at me funny. The little patches of silver gleam on his temples, and he runs his hand through his hair again. My eyes drop to the skin at his hips that reveals itself when he lifts his arm. My throat is tight.

Simone claps me on the shoulder, making me jump. I'd forgotten she was here. "Should we get to work?" She turns to Grant. "Where do you want us, boss?"

# EIGHT
# GRANT

I'VE SPENT the whole day convincing myself that this attraction will pass, and done everything in my power to stop thinking about Fiona, but whenever I'm in the same room as her my whole body seems to react to her presence.

When she turns her back to swap her sweat-soaked tank top for one of the pastel pink work shirts, my eyes linger on the bare skin of her back. My gaze drops down to her shapely ass, and all I want to do is pull her into me and press her back to my front.

My pants are very tight all of a sudden.

This is...not good.

I've been attracted to women before, but Fiona makes me want something else. She makes me want to take care of her, protect her.

After what happened with my ex, I know that's a dangerous road to go down. I can't protect or help anyone unless they want it.

"What's the festival Candice mentioned?" Fiona asks, her voice delicate and musical and apparently directly attached to my cock, judging by the twitching currently happening between my legs.

I shift my pants, glancing over my shoulder at Fiona. "The Fringe Festival. It's happening in three weeks, during the first week of June."

"Shame we'll miss it," Simone says, arching her brows.

I instruct the ladies to start moving things from the desk, as we need to move it all to prep for painting. Instead of helping them, I move to the wall of cubby holes and start taking them apart. I need space. Distance between Fiona and me. A bit of air so I can take a full breath.

When Candice returns with a tray full of coffees and sandwiches, Fiona lets out a little moan that makes my cock stand at attention (again). I grit my teeth, adjust myself (again), and accept a hot coffee from Candice with a nod.

"Candice, I couldn't help but notice your filing system when I was moving things out of the desk," Fiona says, sipping her coffee. She lets out another one of those moans, and I take my hammer to a shelf with a bit too much force. The particle board shelf explodes, bits of wood raining down on me.

After a pause, during which I don't dare turn to look at the three women on the other side of the room, Candice speaks. "My *lack* of filing system, you mean?"

Fiona laughs, causing my core to tighten. Another shelf goes flying.

"Have you ever considered going digital?"

Candice laughs. "Considered it? Yeah, of course. But actually following through is difficult when you're technology-challenged like me. Combined with managing everything to open this café, doing up the yoga studio, taking care of my daughter... updating filing systems is at the very bottom of the list."

"Fi is a whiz," Simone says. "She's an organization queen who ran every major fundraiser for her community club from galas to silent auctions. She could help you with all that, no problem. Could probably manage the café if you're overwhelmed."

I glance over my shoulder in time to see a sexy little flush creep over Fiona's cheeks.

Candice sips her coffee, then tilts her head. "Yeah?"

"I'm not that good," Fiona says, shaking her head.

"Oh, come on, Fi. You started the yearly Christmas Gala at the club and made more money for those people than they do at their day jobs. Remember the silent auction? You somehow wrangled courtside seats to the Lakers' game in less than twenty-four hours. You *are* that good." Simone turns to Candice. "She could help you, and she'd love to do it."

Candice's eyebrows shoot up.

I listen, taking my hammer to another section of the shelving. If Fiona were to stay in Heart's Cove longer than planned...

*No*. I'm not interested. Can't be interested.

"Would you be willing to help?" Candice asks. "I'm not sure I can manage the actual running of the café while the festival is going on, especially with the yoga classes being fully booked. I've finished all the applications and permits to open the café, but I need help. As you can tell by the state of my files."

"We'd only planned on staying here two weeks..." Fiona

nibbles at her bottom lip, and the heat winding through my core grows hotter.

"...but we have no real commitments," Simone finishes. "You should stay."

"What would you want me to do?" Fiona asks.

"Well, if you could take over the café project downstairs, it would free me up to do everything yoga-related. The Fringe Fest is only one week long, so you wouldn't even have to commit to staying much longer at all. We've had more bookings than ever this year, and I'm rushing to get everything ready. Having someone manage things at the coffee shop would be a huge help."

"Fi can do that," Simone says.

Fiona huffs. "Well, I've never done restaurant management before. I don't know..."

"Look, there's no real coffee shop in town. My plan was to have a bit of a hub here. You know, people do yoga first thing in the morning, then head downstairs for a coffee and smoothie. It sounds great in my head, but execution is about a million times more difficult than I expected. We have three weeks to get everything organized, which is tight, but it should be doable. I'll pay you. Maybe not as much as you're used to in the city, but enough to cover your expenses here. We could draw up employment contracts this afternoon." Glancing over my shoulder, I see Candice smile, hopeful.

My heart starts to thump. I've been telling myself to keep my distance from Fiona because I know she's leaving, and I don't want to get involved with anyone—especially not when my body reacts the way it does to Fiona. Too complicated. Too much emotion.

But if she were to stay...

She'd be here until the end of the Fringe Fest, at least. That's four weeks away. A lot can happen in four weeks.

Looking over my shoulder, I see Fiona exchange a glance with her friend.

"You should stay," Simone says. "Weren't you saying you needed a job? Looks like one just fell in your lap."

"But what about..." Fiona glances over at me. I turn my head toward their conversation, my hammer hovering over another shelf. She clears her throat. "I'll need to find somewhere to stay."

"You're welcome to stay at my place as long as you need," I say, turning to face them fully. *Oops*. I hadn't meant to say that.

Fiona's cheeks flush again. She shakes her head. "I can't accept that."

"I insist." *Double oops*. The words just keep falling out of my mouth before I can stop myself.

"She'll pay rent," Simone pipes in, a strange glimmer in her eyes. "Won't you, Fi?"

"Look—absolutely not." She shakes her head, then darts her gaze to me. "Not about the rent. Of course I'd pay rent. But I won't stay at Grant's house."

"Do I smell that bad?"

Fiona's lips quirk, but she shakes her head. "You've been kind enough to us already. I'll find somewhere else. I'm sure the hotel will be fixed up in a couple of weeks."

Disappointment gurgles in my stomach, and I turn back to

the cubby holes. I make quick work of the rest of them as the ladies start moving furniture. It doesn't take long with the extra hands to help. When Candice and Simone move some of the files downstairs, I close the distance between Fiona and me.

"You can stay at my place, Fiona," I say, ducking my head to meet her eyes.

She bites her lip, and my body reacts just as it did before. I'm surprised the zipper on my jeans is still holding strong. "It's too much, Grant. You've been so kind already."

"It's nothing." A desperate kind of feeling winds its way through my chest. "I promise to say nothing in order to maintain my peak hotness status."

Fiona laughs, the sound easing something in my chest I hadn't realized was knotted. She reaches over and puts her hand on my bicep, and a jolt of heat travels straight to my core. She squeezes gently, warmth permeating from her touch. "I'll think about it."

I watch as she picks up a box full of old yoga blocks and follows the other women downstairs, the space too quiet and too empty without her in it.

Just like my house felt after she left in the morning. Just like the porch felt after she went to bed last night. Her absence just highlights how alone I've been.

I rake my fingers through my hair. This is bad. Somehow this woman has gotten under my skin, and now I'm falling over myself to offer her a place to stay. Releasing a long breath, I shake my head. This isn't me. I operate by myself. I take odd jobs and live quietly by myself on the edge of town. I come and go as I please, and I don't invite people into my life.

Especially not women.

"So it's settled, then!" Candice says, bursting through the door into the yoga studio, followed by Fiona and Simone. She wraps Fiona in a tight hug. "This is the best thing that's happened all year! I might actually be able to get everything done." She flashes a smile at me, noticing me watching. "Fiona and Simone are staying!"

"Actually, I have responsibilities to get back to," Simone says, lifting a finger in the air. "Fiona will stay on her own. She needs some alone time, anyway."

Fiona's eyes climb up to mine as she nibbles on her bottom lip. She lets out a sigh, then shrugs. "Might need to stay at your place, after all."

"The only thing wrong with this town is the lack of a good coffee shop," Simone says, reaching for her cup and draining the last of the coffee in it. "Everything else is"—she brings her fingers to her lips and kisses them—"chef's kiss. The people, the scenery, the activities, the men..." She glances at me, winking.

"Simone!" Fiona laughs, a flush rising up her neck. My eyes trace her lips, pinched in mock outrage.

"This is exactly what you need, girl. Now we just need to find you someone to date so you can get over Voldemort, and you'll be all set for a new chapter of your life."

"Voldemort?" Candice asks, dragging the desk across to the corner of the room.

"Her ex-husband."

Candice nods. "Ah. I never had one of those. I was one of the lucky ones."

"Was?" Fiona asks, tilting her head.

Candice looks down at her hand, fiddling with her wedding band. "Paul died a year ago."

"I'm sorry," Fiona says. Simone reaches over to squeeze her hand.

These women are so...easy with each other. Seeing them offer each other support—when they're virtual strangers—makes me feel like an outsider. Maybe I've been wrong to isolate myself, to push everyone away. Maybe being alone isn't the best way to keep my heart and mind safe. Fiona and Simone barely know Candice, but somehow the three of them are able to talk about trauma they've been through.

Me? I bury it all down inside me, thinking it'll help if I ignore it. I don't talk about what Sylvie did to me. What actually caused my heart attack and my subsequent move to Heart's Cove. Maybe because if I talk about what she did, I'll have to face what I did, too. How I caused her to walk away from me without a word. The things I did to push her away without even realizing it.

The destroyed shelving smells like musty particle board as I pick it up, hauling it into a bag to avoid getting splinters. I carry it downstairs to the dumpster I'd organized for the studio renovation. Once outside, I take a deep breath and lean against the green metal.

A hand appears on my shoulder, followed by the sweet scent I'm already addicted to. Fiona looks up at me, eyebrows drawn together. "I promise I'll find somewhere else to stay," she says. "I won't impose on you."

Her words make my chest ache. I shake my head. "Stay as long as you want, Fiona."

Fiona's lips curl into a smile as she looks at me through her lashes. "Simone was right, you know. All this town needs is a nice coffee shop. Maybe this is the start of something good."

As we stand in the mid-morning sun, with the rays making Fiona's dark hair gleam with reddish strands, I have to hold myself back from leaning down and kissing her. Every fiber of my body wants to wrap myself around her and crush her to me. I want to run my hands over her curves and tear the sadness away from her eyes. I want to show her how a real man can treat her. How she deserves to be treated.

But we just stand there, a foot apart, staring into each other's eyes. The words won't come. My walls are too thick.

Fiona might stay for another four to six weeks. She'll hang around, but after that? She won't stay. No one does.

# NINE
# FIONA

BEFORE HEADING to the kitchen for my nightly cup of tea, I slip on my old black one-piece swimsuit with the saggy butt and throw a towel over my shoulder. Grant said something about a pier, and after a day spent doing yoga, renovating, and expanding my mind with art and meditation, I need a dip in the ocean.

The pier isn't visible from the house, hidden on the other side of a small knoll. Trees line the path, but they open up to a small, private beach. It's...perfect. It's like he pulled this property from my mind and created my dream house before he even met me.

And there in the water, as if he needed a dip in the ocean as badly as I did today, is Grant. He's swimming around a far buoy and heading back toward the pier, his powerful body slicing through the waves with ease.

Waves lap the shore as I step onto the pier, my flip-flops

slapping on the wood. I take a deep breath of salty sea air, walking all the way down to the end before depositing my towel on the pier and kicking my sandals off.

Grant approaches and finally looks up, pulling his goggles off to rest on his forehead. "Hey," he says, huffing.

"You mind if I join you?"

He treads water with ease, his powerful shoulders slick with water. He jerks his head as if to say, *Come on in.*

So, without hesitation, I jump.

It's chilly. Refreshing. I kick off the sandy bottom and break the surface, smiling wide. I laugh, spinning around to face Grant.

His eyes soften as he watches me, then he points to the buoy. "I was going to do another lap. Care to join?"

"Race you!" I take off, knowing I won't win. The man is a foot taller than me and made of pure muscle—but I still swim like hell.

I may not be a cycling fanatic, but I do like swimming. Glancing up periodically, I swim freestyle to the buoy, getting there a second before Grant. Laughing, I tilt my head. "You better not have let me win. I don't do well with being coddled."

"Never," he says, huffing. "Although that was my fourth lap, so it wasn't exactly fair."

"Fair shmair. You're a grown man with a swimmer's body."

Grinning, he says nothing as he dunks his head back in and takes off toward the pier again. I yelp, laughing, and swim like hell to catch up. When he slaps the pier with a broad palm, his smile says it all. "How's that for fair?"

All I can do is grin, my breath coming hard and fast. "It's a tie, then."

I don't remember the last time I raced someone like this. The last time I just had *fun*. It seems like the past decade of my life has been spent always trying so hard to be an adult. Going to functions and making small talk with people I'm supposed to impress.

The energy buzzing inside me bubbles up as I put a hand on the pier, letting my feet kick gently to keep me afloat. My lips tug into a smile, and I let out a happy sigh. "Thanks again, Grant."

"For what?"

"For inviting me. For letting me stay at your place. For having the perfect home and making me feel welcome."

He shakes his head. "No problem." In one swift movement, Grant pulls himself out of the water. The pier is high enough to be level with the top of my head, and Grant just lifts himself out without trying. From the water, I watch him stand tall and run his palms over his wet hair, sunlight glinting off the rivulets running down his body. He shakes his head as droplets go flying, his hands smoothing down his hard chest and abs to swipe off most of the water.

All thoughts float out of my head as I watch the show. His muscles flex and contract as he readjusts the waistband of his swimming trunks, and my mouth goes dry.

A boat roars in the distance, and I barely hear it. All my attention is on that gorgeous male body.

I only realize my jaw is hanging when a wave hits my face and salt water fills my mouth. Spluttering, I let go of the pier and splash around a bit, mostly out of surprise. My hands flail, trying to grab the pier again, but all I get is air. Another wave smashes into me—the wake from that damn boat.

Then a splash, and a warm body presses up against mine. Grant's arm wraps around my back as he sears his chest to mine, then slides his hand down to my butt and launches me out of the water.

I land on the edge of the pier with a graceless *oomph*, and kick/pull/let Grant shove his hand on my butt to get myself all the way up. Rolling over, I see Grant pull himself out of the water once more and kneel beside me, a hand on my cheek.

"You okay?"

"Fine," I say, face heated. "I'm fine." I prop myself up on my elbows, shaking my head. "If you didn't look so good without a shirt on, I'd have been ready for that wave."

Grant doesn't seem to hear me. He glances after the boat, frowning, then shifts his gaze to the pier. "I've been meaning to install a ladder for a year and a half, but no one uses the pier except me."

"It's fine, really." I roll over onto my stomach before getting on all fours, and finally standing up. *Smooth, Fiona. Real smooth.* I wrap my towel around myself and slip my sandals on, only to find Grant staring at me. "Tea time?" I ask hopefully, if only to get his intense gaze off my face.

Grant nods, waving a hand. He pauses by the outdoor shower. It's nothing more than a spigot raised up high with a leaning, three-walled shack surrounding it, and as I walk by, I catch a glimpse of his ass as he tugs his swimming trunks down.

My cheeks are so hot they might catch fire. I turn away until

I hear the water turn off and Grant's footsteps bring him beside me, my eyes darting down to the towel he's holding over his hips, a wet swimsuit balled up in his other hand.

Sweet mother of shirtless hunks, he's wearing nothing but a towel.

My steps are jerky as we head to the house, and I mumble something about a shower before running upstairs. When I finally cool off, get myself together, get dressed, and head back downstairs, he's already got the tea prepped and waiting.

I'm in heaven.

We have a quiet mug on the porch as we watch the sunset, neither of us mentioning anything about our swim.

THE NEXT DAY, after more yoga, meditation, and quality time with Simone, I find myself at the pier again before dinner. A smile teases over my lips when I see a brand-new galvanized metal ladder hanging off the side of the pier, fresh screws and pieces of wood bracing it to the structure.

*He did this for me.* The thought jumps through my mind as my stomach tightens. John *never* did things like that for me. He rarely considered my safety or my hobbies or...anything, really. He just worked all the time and dragged me along to stuffy events that I never truly enjoyed.

I swim alone, doing two laps to the buoy and back, then use the new ladder to pull myself out, smiling the whole time.

"You like it?" Grant calls out from the top of the hill, shading his eyes from the setting sun.

"It's perfect."

"Any chance for another race, or are you worried it won't be fair this time?" His grin widens as he approaches, broad body coiled with power and grace. We meet at the start of the pier, him on the sand and me on the timber.

My stomach clenches, thighs squeezing together. Whenever he's close, it's like air becomes harder to breathe. He's shirtless—again—his chest practically begging for me to trace my fingertips over it. I ball my hands into fists and shake my head. "I have dinner with Simone in town. Maybe tomorrow."

Grant's gaze flicks to my lips, then back to my eyes. I can't read the expression on his face, but I see the heat in his blue-grey irises. We stand a foot apart for a few long moments, and I wonder what would happen if I closed the distance. What would happen if I uncurled my fists and gave in to the temptation to touch him?

*No.* It's too soon. I can't find myself if I'm busy exploring someone else.

A noise to my left makes me jump. At the edge of the trees, a bush overhanging the beach rustles violently. Branches sway, and a large crack sounds, as if a huge animal is about to leap out.

Grant takes a step toward me, his hand curling around my side as he nudges me behind his back. His body stills, tension coursing through every hard muscle.

I stare at his back, my face an inch away from all that glorious flesh. Would he notice if I licked it?

Grant's eyes scan the trees, his hand sliding down my waist as he widens his stance. His touch is warm on my waist, steady. Every line of his body is ready to attack. To...protect. Heat licks the inside of my belly as I stand there, so close to the most beautiful man I've ever seen, knowing he'd do anything to keep me safe right now.

Heart thumping, I glance around his broad shoulder at the rustling trees.

A chipmunk jumps out and leaps onto a tree trunk, disappearing into the foliage.

Tension melts off Grant's body as he steps away and turns to glance at me, unimpressed.

I slap my hand over my mouth and laugh. Grant's lips twitch, but he just shakes his head. Before I can stop myself, I reach up and pat his chest. Warm and solid, just like I expected. My cheeks burn, but I manage to keep my voice casual, teasing. "At least you were ready for action."

"I was expecting a mountain lion, or at the very least a raccoon. Could have been rabid." He scowls at the trees.

"Nope. Just Alvin." Still giggling, I step around Grant and start walking up the hill, if only so I can breathe again. Being that close to him...it's a lot. He's all power and sex and pheromones, and I'm just me. I need a minute to compose myself.

"Same time tomorrow?" he asks. "Race ya."

I look over my shoulder and grin. "Wouldn't miss it."

When I finally get upstairs and lock myself in the bathroom for a shower, I bite my lip and close my eyes and let my hand slip between my legs. Sleeping with him would be a bad idea, especially if I'm staying in town. I know I need to focus on me before I can give anything to someone else, but that doesn't mean I can't let my imagination run wild, right?

# TEN
# FIONA

IN LESS THAN A WEEK, I've met a man who makes my body light up like a Christmas tree with nothing more than a look, I've moved into my dream home, and I've gotten a job I can't wait to start. Not to mention I've met half a dozen locals that feel more like friends than any of the people in L.A. that I've known for years.

Basically, I'm dreaming. This isn't real life.

Simone chatters while we make our way to the hotel for a pottery class, and I mostly try to keep myself upright. My thoughts drift back to Grant. Always to Grant.

When we're in the hotel lobby, I spy Dorothy behind the desk, wearing big gold hoop earrings and a kind of flowy boho skirt with a peasant top.

She smiles broadly at the two of us. "Fiona! I hear you'll be staying longer than anticipated. We've heard from the contractors, and your room will be fixed up in four weeks, so if you can bear to stay with Grant for that long, you'll have a place reserved here."

Simone smiles, hooking her arm into mine. "I love this town."

Margaret comes around the corner, wearing a well-tailored pantsuit and her usual string of pearls. Her white hair is twisted into a neat bun at the nape of her neck. She greets us like a gracious host as I lean against the reception desk. "Didn't take you long to settle in," Margaret says with a kind smile.

I shrug. "You all made it easy, although I'm a little nervous about managing the café. I don't exactly have experience with that kind of work, and it feels like it's a bit too late to be starting over so drastically."

Margaret waves a hand to dismiss my fears. "Dorothy and I bought the hotel when we turned fifty. It's been over twenty years now, and they've been the best years of my life. It's never too late."

"What make you want to buy the hotel?"

"An ad in the paper." Dorothy laughs. "We saw a story about the hotel being up for sale, and both had fond memories of being here when we were young. Marge's husband had just passed, poor dear, and I've always been a proud spinster. Somehow I convinced her to give it a try."

"You caught me when I was desperate," Marge grumbles, but there's a hint of a smile on her face.

I shift my gaze to her sister. "Can I ask you something, Dorothy?"

"Shoot."

"What did Agnes do to you?" I ask. "Why the feud?"

Margaret freezes, letting her eyes dart to her sister.

Dorothy's eyebrows draw together. "What did she do to me?" she huffs, then starts repeating the question while she emphasizes different words, as if that clarifies anything. "What did she *do* to me? What did *she* do to *me*? *What* did—"

"You peed in her raspberry bushes, Dorothy," Margaret says as she straightens up a stack of papers on the desk. "You can hardly claim complete innocence."

"First of all," Dorothy says as she raises a finger, "urine is a great fertilizer, and did she or did she not get more berries that year than any previous harvest?" She levels a stare at her sister, who keeps tidying up the desk. "Second of all, she started it! She ran William out of town with her cruelty even though she *knew* we had a thing going on. I think she was jealous that I had a man-friend."

"Then you gave her bookstore a one-star review and called her a vindictive hag," Margaret continues as if her sister said nothing.

"It's not slander if it's true. She told people who came into the bookstore that we had bedbugs!"

"Sorry I asked," I mumble, glancing at Simone. My best friend is red in the face from trying not to laugh.

"Me too," Margaret answers. "You enjoy your pottery class, ladies. Say hi to Grant for me."

AFTER AN HOUR SPENT MAKING a misshapen bowl, Simone hooks her arm through mine as we walk outside, our butt-bruising devices—I mean, bicycles—waiting just where we left them. "This is turning out better than I could have expected," she sighs. "I wish I didn't have to leave."

"Are you sure it's a good idea for me to stay?" I ask, standing beside my bicycle. I squeeze the brakes just to do something with my hands, chewing my lip. "Maybe I should go back to L.A. with you. I don't even know Candice, and I'm supposed to work with her for the next month? I'm taking over a half-baked plan for a café and have to somehow get it running in three weeks, then manage it all through the Fringe Fest? It's the biggest event of the year in Heart's Cove. Everyone says so."

"First of all, you could run a coffee shop in your sleep. Remember when you planned the two-week golf tournament a few years ago? You had to organize all the caterers, the tee times, run the pro shop, sort out the sponsors—a single café will be a breeze."

"Right, but..."

"No buts." Simone nudges the kickstand on her bike, beaming at me.

"You seem to have a lot of confidence in me."

"Only as much as you should have for yourself." She swings her leg over her bike, then stares at me expectantly. "What?"

I shift my weight from one foot to the other. "It's just...I'm not sure I should stay with Grant."

Her brows inch up. "Why not? Cheap accommodation with the town hottie doesn't sound so bad to me."

"He told me he used to be a lawyer before he moved here."

Simone nods slowly, her gaze dull, waiting. "And that precludes you from staying with him because..."

"Well, don't you think it's a bit... *intimate*? Us alone out there on that beautiful property...the ocean...the sunsets... *alone*," I repeat.

"I'm still struggling to find the problem." Simone cracks a grin, shaking her head. "Loosen up, Fi. This is a new beginning. If you're not ready to bang the hottie, don't bang the hottie. But if I were you—"

"You're not."

"I would climb him like a tree. Ride him like a bike. Bang him like a drum. Lick him like a lollipop."

"Did you come up with these lines ahead of time, or...?"

"Paddle him like a canoe."

That one makes me laugh. I open my mouth to tell her I'm not ready, but that feeling is there, just under my skin. Pressure building inside me, needing release. Not necessarily sexual release, but just... I just need to be let *out*. Set free. *Do* something with my life that isn't cowering from my ex-husband or feeling like I'm watching my life pass me by.

Simone grins, jerking her head toward the road. "Come on. We have another week or so together, and I can chaperone for you while you're at that beautiful, romantic seaside property. After that, you're on your own, girl."

"Don't remind me," I grouse, then hop on my bike with a wince as my sore butt hits the seat. We pedal home in the fresh night air, and a part of me doesn't feel like this is a bad idea at all.

I can stay with Grant until the hotel has a room for me. I'll be busy with Candice and Jen, and Grant will probably be busy, too. We can stay out of each other's way, and I might actually have a purpose for a while.

Simone's right. I'm *good* at these things—organizing, managing, directing. Excitement curls in the pit of my stomach at the thought of having a project of my own. It's not John's golf club, or his friend's fundraiser, or his firm's gala.

It's *mine*. This café will be open for the Fringe Festival, and it'll be nothing like the swanky, stuffy affairs I used to plan before.

Despite the fact that I'm not sure about staying with Grant—not sure about my ability to resist my attraction to him—I still can't help the feeling of starting something big. My entire marriage was built on putting myself second. On making sure John was fed and happy. On propping up his career first before I thought about my own—then deciding that my need for a career wasn't important at all.

But he's not here.

There's a coffee shop begging to be opened, and a yoga studio on top of it in need of some new paperwork organization. I have the skills to help with both. I *can* do both, and I can do a good job. I can listen to Dorothy complain about Agnes, and I can make breakfast in my dream kitchen. I can steal glances at Grant wherever he is, and I can inhale fresh, salty air right off the ocean.

I can *live*. If only for a few weeks. And if I decide to stay longer—if Candice wants me to—then I will.

I don't need to paddle anyone like a canoe to be happy. I don't need a man to support me. I can live my life and be independent and rely on no one but myself. And if things progress with Grant, well, who knows? Maybe I can find physical intimacy, even if I'm not ready for anything more.

And after Simone leaves, I can stay here. For the first time in a long time, that thought doesn't scare me. I *can* do this on my own. I can do anything.

What's the worst that can happen? If things don't work out, I'll drive back down to L.A. in a month and leave it all behind. Easy.

# ELEVEN
# SIMONE

DAYS BLEED INTO EACH OTHER. It's nice spending time with Fiona, seeing her come into her own. After she agrees to manage Candice's café for the Fringe Fest, I see a spark in her eyes that hasn't been there in many, many years. I want to pat myself on the back for dragging her on this holiday, even though she fought me the whole way.

We've already been in Heart's Cove ten days, and despite my money stress, I have to admit I feel more relaxed. Even I don't want to leave, but I know I need to get back to reality, and mortgages, and bills...

Texts from ex-husbands.

My phone buzzed again this morning—apparently El Bastardo didn't get the message when I didn't answer his first attempt. This time, his text message sounded suspiciously like begging. *Please,* he wrote. *I want to meet up with you. Let me take you out to dinner.*

Maybe spending all this time next to a hot-blooded man who looks like Grant is scrambling my brain, because I'm actually considering it. Weak, weak woman. Nothing good can come of meeting up with my ex, but it's getting harder to ignore his messages.

In the evening of our tenth day, I leave Fiona in her favorite place of the house—that gorgeous kitchen—and take a walk down to the beach. Grant's property extends all the way to the ocean, with a little pier jutting out from his private beach. I walk along the shore, taking my shoes off to sink my toes in the sand, then putting them back on to climb over some rocks to continue my walk.

Evening walks have become my routine, and more than any of the art classes or meditation sessions, I think they've helped me clear the rubble from my mind. In three days, I'll go back to L.A. and put my house up for sale. I'll rent a place and get a more reliable car with the money I make from the sale, and work on getting my freelance business back to a livable wage. I haven't been putting enough time into looking for new clients, but if I have more of a financial cushion, I'll be able to do it. I'm scrappy, resourceful, and a badass woman who can do whatever she wants.

Seagulls squawk above my head as waves lap on the coast, and I find myself walking in a familiar direction. Maybe part of my evening walks have been motivated by a certain grumpy beast of a man—the thrill of thinking he was going to throw an axe at my head probably appealed to all the broken, masochistic parts of me—but in the ten days we've been here, I haven't seen a hint of Wesley.

Until today.

I round a curve on the coast and see him, knee-deep in the surf, tying an old skiff to his own pier. The fabric of his shirt stretches over his broad shoulders. His body makes me wonder what he did for work before he came back here. Muscles like that are honed over years.

He lifts his eyes when I come closer, his lips pinching in displeasure.

"Nice to see you, too," I call out, planting my hands on my hips.

The sunlight glints gold off his hair as he straightens, the bottom of his t-shirt clinging to those carved muscles I may or may not have dreamed about once or twice since I first saw them. At least he's wearing a shirt today. Makes it easier to think straight.

"You lost again?" Wesley grunts, tying his little boat off to the dock.

"At least you weren't faking your grumpiness last time we met." I take a step onto the pier. "Straight shooter. What you see is what you get." I point finger guns in his direction, because I'm a total dweeb. Somehow, I've walked all the way to the pier without noticing. Traitorous feet.

He grumbles something I don't hear, then heaves himself up onto the wooden slats. I'd forgotten how tall he is, how he towers over me. Green eyes look almost black as they stare at me, making my gut tighten in a way I don't hate. "Is there a reason you're here?"

"Not really. Thought I'd get my daily dose of asshole to remind myself what's waiting for me back in L.A."

A huff escapes his nostrils, and I think I see his lips curve up. Is that a hint of a dimple? Oh Lordy, if this man has dimples, I might as well lie down and die right now. His ghost of a smile is gone in an instant, though, and I let my eyes drift out to the horizon.

"I heard about your parents," I finally say as I watch Wesley secure everything in the boat and haul a bag over his shoulder. "I'm sorry."

"Not your fault."

"Fiona—my friend—she's opening a café in town in time for the Fringe Festival with Candice. Candice mentioned she has the permit for the year, so I'm not sure if they'll close the café after the festival." My shoe scuffs on the worn, grey wood of the pier.

His eyes dart to mine. A grunt is the only reply I get.

"Your parents owned the old café, didn't they? Everyone talks about how wonderful they were."

Another grunt.

"Anyway, I just thought you'd want to know."

"Why would I care if someone opens a café?"

My heart squeezes, heat splattering over my cheeks. Shrugging, I let out a sigh. "I would've wanted to know if I were in your shoes," I say. "She says it's only temporary, helping out for the Fringe Fest, but... I don't know. I think she might like to stay. She seems happier here."

"Good for her."

Throwing him one last glance, I turn away.

I'm almost around the bend when I hear Wesley call out. He's near the tree line, half-turned toward me, as if all he wanted was to walk away but forced himself to stop. His eyes are dark, steady on mine. "Thanks, Simone. For telling me." With a sharp nod, quiet steps carry him into the shelter of the trees.

I stand there for a few heartbeats. Waiting for what, I'm not sure.

One thing strikes me, though—he remembered my name. I don't want to admit how it felt to hear him say it in that gruff, deep voice of his. Best not to let my thoughts linger on that too long.

I go back the way I came, sticking to the coastline so I don't get lost, and I make my way up to the big, beautiful farmhouse with light spilling from its windows. I find my best friend smiling in the kitchen—*smiling*—and accept her offer of wine.

A part of me wishes I weren't leaving.

I leave my text messages unanswered.

# TWELVE
# FIONA

ON SIMONE'S last day in town, I wake up to the sound of a lawnmower and stumble downstairs to find Simone in the kitchen, holding a cup of coffee.

She pours me one, then jerks her head toward the window with a huff. "Why is it that men look more distinguished when they age, and women turn invisible? It's not fair. The man belongs in a lawnmower commercial."

Following her gaze, I see Grant pushing a lawnmower, sweat starting to dampen the space between his shoulder blades. He pauses halfway across the lawn, reaches behind his head to grab the neckline of his shirt with a fist, then pulls it off in one motion.

I gape, drool dribbling down my chin and onto the nice timber floor as his muscles gleam in the early morning light.

"I think that man has M.M.S.," Simone says.

"M.M.S.?"

"Matthew McConaughey Syndrome. Symptoms include not being able to keep a shirt on."

Her impish grin makes me giggle. I shrug. "I'm not complaining."

"Yeehaw." Her eyes glimmer as she brings her mug up to her lips, wiggling her eyebrows. "Remember what I said?"

"'Til the cows come home," I reply with an eye roll. "Something, something, canoeing. How could I forget?"

"You have at least another three, four weeks here, Fi. The Fringe Fest is in two weeks, right?" I nod, and she continues: "Right, so you'll be here for four, maybe five weeks at least. If you decide to stay on to manage the café, which I have a feeling Candice will ask you to do, you could be here for months. More than enough time to go for a test drive."

"What if I don't want to?"

"Don't want to what? Feel that man's rough, calloused hands all over your body?"

I blush furiously, gulping down my coffee. "No. I mean...what if I'm not ready? Look at him, then look at me. How am I supposed to..." I sigh. "You've seen the women at those yoga classes. The other women in town who do art. I'm not twenty-five anymore."

"No. You're forty-five, which means not only do you have the looks to get his attention, you've got the wisdom and intelligence to *keep* him interested."

"I don't want my whole existence to revolve around whether or not a man finds me interesting."

"Good. It shouldn't. But Miss Fifi"—she points to my crotch—"might disagree."

"Miss Fifi doesn't get a vote."

Simone arches a brow. "Are you sure about that? Because judging by the look in your eyes when you stare at that lawn-mower, seems like Miss Fifi knows *exactly* what she wants, and she's plotting big things."

"Who's Miss Fifi?" a deep voice says behind me. "And why does she care about my lawnmower?"

I yelp, red-faced, as Simone cackles behind me. Her hand drops onto my shoulder as she hides her head behind my back, shaking with laughter. I babble some gibberish as I wave to the coffee machine, my eyes drifting down to Grant's pecs, then his abs, and finally, slowly, back up to his face.

Miss Fifi's making herself heard loud and clear right now.

A funny kind of look crosses Grant's features, but he says nothing. He stalks closer—close enough that I can smell the sweat and grass and dirt and manliness on his skin—and pours himself a cup of coffee.

"I'm going to miss this town." Simone sighs.

"Leaving already?" Grant sips, and I'm suddenly fascinated by the movement of his lips around the cup, his fingers flexing, his throat bobbing as he swallows.

Dizzy, I lean against the counter.

*Four more weeks, minimum.*

"It's high time I pushed Fi out of the nest," Simone says, shooting me a glance that says a thousand things and makes images of sweaty cowboys pop into my head. "Time for her to spread her wings and fly."

"I'll be here to catch her," Grant replies with a grin.

"Although if she always talks about herself in the third person, things might get confusing. Miss Fifi?"

"Oh, no, that was our friend in L.A., Fifi. She's...shy." I cringe, squeezing my eyes shut.

"Didn't want to come on a trip with you two?"

"No, she hasn't been on a trip in a long, long time," Simone says, shaking her head with mock sadness in her eyes. "Too long. She used to be a lot of fun back in college, but you know. Life happened. I've been trying to drag old Fifi out to play for ages, but she just wants to stay locked up at home. Alone. In the dark."

"Sounds like Miss Fifi needs to be coaxed out of hiding," Grant says, topping up his cup of coffee. "There's a whole wide world ready to be enjoyed."

"That's what I've been trying to tell her." Simone pats Grant's arm, shooting me a look full of danger and mischief. I want the earth to open up and swallow me whole, right here in this beautiful kitchen. If I have to listen to my best friend and my hot new roommate talk about my vagina needing to come out and play for one more minute, I might spontaneously combust.

Thankfully, the doorbell rings. Grant stalks toward the front door as I let out a long sigh.

Simone cackles.

"You're a pest," I say. "I'm glad you're leaving."

"Don't be mean." She pouts.

Voices float down to us from the hallway, and Grant reappears with Candice and Jen in tow. Candice is carrying a box full of huge binders, and Jen has a folder tucked under her arm.

"I thought we could get started now that you're done with the art retreat," Candice says, dropping the box onto the island. "We have less than two weeks until the Fringe Fest, so we'd better focus on the café for now, then once you've got everything in hand, I can focus on getting the yoga studio ready. Maybe even tackling my filing system." She grins.

"You have a filing system?" Jen asks. I laugh, and Jen blinks at me, confused. Oh. She hadn't been making a joke.

"The painting is done, but we need to set up tables and give everything a clean. The health inspector needs to give us the final sign-off before we open." Candice takes a binder out of the box and places it on the kitchen counter. "I have a checklist."

"You have a *checklist*?" Jen gapes. "Who are you, and what have you done with Candice?"

I grin. "I may have helped with the list."

As Grant mumbles something about heading to the studio to work on the renovations, and Simone says she has to finish packing, I let my feet take me closer to the documents Jen and Candice brought. Despite my apprehensions about staying at Grant's place, I can't help the spark of excitement in my heart.

This is a *project*. And not just any project—not some fundraiser for corporate lawyers with more money than sense. This project is all mine, and I can make something special happen.

Sure, all we're doing is reopening a much-needed café in town for the biggest event of the year, but it's more than that. I get to manage a business, if only for a short time. I get to make decisions that are all my own. I get to live my life with no one staring over my shoulder, telling me I should wear something more appropriate or speak to so-and-so with more respect because he's a major client. Without anyone telling me not to mess up. Without spending long evenings watching my partner flirting with women who are thinner and younger and prettier than me.

No, this is different from the other projects I've had. It's terrifying and exhilarating, and I can't wipe the smile off my face.

Jen goes over the pastry menu she's proposing, and we discuss how many hours she'll be able to dedicate to the café around her regular job. Candice shows me figures from last year's Fringe Festival and we talk about budgets, price points for different coffee drinks, staff we might need.

"Any of you guys know a good barista?" I chew my lip.

"I do, actually," Candice beams. "Sven. He agreed to help out."

Jen makes an approving noise. "And he's got the whole hipster look as well, with big gauges in his ears and a weird haircut."

I hide my smile at her sincerity. "Perfect."

We pore over documents and plans until I hear a knock on the door jamb. Simone smiles at me, eyes gleaming. "You're kind of making me wish I was staying."

Sadness spears my heart, and I realize in a few short minutes, I'll be all alone here. I pinch my lips together. "Me too."

"The mechanic just called. Bertha's all patched up."

"Are you sure she's going to make it back to L.A.?"

"She'll be fine," Simone says, blinking moisture away. She

opens her arms toward me and wraps me in a hug, squeezing tight. "I'm proud of you, Fi. I haven't seen you this excited about anything in a long time. Way too long."

"Fifteen months since this nightmare started," I mumble.

Simone shakes her head. "Way longer than that. It's been years since your eyes have dimmed, your shoulders rounded. Your spirit has been beaten down." She squeezes my shoulders, smiling tenderly. "But I see the old you coming back. This will do you good, and I might have to come back once my stuff is sorted out in L.A.

"Has El Bastardo texted you since the last time?"

Simone rolls her eyes. Her ex has been pestering her, and I'm worried she'll actually meet up with him when she's in L.A. They divorced eight years ago but he's circling again, a shark smelling blood. I don't trust him for a minute.

"He wants something." She nibbles her bottom lip. "I told him I'd have one dinner with him. Just dinner."

"If he hurts you again, I'll murder him."

"I can help," Jen calls out. "We have a meat grinder at work."

Candice wrinkles her nose, laughing. "Gross. Who are you, that creepy guy from *You*?"

"I also know the pig farmer who supplies the pork for the restaurant. I hear hogs will eat through a body in minutes." Jen blinks at the three of us, not a trace of humor on her face.

"Remind me never to get on your bad side," I mumble.

"I'm just sayin'." Jen turns back to the paperwork. "I've never committed or been an accessory to murder, but there are options."

"You watch too much true crime," Candice says. "You've gotten Allie hooked on it, too."

"Your daughter has a morbid streak a mile wide. That has nothing to do with me."

A shadow passes over Candice's face as she shakes her head. "She's had an obsession with death since Paul died. The therapist said it was normal. It'll pass, apparently, although I'm still waiting."

Grant clears his throat behind Simone. He rubs the back of his neck with a calloused hand, flicking his eyes between the four of us. How much of that looney tunes conversation did he hear? "You still want that lift into town, Simone? I was hoping to get started on the renovations soon."

"Meet you outside in two minutes," Simone says, her eyes still on me. As Grant's footsteps retreat, she gives me a hug and whispers in my ear, "You don't need him to make you whole, Fiona, but I bet he'd be fun in the sack."

I laugh, pulling away, and give her one last wave. My best friend walks out the front door and into the sunshine, and I turn back to the papers strewn all over the kitchen island. "So," I say, a smile stretching over my lips, "should we talk about beans? You guys know any local roasters?"

# THIRTEEN
# GRANT

*FOUR MORE WEEKS TOGETHER.* Maybe more.

I've spent the past fifteen and a half years living on my own. When I moved to Heart's Cove fourteen years ago, I thought I'd spend the rest of my life as a bachelor. On my own. Living out my days in the quiet of the woods.

But now...I'm not so sure.

As I pack up my tools and load them into my truck, I let out a long sigh. I spent the day working on a project across town from the café, and couldn't stop thinking about Fiona.

Out of the corner of my eye, I see someone walk toward me. Her hips swing as she approaches, her long blond hair tied up in a high pony. Tessa is fifteen years younger than me, and a month ago we'd been in the middle of a casual flirtation. It was easy with her. She didn't want anything other than physical release. It was enough for me.

"Hi there, stranger," she purrs. "Haven't seen you in the bar for a while. Bartending isn't the same when I don't have your pretty face to look at all evening."

I secure my tools to the bed of my truck and give her a tight smile. "Been busy. With the Fringe Fest coming up, lots of people are looking for odd jobs done."

"And here I was thinking you were avoiding me." She gives me a smile that probably works on a lot of men. The woman exudes sex with every flick of her eyes, every liquid movement of her body.

But somehow, it bores me.

I jerk my head toward the road. "I'd better get back."

"Someone waiting for you at home?"

I snort, shaking my head. "You know me, Tessa. Lone wolf."

She waves her dainty fingers as I get in my truck and drive away, letting out a long sigh. A month ago, I would've probably followed her to her place, had a couple of drinks, and slept with her. It would've felt empty and meaningless, and I would've left after it was over.

As I park the truck in my driveway and see a few lights on inside the house, tension eases in my chest, and I let out a sigh I didn't know I was holding. I'm home. Does it feel more like home now than it did two weeks ago?

Kicking my work boots off, I pad through the house and find the lights on in the kitchen. The open-plan room has a living area attached, and I see a pair of feet hanging over the arm of the sofa. Soft snores sound from the other side of the couch, and a smile teases at my lips.

Stepping closer, I see Fiona with a stack of papers splayed over her chest, a mug of tea forgotten on the coffee table. I touch it—cold. She's been asleep for a while. She looks peaceful like that, spread over the sofa. Sleeping soundly, safe in my house.

My chest stirs, and an odd feeling rises up inside me. Warmth spreads through me as I watch Fiona's chest rise and fall until I have to look away.

She's gorgeous. She's funny, and smart, and obviously hard-working. She makes great coffee and has loyal friends. Everyone in town has basically flocked to her side. The fact that Candice offered her a job within an hour of meeting her says a lot.

Fiona's special…

…so what? I gave up companionship fifteen and a half years ago. I let betrayal soak into my bones and poison my blood. I broke the part of me that craves a woman's company for anything more than physical satisfaction.

That part of me is gone. It's been gone for a long time, and I haven't missed it. Sylvie left me, but I drove her away. I know that, and I have no interest in doing it again.

Glancing at Fiona once more, I feel almost ashamed. Here's this woman, only fifteen months after her husband told her he wanted a divorce, starting over. Smiling. Laughing. Throwing herself into a new project.

It's been fifteen *years* since I felt a similar loss, and I'm still broken inside. Sylvie left me without a word, and I spiraled. I wouldn't have been able to pick myself up the way Fiona has.

I huff out a sigh, moving to the fridge.

"I saved you a plate for dinner," a groggy voice says from the couch. "It's in the oven. Might be cold by now, though. I thought you'd be here sooner." Her head pokes up above the back of the couch, and my heart constricts. Her hair is mussed, sticking out at all angles as she rubs the sleep from her eyes.

I grunt out my thanks and check the oven, using the few moments with my back to her to compose myself. Sure enough, a plate with roast chicken, potatoes, and vegetables awaits.

"This looks good, Fiona." I try to keep the emotion out of my voice. I wasn't expecting her to make any food for me, or even think about the fact that I'd be coming back.

She smiles sleepily, rubbing her eyes. "Jen made it, although I'd love to take the credit. I think she had a heart attack when I tried to eyeball things. Did you know she carries a kitchen scale in her purse at all times?" Fiona laughs. "She's so precise about everything. Even the menu for the café is completely planned out, and it's basically just sandwiches, muffins, and brownies."

"So you're doing this?" I grab a fork from the drawer, digging in. "You're managing the coffee shop for the festival?" *And longer?*

She shrugs, letting out a sigh. "Can't back out now." A smile teases over her lips, and my heart does that funny flip again.

She smiles so easily. Unlike me, who apparently has only laughed twice in the past fourteen years. Well, three times, now. Or is it more? I'm sure I've laughed more in the past two weeks than I have in the years previous.

Standing in the kitchen, balancing a plate on one hand and eating with the other, my emotions run wild inside me. Emotions that I've tried to stamp out like the dying embers of a campfire. Emotions that almost dragged me under when I first moved here.

Flaring bright in my mind over all the other emotions is fear.

Fear that if I let Fiona get too close, I'll be crushed when she leaves. When I drive her away. Not *if*. When.

Four weeks seems like a long time now, but if anything develops between us, it'll be too short. A lifetime would be too short. I keep my eyes on my plate as I eat, swallowing chicken along with the ball of emotion stuck in my throat.

This isn't me.

Fiona stands up, stretching, and my eyes drift over her curves. Womanly. Perfect.

The physical reaction that was missing when Tessa purred at me ignites in my core. I want Fiona more than I've wanted a woman in a long, long time.

She pads toward me, barefoot. I glance at her feet, wondering why it feels oddly intimate to see her without shoes or socks in our—*my* house. When Fiona gives me a sleepy smile, I know this connection isn't the same as what I've had with other women.

I can't sleep with her, then pretend it never happened. I can't spend one night with her and let that be the end of it. If I got to touch her that way, kiss her, taste her—I know I'd never want to stop. I'll get wrapped up in her, and watching her leave...

That might be the thing that truly breaks me. Having another woman leave me without looking back.

Somehow, I need to resist. I need to squash these feelings arcing up inside me. I need to bury them deep and never, ever act on them.

Everything inside me wants to wrap my arms around Fiona. As she stands next to me in the kitchen, close enough to touch, all I want to do is put my plate down and drag her closer.

Then what?

We have sex? There's awkwardness in the morning, she moves out when her room at the hotel is ready, and she leaves at the end of the Fringe Festival?

And I...I stay here. Alone. Sleeping in a cold bed at night, knowing what it felt like to have her warm it beside me.

No, I can't do that. If I sleep with Fiona, it'll ruin me forever. I'd never be able to take a woman like Tessa to bed afterwards, even if Fiona was long gone from Heart's Cove. I can't afford another sixteen years like this.

The best thing for me to do is stay far, far away from Fiona, and never act on these urges.

Not unless I want to destroy myself.

# FOURTEEN
## FIONA

"IS IT JUST ME, or does Grant seem more gruff than usual?" I glance across the half-renovated café toward the big man in the corner. We've finished most of the renovation work and are now putting chairs and tables together, cleaning, and putting the finishing touches on the place before we stock it with food and drinks. After our evening swims together nearly every day, Grant has started avoiding me since Simone left. It's like without her as a neutral presence in the house, our...whatever is going on between us...has become too much for him to handle.

It stings.

Candice shrugs. "He's never been much of a talker. Seems normal to me."

Frowning, I go back to deep-cleaning the display refrigerator next to the counter, pursing my lips. Grant's hardly said two words to me in the past five days. We've worked alongside each other, and he mostly avoids looking at me at all. We open the café in a week, and if I have to spend that time tiptoeing around the house, I might explode.

The three of us look up when the front door opens. Agnes appears in the doorway, planting her hands on her hips and glancing around the room. "So. This is happening, is it?"

I stand up slowly, wiping my hands on a rag. "Yes. We're opening the café for the Fringe Festival. Is that a problem?"

"And I assume Dorothy is happy about it?"

I exchange a glance with Grant, who finally lets the scowl melt off his face. He lifts a shoulder up in a slight shrug. Turning back to Agnes, I clear my throat. "Look, Agnes, I don't want to cause any trouble."

A man appears behind Agnes. Youngish, maybe late thirties, with thick blond hair and a square jaw. Handsome. His sharp blue eyes sweep over the room as he puts a hand on Agnes's shoulder, his gaze finally settling on me. With a fine, straight nose and sensual lips, the man makes something tighten in my core. Not the way my body blazes when I catch Grant looking at me when he thinks I'm not watching, but a kind of echo of that feeling. How any attractive male would make my body react. "Hello," he says softly. "I hope my grandmother isn't bothering you."

"Oh, hush," Agnes says, swatting at the man. "I'm just making sure that hag isn't sinking her claws into every business on the street."

"That hag used to be a good friend, Gram."

"That hag is a hag!" Agnes huffs, shuffling past her grandson.

"Wait, Agnes!" I call out, hurrying to the box of sample

pastries Jen dropped off this morning. "I heard you like almond croissants. Jen dropped these off. Maybe you could taste it and see if it's worth offering for sale?" I tuck the pastry into a brown bag and give it to Agnes with a hopeful smile.

If I can be like Grant and somehow straddle the line of this feud, it'll be better for me—and better for business.

Agnes's eyes narrow, but she huffs, closes the distance between us, and takes the bag from my hands. "I'll let you know what I think."

I grin, letting my gaze drift to Agnes's grandson again.

He nods, a charming smile tugging at his lips. "I'm Rudy. I heard there was fresh meat in town. Hope Gram isn't giving you a hard time."

I resist the urge to bristle at the term *fresh meat*. He didn't mean anything bad by it, I don't think, but it reminds me of the type of thing John would say.

"She's been fine," I say, waving a hand. "Harmless."

"I'm not sure about that." Rudy laughs. He reaches into his pocket and pulls out a card, closing the distance to the counter and handing it over to me. His fingers brush mine as his blue eyes spark, the corner of his lips curling. "Call me if she gives you any grief. Or if you want a night off from renovating. There are a few good restaurants around here. I'd be happy to show you around."

Grant shoves a chair against the wall, dragging a table across the floor. I jump at the sound, then tuck Rudy's card into my pocket. "Thanks. That sounds nice—we've been spending lots of time in here. A night off might be needed." I give him a shy smile. "I guess I'll see you around."

"If I'm lucky." His eye twitches—wait, was that a wink?—then Rudy follows his grandmother down the street.

Candice whistles. "Girl, did you say bedroom eyes? He was basically undressing you where you stand."

I look down at myself—*Heart's Cove Hottie* shirt and all—and shake my head. "Please. He was just being friendly. Probably used to patching over whatever feuds Agnes causes."

"He's never offered to take *me* out to dinner," she laughs, nudging me. "I've always wanted a younger man. I think I'd make a good cougar."

I laugh, wrinkling my nose. "I'm not sure I'm there yet. Younger men... I don't know."

"Younger men all the way," Candice says, returning to her cleaning task. "More stamina."

A bang makes me jump. The back door of the café slams, Grant disappearing behind it.

Frowning, I glance at Candice. "What got into him?"

"Moody fucker," she grumbles. "Probably annoyed that Rudy was flirting with you."

"First of all, we weren't flirting."

"Fiona, he *winked*. He was definitely flirting with you."

"I thought that was a twitch. And why would that make Grant mad? We've barely seen each other. We're like, cordial roommates. Nothing more." I cross my arms, leaning against the counter. "I think this is why I stayed married for so long. I knew my marriage was over, but the thought of dating and dealing with full-grown man-children is too much for me. I can't do it."

Candice laughs, rinsing out her rag as she moves to clean another table. "That's because you're not getting any of the perks." She arches her eyebrows. "Maybe a little romp in the sheets with young Rudy will sort you out."

"You're worse than Simone," I grumble, but still let my lips slide into a smile. The thought of sleeping with Rudy doesn't appeal, but dinner...

Didn't Simone tell me to get out there? To put myself on the market? I pull the card out of my pocket and stare at it, sighing.

Maybe this is what I need. A night off, when I can dress up and feel pretty and let a man take me out. Maybe a date will release some of this pressure bubbling up inside. Make that energy zinging just beneath my skin settle, if only for a few hours. He's young and attractive and interested in me. Isn't that something I'm allowed to enjoy?

Candice and I clean in silence, and Grant doesn't return.

WHEN I RIDE my bicycle home that evening, I park it up near the front porch but I don't go inside. The thought of facing Grant after he stormed out today makes me queasy, so instead I take a walk around the side of the house and down a dirt path leading to the ocean. The pier has become my favorite place on the property, and even if Grant no longer joins me for evening swims, I look forward to them every day. Maybe a small part of me comes to the pier every night hoping he'll join me.

When I get to the pier, the sun is just dipping down to the horizon. I walk down to the end and remove my shoes, letting my feet dangle into the water. Taking a deep breath, I close my eyes and enjoy the last rays of the sun.

This is life, I realize. All the quiet moments in between. All the time I spent waiting for something to happen, wishing my time away in the hope of the next big thing—I was letting my life pass me by. I stayed married to my ex-husband for twenty years, thinking things would get better when it was just a long, slow decline. Even when I knew he was cheating on me, I wouldn't admit it to myself. I wouldn't confront him, thinking it would pass. I *settled.*

But I'm here. I have my feet in the Pacific Ocean and my lungs full of fresh air. I'm *working*—really working—on something I care about for the first time in years.

Sure, I feel like I wasted time with John. I hoped he'd come around and agree to have a baby. I told myself I was okay with not having kids, even though a part of me withered and died because of it. I told myself I didn't want a career of my own, I only wanted a happy life. I told myself I cared about the Mercedes and the shoes and the fancy penthouse.

But this? Sitting by myself with my feet dangling off an old pier—it's better.

Electricity buzzes in my veins as I swish my feet in the water, a smile tugging at my lips. I glance behind my shoulder and, seeing no one, stand up.

One thing I've never done in my forty-five years on this earth is go skinny dipping. I've always been too proper, too afraid, too...encumbered.

Not anymore. I don't need John, or Grant, or Rudy. I don't need a fancy job or car to feel whole. I just need to do things that make *me* feel good. I need to surround myself with people I like, who like me right back. People like Simone and Jen and Candice. Friends.

This pressure building inside me—it doesn't need a man to let it release. *I* have that power all on my own. I can own my body and myself and live my life the way I've always wanted. I can be the type of woman who goes skinny dipping on a Wednesday afternoon just because she feels like it.

I need to strip my clothes off and jump in the ocean, for once, and let the salt water lap at my bare skin. So, tearing off my pale pink shirt and shoving my jeans down, I hardly hold back the bubbles of laughter as I kick the garments aside and stand on the edge of the pier, totally naked.

My cheeks heat, but my smile widens. A soft breeze ruffles my hair, spreading goosebumps over my skin. My nipples tighten in the chill, and I feel fresh air on places that haven't been bare in a long time. I spread my arms, tilting my head toward the sky, and laugh.

Birds cry overhead, flying in a precise formation. Leaves rustle in the trees and waves lap at the shore. The air is just warm enough to be bearable, and I have no doubt the water is just cold enough to make me yelp.

Only one way to find out.

Breasts flying, arms akimbo, I leap.

The water's colder than I expected. It steals the breath from my lungs as I sink down, down, down, freezing my limbs and making everything feel heavier. My feet touch the sandy bottom and I explode upward, breaking the surface with a scream and a laugh that make me feel more alive than ever before.

The pressure inside me releases, just a little. Enough to make me sigh in contentment.

I face the setting sun, smiling wider than ever before as I tread water. It's like a baptism. A new start. A new life.

My body adjusts to the temperature of the water, and I lean back, floating to the surface, naked and free and *alive.*

That is, until a throat clears behind me, and I realize I'm not alone.

# FIFTEEN
# GRANT

I CAME to the pier for peace. To forget about the anger that ripped through my core when Rudy handed Fiona his card. To wipe the memory of her coy smile from my mind.

I'd hoped Fiona was still in town or had finished her nightly swim. After Simone left, coming here with Fiona felt far too intimate for me. Too tempting to let my hands drift toward her, to give in to the stuttering in my chest whenever the setting sun lit up her face.

But she's here.

She spins around, the water lapping the tops of her breasts. My eyes drift down despite my attempts to control my gaze, wishing I could see below the surface. Her wet hair is swept back from her face, water carving rivulets down her cheeks and neck and shoulders.

"Grant," she says, eyes wide. "I thought I was alone." Her cheeks redden, and I don't think I've ever seen someone more beautiful. In the light of the fading sun, she looks like a goddess sent down to earth to remind me that good things still exist. Light shimmers over the surface of the ocean like a million twinkling lights, surrounding her in a pool of magic.

It's her eyes that make me still, though. Heated, teasing, mischievous. There's danger in her gaze, and I know I should walk away. I should forget how she looks, bare shoulders poking out of the water, the swell of her breasts just visible.

I don't walk away, though. I stay rooted to the spot as heat whips through my body like an uncontrolled blaze.

Biting her lip, she waves a hand. "Care to join me?"

My cock is instantly hard. Eyes popping out, I try to think of something to say. Try to think of some excuse why I shouldn't join her, naked, in the water...but I come up empty. I've been trying to convince myself to keep my distance, but can't quite remember exactly *why*. And this afternoon, when I nearly had an aneurysm watching Rudy rake his eyes over her?

Nothing good would come of us hooking up. I'd get too attached. I'd try to be her protector, and she obviously doesn't need someone like me to take care of her. She's strong and independent and capable—but I'd be overbearing and possessive, just like I was trying to help Sylvie through her dark times, and it'd push Fiona away.

I know these things for a fact. It's not worth the pain. If I act on these urges, I will ruin this. Ruin myself.

Fiona sweeps her hand over the surface toward me, sending a spray of water my way. "The water's nice once you get over the initial shock."

"I'm not worried about the water," I answer, my voice

nothing more than a growl. Her gaze drifts down my body, and I wonder if she's picturing me naked. She's seen it all already, so it shouldn't be any different.

But it is.

Posing for a bunch of artists in a studio feels nothing like this. With her gorgeous lips curling into a teasing smile, I know I'm going to lose this battle. I'm going to get in the water. There's no fighting this urge. I spin my finger in the air. "Turn around, missy."

She pops a brow. "Grew a sense of modesty, did we?"

"I don't remember you being this bold."

"Maybe you haven't spent enough time trying to get to know me." Her words are smooth, settling deep in my core. "Seems to me you've been avoiding me, Mr. Greene. Why's that? Something get your panties in a twist?"

I cross my arms and tilt my head in a way I hope screams, *Turn the hell around, woman.*

Eyes flashing, she shrugs and spins herself around.

In just a few moments, I have my clothes off and I'm jumping in the ocean.

Well—she lied. It's fucking freezing in here. Everything shrivels up as I break the surface with a gasp, and I hear the delicate sound of Fiona's laughter.

I could play that sound on repeat and die happy. Turning to face her with nothing but a few feet of water separating us, I shake my head. "I'm still waiting for the initial shock to wear off. Feels pretty cold to me."

"Oh, toughen up, princess." She grins, swiping more water toward me.

I return the favor, if only to hear her laugh. "I haven't been skinny dipping in years," I admit, swimming a few feet away from her. I need distance. If I get any closer, I might feel the need to grab her hand and pull her close, and if I feel Fiona's naked body against mine, it might undo me entirely.

As we tread water, naked, a short distance from each other, I wonder why exactly I'm still trying to resist her. Why do I need to push her away, when for the first time in fifteen and a half years, I feel like I have something to look forward to every day?

Clearing my throat, I glance at the setting sun. There's only a sliver of brightness arching over the horizon, and I know the air will be cold in a matter of minutes. "Sorry about today."

"That little temper tantrum?" Her impish grin slices through my core. "Is there another town feud I need to know about?"

"No," I snort. "I actually like Rudy."

"But...?"

"But I didn't like thinking about him taking you out."

Her eyes darken, silence settling between us. For a moment, I regret saying it out loud. I regret putting words to these budding feelings, regret admitting them to her—and to myself.

"Why's that?" She moves closer, body gliding through the gentle waves.

I hold her gaze, knowing I'm dancing on a very dangerous line.

I can stay on this side of it, where my life is safe. Routine. Lonely. Or I can close the distance between us and *feel* something.

The only problem is that I know it won't be how it is with

other women. I won't be able to go back to how things were before. I won't be able to shut down the part of my heart that's banging to be let free.

And...is it so bad to give in? Would it be a mistake to let myself feel something, for once? To kiss a beautiful woman in the light of the setting sun?

I could forget all the pain that brought me here and shed my memories like an old skin. I could be...better. Maybe I wouldn't push her away, I wouldn't destroy anything.

She moves closer again, another foot, eyes flashing dangerously. "Cat got your tongue?" Her voice is husky, and I wonder if she knows how much it affects me. How badly I want to tug her closer and crush my lips to hers. How her voice seems to have a direct line to my cock.

"I don't want to sleep with you, Fiona," I say softly.

Hurt flashes across her eyes, then quickly settles into a blank expression. "Right. I mean... of course not." She clears her throat, looking at the pier. She wants to get out.

"I don't want to hurt you." I squeeze my eyes shut, treading water in more ways than one. "If we sleep together, it'll change things. I'm not... I can't give you what you need."

She laughs then, but it sounds bitter. "Grant, how could you possibly know what I need? I just got out of a twenty-year marriage with a man who might have only loved me for five or six of them, if he did at all. Maybe all I need is a cock between my legs and someone to remind me that I'm actually a woman. So please, spare me your self-flagellating bullshit. You treat me like I'm breakable. Like you have the power to hurt me because you're such a big, strong man. Fucking *please*."

Fiona makes to leave, but I catch her hand as it sweeps toward me. I tug her closer, hating the pain zinging through my chest. I pull her close, and she lets me. She hooks her arm around my neck and stares at me, a challenge flashing through her eyes.

"All you want is a cock, is it?" My voice is nothing more than a low rasp. I let my anger and hurt settle into something different down in my core. Lower.

If all she wants is a cock, then good. I can provide that. Gladly.

Fiona's lips drop open, fire burning in her eyes. "I don't need you to be moody and possessive, Grant. I don't need you to treat me like I'm some sort of priceless artifact. I don't need you to worry about what'll happen in the morning. I'm a grown-ass woman."

She moves closer then, her chest pressed against mine. Peaked nipples brushing against my skin, sending another wave of desire crashing against me. Our legs move, still treading water, and I know she feels how hard my cock is between us. My hand sweeps down her spine, feeling her skin for the first time. How many times have I thought about this? How many times have I wondered what she'd feel like to touch, to taste?

The broken part of me rears up, but I push aside all the reasons I haven't acted on it. If she leaves, she leaves. If I push her away, I'll deal with the fallout. I've picked myself up off of rock bottom once and I can do it again. Later. In a few weeks.

Right now she's here, pressed up against me, with her gorgeous body and wet hair and heat in her eyes. Whether it's anger or lust, I'm not sure—and I'm not sure it even matters.

"I can't promise you anything other than sex, Fiona," I say, a last-ditch effort to stop this from happening. To prevent myself from ruining it. Her. Myself.

"I'm not asking for anything more." Her voice is a rasp, and the last part of my defenses crumbles to dust.

I sear my lips to hers, shoving my hand into her wet hair as I pull her close. She wraps her legs around me, pinning my shaft between us. I groan against her lips, knowing somewhere deep down inside me that this is a mistake.

# SIXTEEN
# FIONA

ANGER and lust roar in my blood. Anger—because I'm sick of men telling me what they think is best for me. Sick of putting my own needs aside and listening to people who aren't *me*. And lust because, well, I haven't had a gorgeous man naked in my arms in far too long.

When Grant appeared behind me on the pier, I felt a sort of reckless freedom. I was gloriously unencumbered. Ready to dive into whatever abyss opened up at my feet, and do something the old me wouldn't have dared to do.

But then he opened his mouth. Damn him! He opened that beautiful mouth of his and tried to tell me what's best for me.

Didn't I warn him not to say anything after that first day? Didn't I tell him that my attraction to him would fade the minute he spoke?

Sure, that was weeks ago, and my attraction hasn't faded in

all the conversations we've had since then, but this...this feels different.

Like a twig snapping underfoot, something shifts within me.

The hesitations that stopped me from acting when Simone was here, the voice in my head that told me I wasn't ready, all the excuses I've given myself for not acting on carnal urges—they vanish. Grant's fingers sink into my flesh and heat overwhelms me, welling from someplace deep in my core. His lips devour mine, kissing me with anger of his own.

It's reckless. Dangerous. It'll end in ruin.

But isn't that the fun of it?

An almost maniacal need builds in my core, winding its way through my veins as I run my fingers through Grant's wet hair, curling my fist into the dark strands. I answer his kiss with hunger of my own. A deep, endless need to *feel* something. To do something stupid. To make a clean break from the person that settled for less for so long.

I'm not the Fiona who accepted a cheating husband. I'm not the Fiona who thought life ended at forty. I'm not the Fiona who thought she didn't enjoy sex.

As his hands sweep over my skin, pulling me closer, I melt. His tongue dances against mine and his mouth—his beautiful, sensual mouth—crushes me. He drops his lips to my neck and I wonder if he can feel the pulse hammering in my veins. His lips brush against that throbbing pulse, sliding down my neck to my shoulder.

Then, swiftly, he swims to the pier and helps me out of the water. I rush up the ladder he installed for me, feeling his gaze on every inch of my bare skin. There are no words left to speak between us. We've crossed a line—demolished it with a pair of sledgehammers—and the only thing that will stop us now is mutual satisfaction. Or is it mutual destruction?

The outdoor shower leans crookedly on the shore, three rickety walls surrounding an old spigot. Grant tugs me toward it, turning the freezing-cold water on full blast to wash the salt off our bodies.

I gasp at the cold, then gasp again when he drops to his knees and brings his lips to the apex of my thighs. I haven't had a man's mouth there in...years. My fingers curl into his hair as I lean over him, legs trembling, one hand splayed against the unsteady walls as he throws my leg over his shoulder.

Grant's hands hold me up, and that's the only thing to stop me tumbling to the hard ground. His rough, calloused hands slide over my ass and onto my back, holding me in place while he teases me, touches me, tastes me.

My anger has morphed into something else. Something bigger. A ball of heat in the pit of my stomach that demands to be heard. Fire in my blood and ecstasy in my soul. Panting, I grab whatever I can hold onto and ride his mouth, knowing this will end me.

Whatever's happening between us—it's the end. The end of our flirtatious smiles. The end of the simplicity of the past few weeks. The end of the version of me that settled for anything less.

*This* is what I want for my life. I want skinny dipping and oral sex on a private beach. I want a man who looks like a warrior to sink his hands into my hips and moan when he tastes me. Anything less is not enough. It'll never be enough after this.

When Grant slides a finger inside me, curling it just so, sealing his mouth to my bud, I come apart. I cry out, an animalistic sound, not caring who or what will hear us. On trembling legs, I lean on Grant as he stands, nothing but darkness and heat in his eyes.

"House. Now." The command snaps through me, tightening my core and lashing another wave of lust over my skin. Scrambling to grab my discarded clothing, I slip my shoes over my wet feet and walk up to the house, still gasping for breath.

My mind is hazy, and the only word I can think of is *more*. I want more. I want more of the touches he gives me as we stumble up the hill, his hands hungry as they sweep over my hip, my side, my ass. I want more of his mouth on my shoulder when we're only halfway back, his arms wrapped around my body as he pulls my back to his front.

I'd let him take me right here on the grass under a darkening sky. I don't care. And when he pauses halfway up the hill to slide his hand down my stomach, teasing the throbbing space between my thighs, I know he's thinking the same thing.

Somehow, we make it to the French doors leading into the kitchen, but we don't make it much farther. Rough hands push me down onto that butcher's block island I love so much. Powerful legs kick my feet apart.

A growl sounds behind me. "Stay."

Like I'm a dog. Like this is nothing more than a dirty fuck, and he's as angry as I am. Good.

He's gone for a handful of heartbeats, then I hear the crinkling of a condom package being ripped open. My heart hammers in my chest, my forehead dipping down to the countertop as I still gasp for breath, waiting, waiting, waiting.

The first thing I feel is a hand sliding up my spine. The another sweeping up the inside of my thighs. The hand on my back makes its way to the nape of my neck, tangling into my hair. Getting a good grip for what's to come. The hand between my thighs probes the wetness leaking out of me, and a satisfied grunt sounds from behind me.

Then, something else. Bigger. Thicker.

I suck a breath in through my teeth, closing my eyes as I feel him slide up against me. Any voice of reason has long since been silenced, and in these few seconds, the only thing in my mind is contentment. Peace. The satisfaction of knowing that I'm getting exactly what I asked for.

I'm getting what *I* want. What *I* need. I'm doing this for me, and I'll never regret it.

Then Grant pushes himself inside me, and I see stars.

How long has it been since I've felt this? Even with my ex-husband, it wasn't like this. It didn't fill me up. Didn't make my back arch. Didn't steal the breath from my lungs.

Another powerful thrust, and I'm nearly over the edge. I'd laugh at how little it took if I had the breath to spare. A tug on my hair, a retreat followed by hips driving into me, and I'm there. Grant makes a satisfied male sound from somewhere at the back of his throat, and even that simple noise undoes me. From there, I'm boneless, riding whatever wave has decided to sweep me away.

My orgasm shatters me. Breaks every wall I've ever erected, every defense I pretended to have. I scream, wordless, or maybe it's his name, gripping the edge of the counter as I back into him again, and again, and again.

When I feel him getting that little bit harder and feel the insistence in his touch, I know he's close. I shut my eyes and listen to the grunts and groans and moans coming from the beautiful man behind me, and another wave of pleasure crashes into me.

We still, the silence filled with heavy breathing, then he backs away. I stand slowly and turn to see him discarding the condom, his eyes still hooded with lust when he meets my gaze. Instead of backing away from me, though, Grant's steps eat the distance between us and his arms circle my waist. His lips find mine, a tender kiss I wasn't expecting and didn't know I wanted.

"Let's go to bed," he rasps, and I'd be lying if I said those words didn't make me happy.

# SEVENTEEN
# GRANT

I WAKE up with Fiona's head nestled in the crook of my shoulder, her leg thrown over mine. Breathing in the scent of her shampoo, I turn my head and stare out the window at the clear blue sky. I haven't woken up this comfortable in a long, long time.

Last night, I thought I was making a mistake. I thought I'd wake up this morning and feel as empty as I usually do after sex, wanting nothing more than to slip away from Fiona. Instead, I find myself curling my body around hers and pulling her closer. I rest my cheek on her head and inhale her scent in deep, cleansing breaths.

We were feral last night. We had sex twice more after the kitchen, both times as wild as the first. I kept expecting to tire of her, to want her to go back to her own bed, but we'd doze off in each other's arms and I couldn't help the feeling that this is right. I want her here.

And that feeling is dangerous. Cracks appear in the armor around my heart as I breathe Fiona in, and I have half a mind to let that armor fall away. But that armor has been built up over years, inch by inch, carefully crafted by the pain I endured with my ex. She left without a word when I thought I'd be with her forever, and I've always blamed myself for driving her away. Then the heart attack, then the kind of depression that twists your thoughts and makes you wonder what's left to live for. Then a slow decade and a half spent building myself back up.

Am I really ready to risk that for another woman? Do I want to trudge through those long, dark hallways of my mind once more when Fiona inevitably walks away?

Letting out a soft, feminine mewl that has a direct line to the half-hard cock between my legs, Fiona blinks awake. "Hey." She smiles sleepily, and I wonder if she's actually an angel. In this moment, with her features soft and her body plastered to mine, I don't think she'd be able to do to me what Sylvie did. Don't think I'd let myself push her away.

Still, my armor persists. My walls won't fall so easily.

"Morning," I grunt, my throat dry.

"I never prepped the coffee pot for this morning." She rolls onto her back, taking her leg away from mine. I miss the closeness, and I curl into her. Fiona usually sets up the coffee pot with filters and grounds so all I have to do is flick it on in the morning. It's something I've never done but have come to appreciate. She turns her head toward me, nuzzling into my neck. Slow, soft movements that bring us closer together. A hand sweeping up her side. A turn of her head so her lips are an inch from mine.

She opens her eyes, backing her head up an inch to meet my gaze. "You should go down and make some. A nice, strong black coffee with lots of sugar."

A grin teases my lips. "I should, should I?"

"It'd be the gentlemanly thing to do."

"As you wish." I pull away from her, reveling in the soft noises she emits every time she moves. My heart tugs as I pull loose shorts on, and I feel her gaze on my body. "Still like what you see?"

"If I grab a sketchbook does it mean I'm allowed to stare?"

Chuckling, I drop a soft kiss on her forehead and make my way downstairs. My steps are light, lips curled into a smile. I feel...happy. Not at all how I thought I'd feel this morning. There's no regret, no emptiness, no fear.

Still, as the coffee pot gurgles and I lean against the counter, I wonder if this is a good idea. She's leaving after the Fringe Festival, so two or three weeks from now, maximum. Maybe less. The last thing I want to do is get attached. I *can't* get attached. I think that part of me is broken—shattered when I went through that nightmare before. So this...thing...between Fiona and me, I don't know what to make of it.

It feels good—great. But it's...it's dangerously close to intimacy.

She walks into the kitchen wearing one of my t-shirts, her bare legs looking delicious below it, and inhales. "Coffee," she groans. "What would we do without it?"

"Well, you wouldn't be opening a café in Heart's Cove, for one," I grin. "And you'd probably be a lot grumpier in the mornings."

"What do you mean, grumpi*er*? That implies I'm grumpy to begin with." Her lip juts out in a pout that makes me want to tug her close and crush my lips to hers.

I let a grin dance over my lips. "Apart from this morning, you've communicated exclusively in grunts and gestures before coffee."

"Worked, didn't it?"

I pour Fiona a cup with two heaping spoonfuls of sugar, just the way she likes it, and hand it to her. Her fingers brush mine as she takes it with a nod, and a little spark of heat tingles at her touch.

"The Fringe Fest starts in two days and there's still so much to do," she says, eyes taking on a distant stare. "I hope everything goes okay. Candice's barista friend is coming in today to check our setup."

"You'll do great." I run my hand down her back, earning a contented sigh from her. Her head tilts, leaning against my chest, and I wonder if it's always this easy. If I hadn't run away from all those one-night stands, would mornings have been this comfortable?

She glances at me, her eyes sharpening. Here comes the awkwardness. The questions. The labels. "So..."

"Last night."

She nods. "I, uh"—she clears her throat—"I don't want things to get weird between us. You know I'm only here for a few more weeks, and I just got out of a divorce..."

"I'm not looking for anything serious." Words I've said a thousand times sound bitter when I speak them this morning.

"Same," she says, even though her tone makes me wonder if it's true.

"I enjoyed last night."

"Me too." She gives me a tight smile. "I'd like to do it again. And I want you to know that I don't... I'm not really into casual sex. I mean, I know I'm basically saying that I want casual sex with you, but it's not something that—" She inhales sharply, shaking her head. "What I'm saying is if this is going to be a regular thing, I'm not really comfortable with there being...other people. For either of us. Even if it's casual between us."

"Casual and exclusive."

A sharp nod. "Exactly. We're going to be living together, so maybe we can have a roommates-with-benefits kind of situation." Her eyes search mine, and something a lot like disappointment curdles my stomach.

"That sounds wise." My words send a sharp pain rattling through my ribcage.

She lets out a breathy laugh, as if she thinks my words were a joke. "Does it?"

"I appreciate you being up front with me, Fiona."

"I'm a grown woman. I don't have time for games. I like you. I like having sex with you, but I don't want...strings." She wiggles her fingers for emphasis.

I should be happy about this conversation. It's exactly what I've been telling myself all morning—and every day since I met her. I don't want strings, or attachment, or commitment. But somehow, disappointment settles in my marrow. I hide it behind my cup of coffee. "Works for me."

What I want to tell her is I haven't wanted to have sex with anyone else since I met her. Ever since she told me to be quiet after spending an hour staring at my naked body in that art studio, all other women ceased to exist for me. Or maybe it was the moment her eyes met mine under the geyser, when that urge to protect her almost overwhelmed me.

But...strings.

I'd be exclusive with her even if she didn't specify it, but the thought of her leaving, of this being temporary... I don't finish that thought. As I stand here, hot coffee warming my stomach, I know that if she'd asked me for more, I would've said yes. I would have told her I'd be willing to try with her. To date. To break down all those walls I've spent so many years building.

But she wants casual, and I'm the king of casual. It's what I do. I can do it with her, too.

I watch her drain her coffee cup and go back for a second, then tuck a strand of hair behind her ear and steal a glance my way. "I have to get to the café in an hour, but..." Her eyes, more heated than they were a moment ago, carve the lines of my stomach and spark fire in my core. She flicks that teasing gaze back up to my face and nibbles her bottom lip. "An hour's a long time, isn't it?"

I grin, all thoughts of regret evaporating. Setting my mug aside, I cage her against the counter. "You tell me what you want me to do to you, Fiona, and I'll do it."

Casual, but exclusive. A couple of weeks, then she leaves, no strings attached. It's clean. Simple. Easy.

Right?

So, I sink to my knees and make her moan with my tongue, my fingers, then my cock in the same place where it happened last night, relishing every time she tugs my hair, every orgasm she gives me—and I know watching her leave won't be easy at all.

## EIGHTEEN
## FIONA

I PRACTICALLY SKIP through my day, then spend another glorious night wrapped up in Grant's arms. It's scary how quickly I get used to waking up next to him. A small voice in my head tells me I should keep my distance. Logically, I know I should. We barely know each other, I'm only here for a short time, and I haven't been with anyone except my cheating ex-husband in over twenty years. The last thing I should be doing is getting involved with someone else.

But isn't this perfect for me? I can enjoy the physical intimacy without tackling all the wounds that John inflicted on my spirit. I can follow Simone's advice and ride him night and day, until we're sweaty and panting and sated.

WE SAID we didn't want strings, but after three days I already feel tangled up in him. The first morning of the Fringe Festival, before the sun has burned the chill out of the air, I slide out of bed and tiptoe out of the room, needing to put space between me and the hot, hard body I've been sleeping next to all weekend.

I'll throw myself into the management of the café for the duration of the festival, then I'll help with the cleanup and closing, then...then I'll figure out my next steps. Later.

Tents are already being set up down the road, with vendors and artists getting ready to display their wares. There's a stage built on the far side of town with a full schedule of free performances. The Fringe Festival is big, and our little café is part of it.

As I greet our barista, Sven, I inhale the scent of freshly roasted coffee beans and do a slow turn in the café. We've repainted, cleaned, and repaired every square inch of this place. I went bargain-hunting for chairs and tables, and was able to find some knickknacks to decorate the place, too. It looks cute and quaint and completely at home in Heart's Cove.

Even though I know it's only for a week, being in charge of this place fills me with a kind of energy I haven't felt in a long, long time. It's similar to other events and fundraisers I've planned. I have the management skills, and it's not particularly challenging so far, but...

It's *mine.* My project, my partners and employees—and that's enough to put a smile on my face.

It's only mine for the duration of the festival, then... I don't want to think about what happens after. I'll talk to Candice about it after the Fringe Fest. She wants to keep the café open, so maybe she'd be open to me staying, too. That's what Simone said would happen. She's always been good at reading people.

By the time we've set up for the day, given the display cabinets one last polish, and propped the café door open, the sun is baking heat into the concrete sidewalk. A man walks in pushing a stroller with a babbling toddler in it, his eyebrows arching. "Open for business?"

"We sure are," I beam.

Then, it's a flood. I jump behind the counter to help Sven take orders as he makes coffee after coffee after coffee. We sell out of baked goods by noon. Agnes buys an almond croissant (Dorothy tried to buy us out, but I hid the last croissant behind the counter just in case. Yes, I know I'm playing a dangerous game). The café bustles with activity all day. I'm on a high. I've never thought of myself as someone who's good at customer service, and I wouldn't want to do it every day, but on *this* day it's exactly where I want to be. Greeting people, smiling, welcoming people into this little space that already feels like something of my own.

In the early afternoon, my eyes are drawn to a well-cut shadow in the doorway. Grant. Tall, gorgeous, tanned, and so damn sexy he makes me want to melt. A half-grin teases over his lips, eyebrows inching up as he takes in the customers seated at tables, the empty display refrigerator, the sweat dotting my brow.

"Good first day?" His steps are casual, controlled, but his energy fills the room. More than a few heads turn to admire his body, female gazes lingering on the powerful thighs, broad shoulders, oh-so-perfectly tousled hair.

A flush creeps over my cheeks as he leans on the counter, his spicy-sweet smell enveloping me. "Better than expected."

"You left without saying goodbye this morning." His voice is low so only I can hear him. A flash of something crosses his eyes that I don't have the energy to decipher.

I shrug a shoulder, arranging and rearranging the items on the counter. "Keep it casual, right?"

"Grant Greene!" An old man hobbles in the cafe door, liver spots covering his receding grey hairline. "Have you been avoiding me, young man?"

"Of course not, Mr. Cheswick," Grant says, straightening. "I got your message. You need me over at your place?" He clasps the old man's hand in his larger one, eyes widening as Mr. Cheswick pulls him close.

The old man's eyes gleam as he glances at me before leaning toward Grant, speaking in a low, conspiratorial voice. "I've got one for you, Grant."

"Here we go." Grant throws me an eye roll, but there's a hint of curiosity and humor in his eyes.

"The young lady can listen, too," Mr. Cheswick says as he nods to me. It's been a while since I've been called a *young lady*, but sure. Mr. Cheswick starts, rapping his gnarled knuckle on the café counter as Grant leans his lean body against the display cabinet. His shirt strains against his powerful shoulders as he crosses his arms, as if to brace himself for the incoming punch line.

"How do you spot a blind man in a nudist camp?" Mr. Cheswick leans in, and I can't help but hold my breath. His eyes sparkle, and he finally shrugs. "It's not hard."

Even if I hadn't thought that silly, dirty joke was funny, I would've laughed simply because Mr. Cheswick's whole body turns to pure mirth. With a hand on his stomach, mouth open, eyes squeezed shut, he cackles at his joke so hard I fear he'll choke on his own spit.

I giggle behind my hand, cheeks reddening, and Grant shakes his head—although I do see a hint of a smile appear on his lips.

Mr. Cheswick wipes his eyes, letting out a sigh, then orders a peppermint tea. He asks Grant to stop by his place this afternoon, promising as many dirty jokes as Grant can handle. When the old man says goodbye to me with a wink, tea in hand, I arch an eyebrow at Grant.

"Where does he fall in the Agnes-Dorothy divide?" I ask.

"He's Switzerland. Neutral. I think Cheswick is the only person Agnes actually likes, and the twins are loyal customers of his woodworking business." Grant grins. "He's got a good heart. If you're almost done here, you can come with me. I think you'd like his place. It's..." He chews his bottom lip in a way that makes my stomach tighten, then shrugs a massive shoulder. "It was the first place that felt like home to me after I thought I'd lost that feeling forever."

My heart thuds. "I'd love to." I smile, unsure what side of *casual* this is, but unable to bring myself to refuse. Not for the first time, I wonder what exactly Grant went through when he came here. He told me about his heart attack, but I wonder if there was something else. Maybe it wasn't just a stressful job that caused it. By the way his eyes linger on mine, I wonder if we have more in common than I first thought.

. . .

WHEN I FINISH up at the café, Grant stands from the tiny two-seater table in the corner and pushes his chair in. He runs his fingers through his hair and I take the moment to admire the way his shirt hugs the planes of his chest—a chest I can't wait to explore with my hands and my mouth later tonight.

But that can wait. Grant slides his hand to the small of my back, ignoring a glance from the last female customer who can't quite keep her eyes to herself. He leads me outside, his touch lingering on my body. It feels...intimate. When he drops his hand from my back, I miss the warmth and the comfort of his touch. His arm swings next to me, hand brushing mine, and the urge to intertwine my fingers with his is almost too overwhelming to ignore.

We said casual, though. Casual roommates-with-benefits relationships don't include hand-holding. So I let my hand swing freely, and Grant doesn't slide his palm against mine, either. It's better that way. We talk about our days as we amble down leafy green streets, making our way to a two-story weatherboard house a short walk away. The garage door is open, revealing Mr. Cheswick puttering around a remarkably well-kitted-out workshop.

He greets us with an ear-to-ear smile, waving us inside. "Over here, Grant. I need help putting this chest of drawers together."

I run my fingers over a workbench, inhaling the scent of sawdust and steel. Rows of tools are neatly displayed on a pegboard running the entire length of the wall, with stacks of material lining the opposite side of the double garage. I've never been a handy person, but this place feels comfortable. I understand how Grant felt at home here.

Grant grunts as he lifts one side of a tall dresser, fitting mortice joints together as Mr. Cheswick directs. The old man's pressed trousers are worn but clean, and his button-down shirt sleeves are rolled up as if he's been working in here all day. The takeaway cup of tea rests on the edge of the workbench, forgotten.

I wonder if Mr. Cheswick wandered into town looking for Grant, and how he knew to come to the café. Sensing my gaze, he glances over his shoulder and gives me a warm smile. "He's not bad for a grumpy bastard, is he?" Cheswick jerks his thumb at Grant as I fight to keep the smile off my face.

"Grumpy bastard?" Grant says, leaning down to pick up another piece of the dresser.

With his back to us, I steal a few moments to admire the way his broad shoulders tense and move with liquid strength. How his trim waist guides my eyes down to his powerful legs.

Grant is... Well, let's just say I understand why the life drawing class is so popular when he's the model.

Mr. Cheswick clicks his tongue, shuffling toward me as he swipes a chisel off the worktable and slides it into a toolbox. "When he first came to town, Grant didn't say a word for nearly a year. We had to make our own language of grunts and clicks just to understand each other."

"That's an exaggeration," Grant huffs, still not turning to face us.

"Did you two know each other before he moved here?"

Mr. Cheswick shakes his head. "Oh, no. But I gave Grant a bit of work to get him started."

"You did more than that," Grant replies, finally turning. "You taught me everything I know about woodworking, even registered me as an apprentice so I could get my business license. You basically gave me a livelihood."

"Is that gratitude I detect in your tone?" Mr. Cheswick's eyes gleam. "That's new."

"I've thanked you plenty for helping me out all those years," he says, but a smile stretches over his lips as he shakes his head. "But it bears repeating. You pulled me out of a dark hole, old man, and I'm not sure I would have made it otherwise."

Mr. Cheswick turns to another project, waving a hand to dismiss the thanks. "We all need a hand out of the darkness at one point or another." He glances over his shoulder at me. "Life is good like that—it shows you what's important. Lets you know you're stronger than you think."

I want to fidget under the woodworker's stare, but I force myself to stay still. A female voice calls out from the driveway, pulling Mr. Cheswick's wise eyes from me. I loose a breath, hearing a hint of a chuckle from Grant.

He pads over to me, sliding a hand across my lower back. "He's intense sometimes, isn't he?"

I meet his grey-blue gaze, wanting to ask him what darkness he needed help crawling out of, but the words don't come. Instead, we both turn to see none other than the she-devil Agnes gliding up the drive—except she doesn't look like she's about to rip anyone's head off.

She's *smiling*.

"Hello, Chezzy," she croons, holding out a plastic container. "I made your favorite. Lemon meringue pie."

"You are an angel," the old man says, sketching a bow.

I arch my eyebrows, glancing at Grant. "Is this the same Agnes who threw her shoe at Dorothy?"

Grant laughs quietly, nodding.

Agnes's gaze sharpens when it settles on me. She arches a brow. "You're still here. How's the hotel?" She spits the last word, as if the very idea of the Heart's Cove Hotel disgusts her.

"I've been staying with Grant, actually. My room was destroyed by water damage, remember?"

Agnes's eyebrows twitch, her shoulders relaxing ever so slightly. "Oh." Her eyes flick from me to Grant. "Count yourself lucky, then. I heard that hovel has had quite the problem with bedbugs over the years."

I have to bite down to stop myself from laughing. I'll probably never understand her dislike of Dorothy and Margaret, but I can't deny she seems almost...tender...with Mr. Cheswick. As they bend their heads closer, saying words too softly for either Grant or me to hear, Grant touches my elbow and nods toward the street.

Understanding his unspoken words, I start walking away. We say a polite goodbye to the couple and walk back the way we came. I shake my head, huffing out a laugh. "Never thought I'd say this, but I think Agnes has a soft side."

"We all do."

A few steps of silence follow. Then, "How long did you work for him?" A probing question. I know I'm fishing.

"Four and a half years," Grant replies. His eyes take on a

faraway look, and he lets out a long breath. "I came here... I was running away," he finally says. "I'd been in a relationship that ended badly, and was under immense stress at work, and I had the heart attack that nearly killed me. I think Mr. Cheswick saw I was just a shell of a man, and thought he might enjoy building me back up again like he would a piece of furniture."

"Your relationship ended badly..." I shouldn't ask. I don't even know why I'm asking. It's not what a casual relationship would demand, and it's definitely crossing some line.

But I want to know.

"She left me. I can't blame her, really. I was working all the time and I was pushing her..." He takes a deep breath. "She had...problems. Sylvie drank a lot, and I ignored it for a while. But when she started drinking every weekend, then weekdays, then afternoons, then first thing in the morning... I tried to help her. I pushed her hard. Too hard. I tried to get her to AA, to rehab, to anything I could think of. I worked longer hours to pay for treatment which she would inevitably drop out of. I thought"—he shakes his head—"I don't know what I thought. I thought I could fix her. Tried to protect her from herself without ever realizing she might not want my help at all. Then, I came home one day and she was gone."

My head snaps to look at him. "She just left? Without saying anything?"

"Changed her number, took all her things, and disappeared. I thought... I thought horrible things. That she was hurt, in trouble. I thought she'd gone out drinking and got murdered, but that didn't explain her clothes being gone. I thought someone had taken her. I looked for her everywhere, called her a million times, called her family, her friends, until she finally sent me an email asking me to leave her alone. It was over, she said. She wanted out. Then I understood she wasn't hurt or in trouble—she was just sick of me. Just wanted to start over without me."

"Pretty cowardly to not even say a word. Even a text to breakup would be better than disappearing."

Grant sighs, then shakes his head. He gives me a tight smile. "Anyway, that's what put me over the edge. I lost my next case—the biggest of my career—and found myself in the ICU after a severe heart attack. Stress is unhealthy, apparently." He lets out a dry snort.

My hand does slide into his then, and he squeezes my palm in his. We walk the rest of the way in silence, and Grant offers to drive me home. I help him haul the bicycle into the bed of his truck and take a seat in the cab, suddenly bone-tired. We don't say much as we drive home, and when we get there, I find myself reaching for his neck, angling my lips against his.

Grant is the type of man who likes to protect, to care for people. I saw it the day with the chipmunk when he was ready to put his body on the line to keep me safe, and how he installed the ladder on the pier as soon as he saw I needed one. I saw it in the way he tried to keep the peace between the twins and Agnes, and when he offered his place for us to stay without hesitation. How Candice felt comfortable asking for his help to renovate her studio and café, which I found out was done for a fee so small it wouldn't even cover materials. Everything he does is in service to others. I can't imagine how much it must have hurt him to have those efforts thrown in his face when his ex left him. To try to help her and have her just walk away without even a word.

The man has a gigantic heart, and he must have felt like he was starving without anyone to give it to. But am I the person who wants to take it? I'm not ready to fall into anything serious, even if my heart swells every time he enters the room. Even if we have a connection I can't deny.

I've only just started feeling like myself again after leaving a disastrous relationship of my own. Starting something with Grant is irresponsible. I can't give him what he needs. I can't give him *me*, when I've only just started realizing that I have a life yet to live.

But when we make love that night, it doesn't feel casual at all, nor is it feral and wild. It's slow, tender, and makes me feel like we've crossed a line we have no business crossing at all.

# NINETEEN
# JEN

"SO FIONA and Grant are banging, huh?" I ask Candice as I take stock of the baked goods left over as we close the café.

Candice glances up at me, mop in hand. She frowns at the door where Fiona and Grant just exited, on their way to check out the stalls and tents set up for the Fringe Fest. "What do you mean? She's staying at his place. She didn't say anything to me."

"And you haven't noticed the long looks, the blushing, the giggling... All evidence of something else going on. They're definitely sleeping together."

Candice rolls her eyes. "You're the only person I know who would talk about *evidence* when gossiping about other people."

"I'm not gossiping. I'm stating facts."

I jot down notes based on the few pastries left in the display case next to the cash register. The brownies have been popular —my mother's recipe—and we have a few blueberry muffins left over, but it'll be another long night of baking well into the early hours of tomorrow morning. Providing the food for this café as well as holding down my regular job has been harder than I expected.

I'd planned my schedule for this week down to the hour, all color coded and labeled in my planner, but I hadn't expected to have to bake so much for the café every day. Hadn't expected the pastries to be so popular. Hadn't expected Guillaume, my French boss/slave driver at the restaurant to keep me back every night this week to work on a new, experimental recipe.

A miscalculation—and I'm paying for it.

"Jen"—Candice levels a stare at me—"you're gossiping."

"Gossiping would imply some level of glee about either outcome. I don't care if they're together or not, therefore I'm not gossiping."

"You sound like a robot. Or a high school kid trying to write an essay."

Huffing, I stuff my notebook in my bag and sling it over my shoulder. "All I'm saying is Grant hasn't had stars in his eyes in all the years I've known him. This is going to fall apart when Fiona leaves."

Candice straightens up, nibbling her bottom lip. "I was thinking maybe she could stay. We could keep the café open and maybe even expand to serving brunch. We'd need a bigger space, somewhere with a kitchen."

My eyes snap to hers. "You want me to keep baking this much every day? Would you hire another chef? Candice..."

"We could figure something else out. Offer fewer baked

goods, or buy them from some other supplier. And yes, I'd hire someone else. I wouldn't ask you to give up your job for me."

"You want to *buy* pastries when you know they won't be anywhere near as good as mine?" I shake my head. "Wait. Back up. You want Fiona to stay on permanently?"

"I haven't talked to Fiona about it yet, but...yeah." My oldest (and only) friend gives me a tentative smile. "It's going well, don't you think? And Heart's Cove needs a coffee shop."

"While I don't deny the truth of that statement—"

"Robot."

I ignore Candice and continue, "I'm not sure we've prepared properly to keep this place open, let alone expand. You told me last week you only ordered enough coffee for two weeks, and I've planned my schedule around closing up after the Fringe Fest is over."

"I know." She sighs, staring at the big windows opening onto the street. "But don't you think this is a good thing? Don't you feel something...special?"

"I feel tired."

Candice sighs. The broom slides when she tries to prop it against the wall, hitting the corner with a dull *clack*. My best friend walks over to me, combing her fingers through her hair. "I won't ask you to stay up until two o'clock in the morning baking for me every day, Jen, but I think you know as well as I do that this feels right. This café, this partnership with Fiona...it could be *good*, Jen."

"The figures are good. We're making money."

"Not just money. Community. You've seen how many

people already stop in every day. How much they love Fiona. We could contribute to this town—create a space where people gather."

"You've always loved that hippie, universe-loving stuff," I grumble, earning a punch in the arm from Candice. I yelp. "What? It's true! You're always talking about abundance and positivity and shit."

"Don't be a dick."

I open my mouth to tell her that I don't understand how I can be a dick for saying something true—she *does* love that hippie stuff, what with all her candles and *ohms* and yoga—but decide to snap my mouth shut again. I'm not the best at reading people, but I do know when my comments aren't appreciated. Even if sometimes I realize *after* they come out of my mouth.

Candice squeezes my forearm. "I know the restaurant is your dream, and you're working under Guillaume and he's the best in the country, but... Jen, I just feel like we could create something special here."

I want to tell her about the screaming that goes on in that kitchen, or the fact that every day, when I pull off my uniform and take a long shower, I wonder if working for Guillaume is still my dream. If I still want to bake pastries in Paris, if I want to spend my life in a kitchen with puffed-up Frenchmen telling me I don't know how to make crème patissière... I'm not sure anymore.

I grew up wanting to be a baker, but chose computer science instead. Then I realized I hated my life and figured screw it, I'd start over. Here I am, five years later, supposedly living my dream. Paris is in sight, and my slave driver boss actually complimented my work last week. But...ugh. I guess I thought once I got to this age I would know if I was on the right track or not. I'd know what my dreams were. I'd know what to do with my life.

I still feel the same as I did twenty years ago, except now my knee hurts every time a storm is on the way and I'm pretty sure I've developed early onset carpal tunnel from typing so much in my early years.

My dream isn't so much of a dream anymore—or maybe I just don't know if I have what it takes to pursue it. But I glance around this café, looking at the empty display fridge, knowing real people ate my pastries today, the same as yesterday, and every day since we opened the doors. People came back for more. Isn't that what I always wanted? To bake things that people actually *enjoyed*?

Not struggle through tasting menus using tweezers to put edible flowers on experimental desserts, even if it will eventually land me in Paris or New York with a recipe book deal.

Sighing, I give Candice a smile. "Fine. Tell me what you need me to do, and I'll do my best to keep baking. But you need to pay me more. I'm spending way more time on this than originally anticipated."

A low *oof* escapes my lips when Candice nearly tackles me with a hug. "Thank you, Jenny. You're the best pastry chef for a hundred miles, and you make this place special."

"I know."

"And modest, too." She laughs, shaking her head. "I'll ask Fiona if she wants to stay when she gets here tomorrow morning."

"She'll say yes," I reply, heading for the door. "She wouldn't want to leave Grant so soon. I've seen him in art class. The man has a huge dong."

Candice clicks her tongue, but I don't have to look at her face to know she agrees.

# TWENTY
# GRANT

IT'S strange to be enjoying every minute of my days while never wanting them to end. As the Fringe Festival marches onward, a week seems so very short. Fiona's already been in town for nearly six weeks, but we've only started this...intimacy...about a week ago—and only one more week until the end of the festival and the end of our romance.

A weight settles in my gut every time I think about it. My chest is tight, and it's hard to focus on anything other than the desire to soak up every minute I can with Fiona.

Because after the Fringe Fest is over, she'll leave.

Of course she'll leave. Like everyone leaves. At least she's had the decency to be up-front about it, right? She won't disappear in the night and leave me to pick up the pieces. I hope.

But then, on the seventh day of the Fringe Festival, Fiona comes home with a blinding smile on her face. She wraps her arms around my middle and tilts her head up toward me, a silent demand for a kiss.

Who am I to refuse?

I take my time, kissing one corner of her mouth, then the other, reveling in the soft noises slipping through her lips. Every time I kiss this woman, it feels like she's unknotting something inside me. There's a lightness to me that I haven't felt...maybe ever. Not since before I finished law school or longer. Decades.

As Fiona pulls away, the sun gilding her hair and setting her skin aglow, I know she's trying to find the words to say something. She takes a step back, leaning against the kitchen island, and stares out the window with a faraway look in her eyes. Nibbling at her lip and letting out a sigh, her expression doesn't fill me with hope. She probably wants to prepare me for her eventual departure. Wants to let me down easy. *It's been fun, but...*

"Candice told me she wants to keep the café open." Fiona lifts her eyes to mine. "She offered me the job to stay on to manage it, and I accepted."

I'm not sure how long I stand there, unmoving. While my past rears up inside me, my fears whistle in my ears, while I wrestle with them all and realize Fiona wants to stay.

She's *staying*.

I won't have to watch her walk away—well, not yet, at least. I won't have to go back to life without her, wondering how it is I even survived in this town with no one to share it with. She feels it too, even if we said this was casual. Even if we promised there weren't any strings attached.

She wants to *stay*. Here. With me.

Nudging her toe against the edge of the island, Fiona takes a deep breath. "I spoke to Dorothy, and she said my room at the hotel was ready..."

My heart falls. "You don't want to stay here."

"I don't want to impose," Fiona says, her eyes still on the corner of the island that her toe runs along. "It was already generous of you to offer Simone and me a place to stay. Then it was even more generous of you to say I could stay for the renovations of the café and the festival. But I just want to make sure you aren't sick of me."

When she lifts her gaze to mine, I see hope flaring there, and I can't stop the smile from breaking across my face. "Never," I answer, and it's true. I don't see how I could ever be sick of her. Even when she's grumpy in the mornings. Even when my own fears stop me from telling her how I feel.

"You don't mind me staying here? For a while longer... Maybe a couple of months or more?"

I cross the space between us and wrap my arm around her waist, dropping my lips to her neck. I brush her skin softly, softly, inhaling her scent. Inhaling *her*. "I *want* you to stay, Fiona." I tighten my arm around her and drag her closer, pull her into my chest and run my hands over her body.

Her lips find mine and she kisses me. Warmth unfurls in the center of my chest, sinking lower as my hands drift over her beautiful body. This woman, this goddess—she's staying. She's mine.

I pull my lips away, resting my forehead against hers. "I like having you here, Fiona. More than I can say. More than I ever thought I would."

"Gee, thanks." She swats at my arm, but her eyes soften, searching mine. "I like it, too."

*I don't want this to be casual.*

*I want strings—all of them.*

*I want* you.

A lump in my throat chokes the words, and all I can do is give her a crooked kiss before pulling away. "Should we celebrate the café staying open? We could go out for dinner."

"Grant Greene." Her eyes gleam. "Are you asking me out on a date?"

My gut tightens at the sight of the mischief in her eyes, and I shake my head. "Just dinner."

"Good, because I haven't been on a date since I was twenty-two years old. I think the nerves would kill me."

I laugh, reaching over to tuck a strand of dark hair behind her ear. My thumb brushes her lips, tracing the outline of them as my heart thuds. She lets out a soft sigh, tilting her head into my touch. "I'm glad you're staying, Fiona. It was killing me to think of you leaving."

Her gaze finds mine, a tentative smile on her lips. "Let's go to dinner."

FOOD, wine, and a beautiful woman across the table from me. What could possibly be better? We don't talk about the fact that this is most definitely a date. We don't discuss the knowing looks that Heart's Cove locals give us as they see us together, or the way this feels so completely right.

For once, I don't listen to the voice that tells me this is a bad idea. I don't think about Fiona leaving, because she told me today it's the last thing she wants to do. She carved out a job for herself and excelled at it, and she's *staying*. She showed me how good it feels to laugh, to have something to look forward to when I get home at night.

It's been nearly sixteen years since I felt like that. Probably longer. I'd forgotten how good it feels to have someone. To have a person that gets me, that cares. Someone who accepts my affection and my attention and doesn't make me feel like a freak for wanting to take care of her.

And there's something else, too. Fiona isn't helpless. She doesn't need me to be her champion—she can take care of herself. I never realized how much I appreciated that in a woman, or how much of a drain it had been with Sylvie.

"Dessert?" I ask at the end of our meal, not wanting this night to end.

Fiona puts a hand on her stomach, groaning. "I'm full. These days if I even *look* at a dessert, I gain five pounds. It's the one thing I don't like about working at the café." She shakes her head. "Seeing all those treats in the display cabinet and not being able to eat them is torture."

"I like a woman with a bit of meat on her bones."

"This wouldn't be meat, I guarantee it." Fiona sighs, then with a flash in her forest-green eyes, plucks the dessert menu from the edge of the table. "But we could have a cheeky little look, couldn't we?"

My cheeks hurt. I haven't smiled or laughed this much in a long time. But every time Fiona looks at me with a sparkle in her eye, my lips start to curl. Every time I hear her laugh, it sends a jolt of heat right through the center of my chest.

I'm *tired* of being aloof, alone. I'm tired of keeping every feeling locked down because I'm afraid of being hurt. Sitting across from Fiona, I realize that there's more to life than what I've been doing. Maybe all my years here starting over—maybe I wasn't just existing, surviving. Maybe I was waiting.

For her.

When we finally make our way home on foot, Fiona's arm is hooked through mine, her head resting on my shoulder. Wine and food and laughter have given her cheeks a beautiful pink flush, and I find my eyes drifting to her perfect rosebud lips. Pausing on the edge of town, I pull her close and kiss her. I take my time, loving the way she opens for me, loving the way she tastes and sounds and smells.

Yes, I was waiting. I built a house—her dream house, she calls it—and a part of me wonders if it was meant to be. I built a house not just for me, not to run away... but for her. For us. Knowing deep down, somehow, she'd find me.

When I pull away from her, my hand stroking the side of her face, I have to reel in the words and feelings that threaten to spill out. Words that go against what we agreed on only a week ago.

*Let's keep it casual.*

What does that even mean? I clamp down on my words and force myself to smile. "Let's go home."

Her lips curl and she nods, drowsy. "Home."

We walk in silence, enjoying the sounds of the forest and each other's presence. My mind runs wild with all the things I plan to do with her when we get back to the house—and if we'll even make it to the bedroom. All the ways I'll show her how I feel, even if I can't find the right words. Even if I have no right to say them.

My hand tightens around her waist, and she melts against me, then stiffens when the house comes into view. I follow her gaze, suddenly alert. A threat, or an intruder...

A girl stands on my front porch, a backpack slung over one shoulder and an old duffel bag at her feet. As we approach, I see the holes worn through her old flannel shirt and the dirt caked onto the bottom hem of her jeans. She's wearing a baseball cap low over her eyes, and her hair looks almost matted. She's...fourteen? Fifteen? Older?

"Can I help you with something?" I ask, my voice gruff, almost threatening.

"Are you Grant Greene?" The girl's eyes dart from me to Fiona, who's straightened herself up and dropped her arm from around my body. There's fear in the girl's gaze. Hesitation. Then her face hardens and she throws her shoulders back, her chin jutting out. Pure teenage attitude in one movement.

I nod. "Yeah. Why?"

The girl's flinty stare meets mine, nothing but defiance in her eyes. "I'm your daughter."

# TWENTY-ONE
## FIONA

AS SOON AS the girl lifts her face enough for the porch light to illuminate it, I know she's telling the truth. She has the same grey-blue eyes, the same long nose, the same broad cheekbones. Her hair is blond, but there's no denying it.

She's Grant's daughter.

My heart stops. He never told me about a daughter. Why would he lie?

Swiveling my head, I take in Grant's reaction. Wariness, confusion, then shock. Pure, blind shock. He opens his mouth, then closes it, then opens it again, his feet rooted to the spot.

*He didn't know.*

My heart takes off, mouth drying up in an instant. Holy shiitake. He didn't know he had a daughter. His ex left without a word nearly sixteen years ago... Oh my goodness. My thoughts whip through my head, heart pounding in my chest.

The girl watches him, waiting. By the set of her jaw and the tension in her shoulders, I can already tell she hasn't had an easy life. There's anger coursing through her. Defiance.

My own shock percolates through my veins, gaze flicking between the two of them. I need to do...something. Clearing my throat, I gesture to the door. "Should we go inside?"

A grunt comes from Grant as a way of agreeing, and I make to grab the girl's duffel bag. She beats me to it, throwing me a threatening glare and baring her teeth. Well, all righty then. I curl my fingers back up and give her a tight smile, heading for the door.

My steps are mechanical. Adrenaline dumps into my blood. This is *not* how I thought tonight would go. Ten minutes ago, I was ready to take the word *casual* and rip it up into a million pieces. But now...

We shed our shoes and light jackets as the girl—shit. "What's your name?" I try to keep my voice light.

"Clancy."

"I'm Fiona. You can call me Fi. That's Grant." I shake my head, flushing. I had too much wine for this. I can't think straight. "But you know that already. Come through to the kitchen. Are you hungry?"

"I'm fine."

I keep my steps even as I walk to the kitchen, rustling up some food from the fridge anyway.

Grant stands by the entrance of the kitchen, unmoving. Still unable to speak. Still staring at the girl like she's an alien.

"Here we go. How do you like your sandwiches? You like mayo? Mustard?"

"Bit of butter if you've got it."

"No problem." My voice is clear. Bright. Doesn't betray the absolute hurricane of emotions rushing through my body.

Grant has a *daughter.*

*Shit shit shit shit shit.*

My movements are steady as I butter both pieces of bread and start assembling a sandwich. An uneasy silence settles over the three of us, and I tell Clancy to help herself to a glass of water.

She moves quickly, quietly, barely making a whisper of noise as her socks pad over the timber floors. As if she's used to moving quietly. Used to not being seen—or not wanting to be seen.

The lines bracketing the girl's mouth, the hollowness of her cheeks, the haunting aggression in her eyes—it makes my chest ache something fierce.

And Grant... He didn't know about her? I glance as he takes a step closer, sliding onto the nearest stool on the opposite side of the island. Judging by the slackness of his jaw and the wide-eyed stare that follows Clancy around the kitchen, no. He didn't know. That reaction could only be genuine.

My heart thunders, but I focus on the sandwich.

I told Candice I'd stay. I already called Simone to tell her, and the decision had been so, so easy. I *want* to stay here, with Grant.

But now...

Complicated—it's complicated. How am I supposed to keep things casual with Grant when his kid just walked into his life, our lives? How can I pretend I'm not falling for him when things have just changed so drastically?

And maybe the scariest thought of all—will I be able to take that room at the Heart's Cove Hotel if he decides he doesn't want me to stay while his daughter is here? Will I be able to walk away from him, to know that I don't belong in this house?

Today, I was ready to tell him that these feelings I have are growing. At dinner, seeing him across the candlelit table on the restaurant patio with a soft evening breeze ruffling his hair made me think...made me think all kinds of things I never thought I'd think again. Not after John. I wanted to tell him it wasn't just the café keeping me in Heart's Cove, and that it had been killing me to think of leaving after the Fringe Fest because I couldn't bear the thought of leaving him.

But now...

I flick my eyes to the teenage girl across from me. To her rounded shoulders and fidgeting hands. To her greasy hair, dirty clothes, to the aggressive, scared look in her eyes. He has a *daughter*—and where does that leave me?

Does it make me a selfish asshole to worry about that?

Brushing my thoughts away, I finish the sandwich, cut it into two triangles, and slide it across the island. I point to a stool. "Sit."

Clancy obeys, shimmying into the stool and devouring the sandwich in half a dozen hungry bites. She's starving.

Without asking if she wants any, I pull out some grapes from the fridge and some cheese and crackers. Things to nibble on if she's still hungry.

She finishes it all, then wipes her mouth on her dirty sleeve and finally lifts her eyes to mine. "Thanks," she mumbles.

"Of course." I nod, giving her what I hope is a friendly smile. Feels a bit like a grimace. I take a deep breath, stealing a glance at Grant. He still looks shell-shocked, watching every movement Clancy makes with a strange sort of awe in his eyes. "So, Clancy," I start. "First thing's first. Does your mother know you're here?"

The girl crosses her arms, burying her chin in her chest. "She won't care where I am."

"She most certainly will."

"I'm not talking to her."

Taking a deep breath through my nose and letting it out through my pursed lips, I brace my hands on the counter. I'm not prepared for this. I never had kids. Never had a teenager. I'm completely out of my depth, and judging by the look on Grant's face, he's not dealing with this any better than I am. Worse, actually. Quite a lot worse than me. I ask softly, "Do you have anywhere to stay?"

She shakes her head, barely moving it side to side. If I'd blinked, I would've missed the movement. Her eyes lift to mine, so full of fear I want to run to her and wrap her in my arms. When she drops her gaze again, I glance at Grant.

He clears his throat, finally speaking. "You can stay here tonight, but you have to call Sylvie in the morning."

Clancy just nods, her shoulders sinking inward, as if the weight of the world rests on her narrow frame.

I watch Grant's hand stretch toward her, then his fingers curl back into themselves and retreat to his lap. My heart aches for him, for the girl, for whatever happened to lead them to this moment. A million questions bubble up in my mind, but

Clancy yawns, and there's no missing the deep purple smudges under her eyes.

"Right. Let's get you set up in a room." I straighten up, grabbing her plate to put it in the sink. "There's a bathroom upstairs—and no offense, girl, but you need to take a shower. My eyes are watering." I pinch my nose, earning a ghost of a smile from Clancy. Barely a tug at the corner of her lips—but it's something.

She slides off the stool, hugging her arms around herself as Grant grabs her things. They both trail behind me as I lead them upstairs, stopping at the linen closet to grab some sheets.

I give Clancy Simone's old room, waving to the bathroom across the way. "In there should be everything you need. Toiletries, towels." I lift my eyes to hers. "You got clean pajamas?"

Clancy's face reddens, shame rippling through her features, and I wish I hadn't asked.

"I'll leave some on the bed for you. Is it okay if I do your laundry?" I nudge the duffel bag with my foot.

The girl nods again, finally pulling her hat off to drop it on top of the bag. To wash, I realize. Without it, she looks even younger than I first thought. How in the world did she make it here? How the hell did she find this place? Find Grant?

Without sparing either of us another glance, she disappears into the bathroom with a soft click of the door. We stand there for a few moments, then I let out a long sigh and grab the bag. "Better get these washed tonight so she has something to wear tomorrow," I say.

Grant's eyes meet mine. They're unreadable. Pain or pride

or gratitude or shame, I don't know. There's too much swirling in those grey-blue irises. Too much for me to understand, to carry.

As I start the load of laundry, my heart breaks all over again when I see the worn-out, ripped, filthy clothing Clancy brought with her, Grant boils the kettle. I hear it clicking off as cups clink against the countertop, and see him spoon sugar and place a tea bag in my mug before pouring the water in.

He hands it to me, and we sit on the Adirondack chairs outside, watching the stars shining in the sky as night deepens around us. Shadows pool under the canopies of nearby trees, and even the crickets seem to quiet down, as if the whole world is holding its breath.

Finally, Grant turns to me. "Thank you," he rasps, emotion tearing his throat raw. "Thank you. I wasn't... I didn't know how to act. You... I couldn't have done what you did in there."

"Make a sandwich?" I try a smile, but it falls flat.

Grant just reaches over and curls his fingers around mine, bringing them up to his lips. My heart tugs again, half of it wanting to run away—run from the complicated and the painful—and the other half wants to stay. To help. To heal.

"This isn't how I thought today would end," I finally say.

Grant huffs out a laugh.

I glance over at the beautiful, strong man beside me, and for the first time I see his vulnerability. His pain. "You didn't know about her?"

A shake of the head. "How old do you think she is?" he asks.

I gulp. "At first, I thought sixteen or older. But when she

took her hat off..." I nibble my lip. "Fourteen? Fifteen? Young. When did you say your ex left you?"

He closes his eyes. "Fifteen and a half years ago. The timing fits." Puffs of steam curl out of his mug, dissipating in the cool night air. A breeze ruffles his hair, and he doesn't bother pushing back the strands that fall across his forehead. Staring out at the distant horizon, Grant sighs as he shakes his head. "That's why Sylvie left. Because she got pregnant, and we'd talked about not having kids. I told her I didn't want any. I thought I wanted to focus on my career. She must have thought I wouldn't want her."

His words sink like stones to the bottom of a pool, one after another. Down, down, down, they plummet. And when they hit the bottom, he drops his head in his hands and weeps.

# TWENTY-TWO
# GRANT

THERE'S one thing I know for sure as I sit in my favorite chair on my back porch: I could not have survived this evening without Fiona. I would've handled it all wrong. I would never have thought about showers and pajamas and food. Instead, I would've demanded answers, been aggressive, caused a scene.

Fiona's hand is warm as she slides it over my forearm all the way down across my palm.

I intertwine my fingers with hers and lean back in my chair, watching more stars wink into view in the night sky. It's the space between the stars that holds my attention, though. That infinite emptiness.

"You probably have questions for me," I finally say, knowing Fiona's waiting for me to break the silence.

She takes a deep breath and releases it slowly, staring into the distance. "I have a lot of questions, but I can't quite think of any particular one right now. I'm a bit shocked."

I huff, shaking my head. "That makes two of us." She turns to meet my gaze when I squeeze her hand, and I almost can't handle the hesitation swirling in her eyes. Forcing myself to meet her gaze, I give my head an almost imperceptible shake. "I didn't know about her, Fiona. If I had, I would've... I would've talked to her. Been part of her life. I would've moved back to New York instead of staying here."

"Does her mother still live in New York?"

"I don't know." My voice is strained, the shame of my failures weighing heavy on every bone, every muscle, every tendon of my body.

I don't know when Clancy was born. Where she was born. How the first—what, fourteen, fifteen?—years of her life have been. I don't even know *how old my daughter is.* I don't know her damn birthday.

Fiona's hand sliding across my shoulders is the only thing that makes me realize I'm hyperventilating. She makes soft, soothing noises and rubs her hand over my back, shifting to sit on the arm of my chair. I lean my elbows on my knees and scrub my face, letting out a long sigh.

"We'll figure it out, Grant," Fiona says in a soft, sure voice. "Tomorrow, we'll call her mother and tell her she's safe. Then we can give her the choice of spending the day here with you or coming to the café with me. Candice told me her daughter would be helping out tomorrow, and she's about the same age as Clancy. We'll sit down—either the three of us or just you two—and find out how she got here and what her plan is."

"The three of us," I blurt out. "I..."

*I need you.*

Fiona's hand rubs my back, never pausing for a second.

I let out a long breath and finally lean back, lifting my eyes to hers. "I'm sorry to drag you into this."

Fiona's smile is pinched, but her eyes are sincere. "I'm just glad your life is as big a mess as mine is. Makes me feel better about myself."

Laughing, I shake my head. The cool night air fills my lungs and purges some of the darkness from my heart. Fiona's right. We'll figure it out. Clancy will call Sylvie, then we'll... I don't know what we'll do. We'll survive.

Intertwining my fingers in Fiona's as I stand up, I drag her to her feet and wrap her in my arms. This woman who drifted into my life just over a month ago has become my rock. My anchor. A light in the darkness. I bury my face in her neck and inhale her, letting my fingers sink into her body as she strokes her hands through my hair.

She pulls back to look in my eyes. Her lips are velvet-smooth and warm when she brushes them against mine, the touch gentle, soothing. As if she's saying, *I'm here. I'm staying. I'm with you.*

JUST AFTER DAWN, I hear an unfamiliar set of footsteps padding down the hallway to the kitchen. Clancy appears in a pair of pajama pants and a *Heart's Cove Hottie* t-shirt, rubbing the sleep from her eyes. I'm surprised to see her up so early.

"Morning," I say. *Keep it casual. This is normal. This is totally, completely normal.*

My daughter—*daughter*—grunts in response and heads for

the sink to pour herself a glass of water. She turns to lean against the edge of the sink as she crosses her arms, and I see so much of Sylvie in her movements that it makes my heart ache.

The coffee machine gurgles, the fresh roasted scent filling the room. "Coffee? Wait—do you drink coffee? You're too young, aren't you?" I resist the urge to punch myself. I don't know anything about parenting, about teenagers.

Clancy just wrinkles her nose. "Coffee's gross. Smells okay, though."

We move in silence. I take out some bread and point to the toaster, and Clancy helps herself to some jam from the fridge. At least she's comfortable enough to do that. That's a good sign, right?

Another, more familiar set of footsteps enters the kitchen, and another grunt greets me. Wonderful—they have that morning cheeriness in common. Fiona's bleary-eyed stare doesn't even move from the coffee machine as she shuffles past me, and I know she won't say a word until half her cup is drained.

So, the three of us sit around the table and have breakfast in relative silence, until Clancy speaks.

"I"—she clears her throat—"I wanted to say thank you. For the clothes and the food, and..." She trails off, not meeting either Fiona's or my eyes.

I nod. "Of course."

"I'm guessing you want me to call my mom now, huh?"

Another nod. "Yes. Does she know where you are?"

Clancy shakes her head.

I push my chair back and grab my cell phone from where

it's plugged in on the kitchen counter, unlock it, and slide it across the table toward my daughter. She runs her fingers through her hair, and my heart clenches when I see myself in the movement. "Use my phone. I'll have Sylvie's number then."

Clancy dips her chin down once, an almost imperceptible nod.

I've missed so much. Damn everything to hell. I've missed my daughter growing up while I was sulking in this town, thinking I'd lost everything. If I'd only *tried*—

"Hey," Clancy says in the phone, turning away from Fiona and me. "Yeah, I'm fine. I'm with Grant. Uh-huh. California."

*Grant.* Not Dad. My name hits me in the gut, but why would she call me anything other than my name? I haven't earned the title of Dad. I haven't been a father to her.

Guilt rakes its claws down my spine, and all I want to do is submit to it. Let it swallow me whole and never come back up for air. Sylvie left, yes, but I didn't look for her after she sent me the last email. I left too. I wallowed for *years*. And wasn't I the one to push her away? I pestered Sylvie for years to get help, to pull herself together. I was overbearing. Pushy. I told her I didn't want kids until she sorted herself out. Every time she started drinking again, I wanted to scream. She must've felt like she *had* to leave.

*My fault my fault my fault.*

When Clancy hands my cell phone across the table to me, she steals a glance at my face, at Fiona's. "She wants to talk to you."

*Oh.* Of course. I knew I'd have to talk to the woman who

broke my spirit, but I hadn't actually prepared for it. Bracing myself, I put the phone to my ear. "Hello?"

"So," a raspy voice says, "Clancy made it across the country on her own, did she?"

"She's safe. She was very resourceful to make it here by herself." I give my daughter a smile that she doesn't return. I guess I'll have to get used to teenage scowls.

"That little bitch s-stole my credit card, that's how far her *resourcefulness* goes. I expect her to pay back every fucking penny she ch-charged to it."

I bristle, a warning noise coming from the back of my throat. "I'll pay back what she owes you," I say, anger winding its way through my core. Does Sylvie call her a bitch to her face? A *child*? I steal a glance at my daughter, who's hunched over the table, her eyes glassy. "I'll pay for her flight back, too, when the time comes."

"She was dying to meet you, and you want to s-send her back so soon?" Sylvie's voice is so soaked in bitterness it almost knocks me back. There's something else in her voice—slurring. As if she's been drinking.

I check the clock—just after six o'clock, which means it's nine o'clock in New York. Too early to be drinking.

My heart sinks. So having Clancy wasn't a turning point for Sylvie. All the help I tried to give her did nothing. She kept drinking, kept spiraling down.

Frowning, I stand up to look out the window. "She's welcome to stay here as long as she wants, but I just figured you'd want her back. I thought you'd be worried."

A male voice shouts something in the background. Sylvie

shuffles, then her voice comes back on. "School doesn't start till September." *Click.*

I stare at the phone, jaw hanging open. Is that the woman who broke my heart? A woman who sounds so broken, so bitter, so...*awful.* She's who I was pining over when I landed in the hospital? She's who I went mad trying to protect? She's who's been *raising my child*?

Slowly, so slowly, I turn around to look at the two women sitting at the table. Fiona's face is pinched, but it's not her usual morning grumpiness. Worry lines her features as she meets my eyes, then shifts her gaze to Clancy.

Clancy's just staring at a spot on the table, hands tucked under her thighs, unmoving.

I clear my throat, but Clancy speaks first. "She didn't want me to come back."

The pain in that little girl's voice nearly breaks me all over again. What the hell happened these years? Why couldn't I do anything to prevent it?

Sliding back into my chair, I resist the urge to reach across the table. I've seen the way Clancy shies from my touch, skirts around the edges of the room to avoid coming too near. I don't want to spook her. So, exchanging a glance with Fiona, I try to keep my voice steady. "Fiona and I were wondering what you'd like to do today. You can go with Fiona to the café in town to help out, bussing dishes and delivering drinks to tables, cleaning"—my eyes dart to Fiona, who nods—"or you could stay here with me. I have some things to fix up in the garage that you could help me with."

"I'll go with Fiona," Clancy says, still not meeting either of our gazes.

It takes a second to swallow back my disappointment, but Fiona slides her hand over my thigh and gives me an encouraging nod.

"That's great, Clancy," Fiona says, her voice brighter than I've ever heard it at this time in the morning. She's trying hard. "We could use the help. It's the last day of the Fringe Festival and it's going to be busy." She squeezes my thigh as I slide my hand over hers, heart thumping.

No, I couldn't have done this without Fiona. I would've made a mess of it. Looking at the woman next to me, something unfurls in my chest. Warmth and gratitude and something deeper. Something I don't want to look at too closely, because even the whisper of it scares me to death. The last time I felt something even close to this, I squeezed it so tight Sylvie broke. *I* broke her. Look where that got me.

Fiona stands up and clears the table, then instructs Clancy to get dressed in that no-nonsense voice she was using last night.

I help her with the dishes and catch her hand as she heads for the stairs. "Fi," I rasp. "Something was wrong with Sylvie. She didn't...didn't seem to care."

Fiona glances at the stairs, then swings her gaze back to me. She gives me a sad smile and shakes her head. "I knew that the minute I saw Clancy's clothes. She's had a hard life, Grant."

"I'm sorry to drag you into this."

"You're not dragging me into anything." She stands on her tiptoes and kisses me. "I know there's a room at the hotel for me, but I'm here. I'm choosing to be here." Her fingers brush my cheekbones as my eyes flutter closed. She smells sweet and fresh when I pull her close, her body fitting perfectly against mine.

Pulling away, Fiona gives me a rueful smile. "This wasn't in the roommates-with-benefits handbook, but I think we both know we're past that now."

Tightness eases in my chest as I brush the backs of my fingers along her cheek. "I'm glad you decided to stay." It's not an overwhelming confession of my feelings, but it's something. I hope Fiona understands the meaning behind the words. How much it means that she would stick by my side.

"It was mostly this beautiful kitchen that convinced me. Couldn't go back to using a regular-sized sink when I have access to that one." She jerks her head to the deep white sink that nearly took my fingers off when I installed it.

Grinning, I nip at her lip with a growl. "I'll come by the café this afternoon. Take care of her."

"She'll be fine." With a pat on my chest, Fiona pulls herself away and walks up the stairs to our room. *Our* room, because we haven't slept apart since that first night.

# TWENTY-THREE
# CANDICE

THE ONLY WARNING I get that Grant's daughter will be joining us is a rushed text message ten minutes before Fiona arrives with the girl in tow. Glancing at my own daughter, currently redoing the artwork on the blackboard propping the door open outside, I suck in a breath.

"Hey, Allie?" I call out.

My daughter's blond curls gleam in the morning sun as she looks up at me, shading her face with her hands. My husband's eyes stare back at me, and for a moment I forget what I was going to say. It's been a year since he passed, but once in a while the pain of his death still hits me right in the middle of the chest.

Like now, when Allie stares at me, chalk in hand, her eyes dimmer than they were a year ago. I miss that crooked grin she used to give me before...*before*. Because that's my life now, forever cleaved in two distinct parts—Before Paul's death, and After.

In the After, Allie's crooked grin doesn't exist. The grin that was on her face from the moment she was born that never failed to remind me of the man I loved—still love. I haven't seen that grin in a year, and sometimes I wonder if I miss it more than I miss Paul.

My throat is tight when I gulp past a lump, and I force a smile of my own. "Grant's daughter is coming to help us out at the café today, and I'm going to need you to show her around, okay?"

"Grant has a daughter?" She arches a brow with the sass that only a fourteen-year-old can muster. "Since when?"

"Since yesterday, apparently."

She shrugs, going back to the blackboard. I know she'll come up with something creative and beautiful, because my teenage daughter is an artistic genius who never fails to impress me. In fact, a few minutes later I'm staring at her work—wide, swooping letters with complicated and colorful chalk shading that I don't know where she learned to create—when Fiona rings a bicycle bell, a scowling girl trailing behind.

Maybe she and Allie can have a glare-off. They'll either get along like a house on fire or absolutely hate each other. Lord help us either way.

Fiona locks both bikes up on the stand outside the shop and motions for the girl to approach. "This is Clancy. She'll be helping us out. Clancy, meet Candice and her daughter, Allie."

*Grunt.*

Lovely. She and Allie can invent their own language, too.

Fiona gives me an apologetic glance, and I shrug in response. I'm used to it.

Clancy wanders over to the blackboard and Allie stands up, wiping her chalk-covered hands on her brand-new black shorts.

I curl my hands into fists to stop myself from making a comment.

"I didn't know Grant had a kid," Allie says as a greeting, folding her arms.

Fiona stiffens beside me.

Clancy arches a brow—rivaling Allie's sass—and cocks her hip to the side. "He abandoned me before I was born." Her chin juts out. A challenge.

Allie holds the girl's gaze. "My dad's dead."

A beat of silence, then the two girls nod to each other, some sort of psychic teenage understanding flowing between them.

I try my best not to let terror flood my veins. Fiona and I exchange a glance, my new friend looking as worried as I feel.

But, soon enough, the day marches on and the morning rush starts, and I'm too busy to worry about the scars on Allie's soul and whether Clancy's presence is good or bad for her. Sven has a day off today, so I'm on barista duty with Fiona taking orders. We work well together, and it makes me happy to think about her staying in Heart's Cove. This café...it means a lot to me. More than I thought it would.

Ever since the Byrons died and their café down the road closed down, I've known I wanted to fill that gap. To give this town somewhere to gather on a Saturday and Sunday morning, just like Mr. and Mrs. Byron used to. Now that Fiona's here, it actually feels possible. It's not as overwhelming to think about running a café and a yoga studio and making sure Allie is fed and happy—well, if not happy, at least alive and unhurt.

Fiona doesn't say much, but I see the way her eyes dart to Clancy every few minutes. How she speaks to her with firmness and respect, keeps her busy cleaning and bussing and running drinks to tables.

"You okay?" I ask during a lull when Clancy and Allie have gone out back to take out the garbage. "How... Where did she come from?"

"New York, apparently. Showed up on Grant's doorstep last night."

I blow out a breath. "Dang."

"I have no idea what I'm doing, but she seems so...small. I want to help her, but I'm worried I'll do more damage."

"Girl, same." I laugh. "I think that's parenthood in a nutshell."

Fiona pinches a smile and shakes her head. "I'm not her parent. I don't want to overstep."

"She chose to come here, right?"

Fiona nods.

"So she feels safe with you. You're neutral. She probably doesn't know what to think about Grant, is angry and hurt and lost. So you're the life raft." I grin, arching my brows. "I'm guessing it's not what you signed up for when you took a room at Grant's place."

"Grant and I have been...involved," she admits.

I hide my surprise. So Jen was right—I should have known.

Fiona stares at the back door of the café, shrugging. "I don't mind Clancy being here. I just don't want to get in the middle of anything."

"You seem to be doing okay."

"It's been less than twenty-four hours."

The two girls burst through the door again, and I hear a sound I haven't heard in a long time. Bright, ringing laughter. Specifically, Allie's laughter. She turns the corner, and my heart stutters as I see not just a crooked grin on Allie's face, but a full-blown smile. Gripping the counter for support, I watch as she turns to Clancy and whispers something in the other girl's ear, the two of them falling into a fit of giggles.

Fiona stares at me, wide-eyed.

Friends, then. Two hurt little girls who might understand each other better than Fiona or I ever could.

# TWENTY-FOUR
## FIONA

I'M SO COMPLETELY unprepared for this. I don't know how to talk to a teenager and I don't know how to talk to Grant about it, but somehow we make it through the day and dinner, then Clancy tells us she'd like to spend some time in her room.

Her face isn't as lined as it was yesterday, and there's a brightness in her eyes that wasn't there this morning. I'm not so naive to think that fourteen years of what mostly likely was a traumatic upbringing can be healed in one day, or ever, but a bit of tension between my shoulders relaxes. Clancy disappears up the stairs, and I curl up on the couch beside Grant.

He wraps his arms around me and pulls me close, and after a long moment of silence he finally speaks. "I can never thank you enough for today, Fiona."

Leaning my head against his chest, words fail me. I want to tell him that even though I feel like a ship tossed out to sea in the midst of a storm, I also feel *good.* Today filled up some part of me I hadn't realized was empty.

I know I can't step in and act as Clancy's mother. It's not my place. I know she's a teenager and she's hurting, and neither of us even know how long she'll stay. But spending the day with her, seeing her with Allie, watching Grant stand by the grill as Clancy set the table earlier...it felt comfortable. Nice. It felt like something I've been looking for my whole life.

I lean my head against Grant's shoulder. He smells like sweetness and sawdust and cut grass. "Will you talk to her?"

Grant nods, his chin brushing my cheek. "I'll give her an hour to herself and then go see her. Thank you for bringing her to the café today, for knowing she needed a choice."

"Stop thanking me," I say, smiling, even though his words warm me all the way to my toes. That's one thing John never did—he never understood the million big and little things I did to make his life easier. He never looked me in the eye and told me he appreciated me.

Nuzzling against Grant's broad chest, I let my eyes drift closed, just enjoying the beat of his heart against my ear. "She's a good kid," I say.

"I want—I *need* to know what happened. I spent all day today itching to jump on a plane and bang Sylvie's door down to ask her what the hell she was thinking. Why the hell Sylvie didn't tell me, why Clancy just ran away. I feel...robbed. I could have been a father, and instead I was just here, sulking. Thinking I'd pushed Sylvie away and was destined to be alone."

"That's dramatic." I grin. Grant's shirt wrinkles as I curl my hand into it, a sliver of his chest appearing as the fabric moves. I let out a long sigh, tilting my head to meet his eyes. "She's here now. I think she needs you. Needs to know you're here for her."

"What do I do, Fi? Do I let her stay here for three and a half more months? Until September? Then I just ship her back to her mother, who might be drinking or doing drugs and obviously doesn't care about her own daughter leaving home? How can I go back to living here like I did before now that I know Clancy exists?"

My lips brush over Grant's stubble, tracing his jaw. He turns his head and lays a soft kiss on my lips, gripping my face with his hand to deepen the kiss. There's something growing in my heart. Expanding with every moment we spend together.

Last night, I thought Clancy's appearance would be a wedge between Grant and me. Selfishly, I thought it would end us.

But now I feel closer to him than ever.

His long, languid kisses make my toes curl. We stay tangled in each other on the couch for an hour, breathing in each other's scent and feeling each other's heartbeat.

We're long past casual now, and I'm not sure I care. It's too early to call this a family. Too soon to know it won't all fall apart, but...

No. I won't do that to myself. I won't latch onto the first man who comes along, the first person who makes me feel anything. I just got divorced and I'm recovering. I'm finding myself—whatever that means. I'm not looking for anything serious, and I'm definitely not looking for a whole new family.

That's what I tell myself when Grant's hands slip up my shirt and sweep over my skin, his calluses spreading goosebumps over my flesh. It's what I tell myself when he slides his tongue over mine and lets out a low groan. When he pulls away and stares into my eyes like he sees the whole world in my gaze.

"You should go to her," I say, and I know it's only to stop myself from saying something I'll regret. From voicing these feelings I have no right to feel, from telling him what's in my heart.

Grant nods. "Maybe I can bring some cookies up to bribe her to speak to me."

I laugh as I pull away, nodding. "You should, but I'm not sure you'll need it. She wants to be here. Wanted to get to know you."

His lips pull into half a smile as his long, muscular body unfolds itself. Standing above me, he grabs my hand, turns it over, and presses a kiss to the inside of my wrist.

My heart clenches, flips, and screams at me to tell him those three little words that shouldn't be anywhere near my tongue. Instead, I just give him an encouraging nod and watch him walk toward the stairs.

## TWENTY-FIVE
# GRANT

MY TOES SINK into the thick carpet outside my daughter's room. I raise my fist and let it hover, noticing a few chips in the paint on the door jamb. I'll need to fix that. There might be some leftover paint in my workshop, and if not, I definitely wrote down the name of the shade in one of my old notebooks—

I'm stalling.

Squeezing my eyes shut, I take a deep breath and will my fist to knock. Once, twice, pause. A small voice answers to come in as I realize my throat is completely dry. I should have brought glasses of water for this conversation.

Clancy is sitting on the bed, her back propped up against the headboard, a sketchbook lying in her lap.

Letting the door close behind me, I give her what I hope is an encouraging smile. "Hey."

She meets my gaze with those grey-blue eyes of hers—my

eyes—and there might be a bit more lightness in them than yesterday. Still dull, though. Suspicious.

Her pencil starts moving again as she turns back to her sketchbook. "Hey."

"You have a few minutes to talk?"

Clancy shrugs, eyes on her book, and I figure that's as much invitation as I'll get.

My palms start to sweat as I glance around the room, not seeing a chair, so I pad to the bed and sit near her feet.

She shifts to give me more room—or is it to move away from me?

I lift my knee up onto the bed and turn to face her, glancing down at her drawing. She's...*good*. "Allie likes to draw, too." My voice is raspy, so I clear my throat.

Clancy doesn't look up when she nods. "I know. We're going to a drawing class at the hotel together on Monday. She said it's free."

"Oh." My eyebrows jump up. "Right. Well, that's good."

She has a friend. She's already made a friend within twenty-four hours. It reminds me of Fiona's arrival in town, how she was able to slide into Heart's Cove with so much ease it felt like she'd always lived here. Nothing like my arrival, when it took months—years—of coaxing from Mr. Cheswick to finally feel like I belonged.

I did that to myself. I held myself apart from everyone, afraid of pushing them away. Afraid of caring too much.

"Your mom said you could stay here until September. I contacted a lawyer today to make sure we're not breaking any rules with custody and all that. I...I'm not sure how it works. They said we might need temporary custody and permission from Sylvie to let you stay here that long."

Clancy nods, her face an unreadable mask. "Okay."

I take a deep breath, turning to look at the wall. Her pencil scratches against the sketchbook, and for a few moments that's the only sound in the room. This is harder than I thought it would be, and I haven't even broached the hardest subject.

I'm the adult here. I should be able to talk to this girl about her mother, about her upbringing. When I look at her all I see is all the years I missed. It's hard to look at this girl who's so close to being grown and wonder how she would have turned out if I'd known she existed.

Stealing a glance at her, I take in the rounded shoulders, the curtain of hair covering part of her face, the short, steady movements of her drawing. Maybe that's where I should start—with the truth. Before I ask her anything about her, I should tell her about me.

"I want you to know that you're welcome here, Clancy," I say softly. "And if I've been...quiet...it's only because your arrival was a shock."

"You didn't think I'd find you?" Her words bite as she flicks her eyes to me, fire flashing in her irises.

"I didn't know you *existed.*"

Her pencil stills. "What do you mean?"

"I mean your mother left me without a word and... I guess it was when she found out she was pregnant. I don't know why she didn't tell me." I close my eyes, letting out a long breath. "I wish she had. I've missed so much, Clancy, and it kills me to think that you grew up without knowing me at all."

The pencil still hovers over the sketchbook, head tilting slightly. Clancy's eyes narrow. "She said you left her when she told you about me."

"*No.*" My breaths grow shorter, faster. "No, that's not what happened. I swear it on, on, on...on my life, Clancy. I didn't know about you."

Clancy holds my gaze, and I don't feel like the adult in the room at all. She holds all the cards here. She's in control of this conversation, and I'm not sure how to change that—or if I should.

I gulp. "Fifteen years ago, I came home to find your mother gone. I looked for her, desperate, until she sent me an email to tell me to stop." I suck in a breath, wondering if I should even tell her any of this. What if she's too young to know? But she's staring at me with bright eyes, intelligence written all over her face. She's had a hard life so far, short as it's been. She deserves for me to be honest, to treat her with respect. So I continue. "I ended up having a heart attack due to the stress from work and your mother leaving. Was in the hospital for a while and decided to leave my job and move here. Been in Heart's Cove ever since. I didn't know. I thought your mother was sick of me. Thought I'd been too pushy about helping her, wanting to fix her. I thought she left because of me."

Clancy just stares at me. Seconds tick by. Time drags on, and on, and on. It might only be a few moments, but it feels like an eternity. I need her to understand that I didn't know. I didn't leave my own daughter to fend for herself.

I close my eyes, shaking my head. "I should have pursued her harder, Clancy. I shouldn't have taken that email as the end, but after the heart attack, I just... I took it as a sign that it was over. That I needed to change. I'd been too overbearing, I'd pushed her away, my life fell apart and it was my fault. I'd tried to help her, wanted her to be something she wasn't. I broke whatever we had. That's what I thought. So I moved away and tried to start over."

Moving slowly, Clancy tucks the pencil into a pouch on the nightstand and closes her sketchbook. She tucks her knees into her chest and wraps her arms around them, staring at the bed. "She told me you never wanted me."

"No," I whisper. "I don't want to...pit you against your mother or anything. I don't want to come between you, but I swear, Clancy, I didn't know about you. I would have stayed."

"Your life would have sucked if you did." She lays her cheek on her knees, and all I want to do is wrap my arms around her. My flesh and blood. My little girl.

A part of me thinks I don't have a right to think of her as my daughter, I don't have a right to parent her—but the feelings roar through me. There's no stopping the protectiveness, the...love.

I want to drag her close and hold her tight and make her forget whatever's caused her eyes to be so empty. Whatever's made her face lined with worry and suspicion. I want to throttle Sylvie for what she did to her. To me.

"Mom was drunk when I spoke to her this morning," Clancy says, still not looking at me. Her head rests on her knees as she hugs them close, as if she's trying to fold herself into nothing. She stares at the wall or at a distant spot within her own mind.

I gulp. "I...I thought she sounded...off." Words are so hard. I'm not prepared for this.

Clancy's lips curl into a bitter grin. "Yeah. *Off* is a more polite way of saying it."

"Does she drink a lot?"

"It would be easier to talk about when she doesn't drink."

Emotion clogs my throat. Anger and hurt and protectiveness and—*betrayal*. Sylvie robbed me of a relationship with my daughter. She stole this from me, and she gave this little girl an upbringing that no one deserves.

And she had the gall to blame *me*. To say I drove her away, I drove her to drink.

Clancy shifts, resting her chin on her knee as she levels me with that unflinching stare. As if she's seen it all, and nothing will ever scare her. "Will you want me to go back there come September?"

"Would you want to stay?"

"You first."

A grin tugs at my lips. "Fine. No, I wouldn't want you to go back, not if you didn't want to. I mean, I'm not... I don't know how to be a father, but if it's not a good environment for you in New York, you'd be welcome to stay here."

Her eyes dim. "But you'd prefer it if I left."

"No." I inhale sharply, rubbing the heels of my palms into my eyes. Everything's coming out wrong.

"I'd be messing up your life with Fiona."

"Fiona and I..." Are what? Casual? I can't get the words out, and I doubt it's an appropriate thing to tell a teenager.

"It's fine. I get it."

"No, Clancy, listen." I scoot closer, and my daughter's eyes narrow suspiciously. I stop my hand before it reaches her, leaving it on the bed halfway between us. It's there if she wants to take it. "I want you here. I would have wanted you here when you were a baby, and I want you here now. Okay? We can talk to your mother and the lawyer about what happens in September, but if you want to stay, I'll do what I can to make sure you can. Let's just see how you like it, yeah? It's only been one day. You might be sick of us in a couple of months."

A tiny nod. "Maybe."

"When's your birthday?" I blurt out.

"July twenty-second."

"You'll be fifteen?"

She nods.

"That's a big year. And your first birthday in Heart's Cove. Your first birthday with...me."

She chews her lip, something softening in her eyes. "You really want me to stay?"

My heart hurts. I lift my arm in a silent invitation, unable to speak, and almost break down when Clancy scoots closer to me and wraps her arms around my middle. It's the first time she's come close enough to touch. The first time I've been able to hug her—hopefully not the last.

We talk for an hour or longer about everything and nothing. She likes to draw and gets pretty good grades. Her favorite subject is art, obviously. I get an eye roll with that answer. It makes me smile and fills me with more than a bit of fear for the amount of sass and attitude to expect over the next few months.

She's never played team sports but likes to run. She'd be interested in spending time in my workshop with me, and enjoyed working at the café with Fiona. She likes chocolate cake.

I tell her about my first years here, about learning to be a carpenter. She asks me about the life drawing class (I blame Allie for telling her about that) and wrinkles her nose in absolute disgust, promising to never, ever, ever go to that class.

I'm laughing when a soft knock sounds on the door. Fiona pokes her head in with a stack of clean, folded laundry. The sight of Fiona's dark hair, kind eyes, and the laundry that is such a small part of what she's done for Clancy over the past twenty-four hours makes my heart clench. She's brave and unflinching and kind, and I'm not sure I deserve her.

She slides it onto the dresser with a smile. "I noticed you don't have any shorts, Clancy. It gets pretty warm here. Would you like to go shopping for some tomorrow?"

Clancy stiffens. "I'm not... I don't..."

I frown, not understanding, but Fiona grins. "Grant missed out on buying you clothes for the first fourteen years of your life. I think he's dying to spoil you. Aren't you, Grant?"

Clancy was worried about *money*. Fiona could tell within seconds, and I had no idea.

I nod, forcing a smile as I give Clancy's shoulder a squeeze. "It's the least I can do, but don't expect me to try to buy your love with a bunch of fancy clothes."

Clancy grins, as if it's a challenge. But she's smiling, and the sight of that smile sends a lightning bolt through my chest.

I leave her after one last hug, then follow Fiona into our room.

She beams at me, eyes bright. "That looks like it went well."

"Yeah." I slide my arms around her waist, knowing it would have been infinitely harder without Fiona here. "It did."

# TWENTY-SIX
## FIONA

THE FIRST WEEK Clancy stays with us is an adjustment period. I'm not sure where Grant and I stand, not sure what my role with Clancy is, and not sure how Grant and Clancy's relationship will develop. Mostly, I try to stay out of the way while offering support.

The logical thing to do would probably be to step aside, to give them space. But Clancy seems to enjoy coming to the café, and Grant always tells me how much he appreciates my help. The three of us fall into a routine together, and it doesn't take long for it to feel natural. Comfortable.

Like a family.

It's silly to think that way. Every night, when Clancy's gone to bed and Grant and I have our nightly cup of tea on the back porch, I keep telling myself I should take a step back. I wanted things to be casual with Grant, and I'm in no place to be a parent to that little girl.

I just got divorced, and no matter how natural it feels to be here with them, they're not my family. I've known Grant a couple of months and Clancy only a week. The last thing I should be doing is falling into a complicated relationship when my marriage officially ended only months ago. Sure, it was a year and a half ago that John told me he wanted a divorce, and probably four or five years since our marriage truly deteriorated, but still. It feels so soon to be jumping into...whatever this is. Something more serious than I anticipated.

I don't care anymore that Grant used to be a lawyer. It's obvious he's different from John in a million ways. He's more caring. He notices all the things I do for him. He does little things for me—making my tea and coffee, driving me to the café, making sure there's a fresh bouquet of flowers in the entryway every week.

Just because he was a lawyer in a past life doesn't make him like John—I know that now. Still, do I really want to pursue this? And Clancy... Is it fair to her for me to be involved when Grant and I aren't even officially together? The last thing I want to do is be another person in her life who lets her down.

Still, as days pass, I stay at Grant's house. We officially hire Clancy to help out at the café, and her eyes go wide when I tell her how much she'll be paid. Minimum wage, and only part time—but evidently more than she's ever had.

Grant takes her to open a bank account in her own name, since she's never had one before. When I watch them walk out of the bank together, a huge smile on Clancy's face as Grant puts his arm around her shoulders, my heart squeezes so hard it hurts.

She needs this—him. Maybe even me. She needs stability.

But, but, but...

Do I really fit into their story?

WEEKS BLEED INTO EACH OTHER. Even after the Fringe Festival ends and all the tents and stalls are packed away, I'm glad I decided to stay. Candice, Jen, and I keep the café open, and with fewer tourists in town, things slow down, but don't stop. We already have regulars.

This project that felt like it was all mine is starting to feel like *ours*. Heart's Cove is starting to feel like home. It happens naturally over the course of hours, days, weeks.

Clancy works hard and earns her pay. She spends more and more time with her dad, which warms my heart, and does art classes at the hotel with Allie. She's still moody and suspicious, but less so. She laughs more. Her sassiness is off the charts, and she has the snarky eye roll down to a science. I try to keep my thoughts at bay and just enjoy the summer, enjoy the moment. The feeling of belonging, of having a project of my own with this café, of having a family to go back to every evening.

Three weeks after the end of the Fringe Festival, I get a message from Simone to tell me she's on her way back, and she's bringing my car. I show Grant the message and grin. "I'd gotten attached to my bike, but it looks like I won't need it much longer."

He runs his hands down my sides as he pulls me close, sliding them around to rest on my ass. With a little squeeze, he cocks a brow. "I've gotten attached to the bike, too, and how perky it's made one of my favorite body parts of yours."

Laughing, I tilt my head up and let him brush his lips over mine. We're past pretending that this is a roommates-with-benefits situation, but we haven't actually broached the subject. Not that I want to. I like how things are. I like these feelings. Talking about what will happen in the future, especially with Clancy here, seems far too difficult for me to tackle right now.

Grant nuzzles my neck, nipping at my ear. "Clancy won't be back from her art class for a couple of hours," he growls, his words sending heat tumbling through my veins.

It doesn't take long for us to stumble up the stairs and end up tangled in the bedsheets. When he holds me, his powerful body arched over mine, the heat in his eyes fans the flames in my gut. My toes curl, my back arches, and I lose myself in him. For those long moments, when we're tangled in each other, I forget about my reservations. I lap up his affection, his emotion, and I let it break me then put me back together again.

"Fiona," he groans, his breath warming my neck. My name sounds like a prayer on his lips, and my heart feels so full I'm afraid it might burst out of my chest. I rake my nails down his back and come apart in his arms, clinging onto him until he finds his own release.

When we catch our breath, I turn my head on the pillow and let my arm fall across his chest. "I'll never get sick of doing that with you."

Grant catches my fingers and brings them to his lips. "Good. Me neither."

I'm an adult. I can do this. Sucking in a hard breath, I force the words out. "Should we talk? About us?"

He meets my gaze, his eyes soft. "Probably. I know this situation isn't what you asked for, Fiona, and I don't want you to feel uncomfortable. But I like having you here. I like...this. What we have."

I nod, breath catching. I can see two paths stretching out before me. One of them includes afternoons like this, tangled in Grant's arms. It includes family and Clancy and letting go of all my fears about committing to a relationship with someone again.

It includes the café. Candice and Jen and maybe even Simone, if she's wanting to stay. It's the fresh start I was looking for.

And the other path has me walking away. Staying true to the commitment I made to myself to stand on my own two feet and find myself. Distancing myself from men and all the complications that come with them.

As Grant wraps his arms around me and pulls me into his embrace, I know which one I want—I want *him*. I want this. I want to be happy, finally. I want to believe I could have all the things I never thought would come to me.

Still, a part of me holds back. A corner of my heart that was hurt most when John betrayed me. A slice of my mind that's trying to protect me. I shouldn't let myself fall for another man so quickly. Right?

Maybe, in time, that hesitant piece of me will disappear.

Grant lays a soft kiss in my hair, and I want those doubts to melt away. I want to be able to give him everything, but I can't quite shake the feeling that it's too soon. It's too much. I can't give him my whole heart—not yet.

"Clancy's birthday is at the end of July," he says after a while. "The twenty-second."

I do mental math—seven weeks away. "We'll have a party."

He grunts. "You want to?"

"Event planning is my jam. I bet she'd love feeling special, for once. We should invite everyone, make it a big get-together. Simone will be here, and she told me she's planning on staying. It can be a birthday party and a welcome and a celebration of the café's success this summer."

He stills. "Maybe we should do something small. We don't know what Clancy wants."

I tilt my head toward his, smiling. "That girl loves being spoiled. She'd like seeing everyone come together."

He squeezes me close, and when he speaks, his voice is choked. "Okay."

"Have you talked to the lawyer? Are you still hoping to get visitation rights?"

He's silent for a long while, then lets out a breath. "I've been talking to him about full custody."

"You want Clancy to stay?" My eyes widen, and Grant's fingers start making small, soothing circles over my back, as if he wants to keep me calm.

"I can't let her go back there. Sylvie called her a bitch when I spoke to her that first morning. She's a kid! The lawyer said I could get custody if the judge in New York determines that

Sylvie isn't fit to parent. If we can prove that she drinks and doesn't take care of Clancy, we might have a chance. He said courts hesitate to take children away from their mothers, though, and it doesn't help that we're in a different state. I might have to go over there. The timeline is tight, especially with school starting in September."

I nod, heart squeezing. "Does it help or hurt that I'm living with you?"

His hand freezes. "What do you mean?"

"Well, we only met a few months ago. On paper, it doesn't exactly tell the story of a stable household for a child to move into."

His arms tighten around me, as if he's afraid to let me go. "We'll cross that bridge later."

I nod, running my fingers over his jaw in smooth strokes. "You're doing the right thing," I whisper. "Let's just make her feel welcome, and we'll deal with the legal stuff as it comes. Maybe her birthday party will be a custody celebration, too. We'll figure it out."

Grant's eyes soften as he looks at me, his forehead resting on mine. "You mean that? *We*?"

Throat tight, I nod. In that moment, I choose which path I want, even if that little corner of my heart and my mind still scream at me to be careful. I can't let my fears hold me back when I know the right thing to do—not just for me and Grant, but for Clancy, too. I brush my lips against Grant's, feeling the weight of my decision settle over my bones. "Yeah," I murmur. "We."

. . .

AT THE BEGINNING OF JULY, Simone arrives in Heart's Cove with a trailer towing all the stuff I'd put in a storage locker after moving out of John's penthouse—and all of Simone's things, too. She pulls up outside the café just as I'm locking the door for the day.

"Surprise!" Her arm hangs out of the driver's window, a cheeky grin on her face. "I figured if you like it so much here, I might as well give it a try."

"What about your house?"

"Put it on the market, got an offer, closing on it in a month. I'm free, baby."

My eyebrows climb up, up, up. "You've really sold your house? Isn't that a bit...drastic?"

"One woman's drastic is another woman's fresh start." Her smile widens, a challenge brimming in her eyes. Something she's not telling me, then.

"You staying at our place?"

"*Our* place?"

I bite my lip. "Things may or may not have progressed with Grant. After his daughter got here, everything's moved pretty quickly."

"And all this from little miss I'm-not-ready."

"You want a room, or no?" I cross my arms.

Simone shakes her head. "I booked our never-used honey-moon cabana at the hotel. Going house-hunting as of tomorrow morning."

"Buying?"

Another shake of the head. "Renting. Turns out rent is a *lot* more affordable in a small tourist town up the coast than it is in L.A. Need to fill up the coffers again. Work has been slow."

"You seem oddly okay with uprooting your whole life."

"Maybe my roots weren't all that deep. Don't pretend you're not happy to see me."

I laugh, nodding. "Will you at least come to dinner tonight? You can meet Clancy."

Simone's smile widens as her chin dips down. "Hop in. I'll check in with Dorothy, unhitch the trailer, and we can drive over together."

"What happened to Big Bertha?"

"Laid to rest after eleven years of loyal service."

I scrunch my nose. "Sorry about that."

"This Merc is much nicer. Weren't you saying how much you enjoyed the bicycle? Maybe you could donate Voldemort's car to a good cause. That good cause being me."

Grinning, I slide into the front seat and jerk my chin toward the hotel. "Come on, you loon. Let's go."

Instead of driving forward, though, Simone just stares at me for a long moment. "You look good, Fiona."

"Don't sound so surprised."

Her eyes soften. "I mean *good.* Your eyes are full of light and your skin is flushed. I haven't seen you like this in a long time."

"Heart's Cove agrees with me."

"Or a certain Heart's Cove hottie." She laughs, putting the car in gear, ready to head home with me.

*Home.* Because that's what Grant's place has become, whether I'm ready to fully accept it or not. It's home with him and Clancy every evening, with our meals in that Pinterest-worthy kitchen and comfortable yet masculine design. Finally, after feeling restless and dissatisfied for so long—longer than I want to admit—I've finally found somewhere to settle.

## TWENTY-SEVEN
## SIMONE

FIONA IS A GREAT HOST, and I can tell things have changed between her and Grant in the past month. They're both a lot more comfortable around each other. I see the little smiles they give each other, the touches they think nobody will notice. There's intimacy between the two of them that I never saw between my best friend and her ex.

She deserves it.

I can't remember the last time I had a family dinner. Dinner parties with girlfriends, yes. Dates—mostly first dates, because I haven't found anyone worth a second—sure.

But an actual sit-down dinner where people talk about their days? Laughter and companionship and a deep feeling of *home*? A teenager? A *pass the salt and pepper* kind of meal?

Years. Probably not since I was a kid. My ex-husband and I never had anything like this, yet somehow, within a couple of months, Fiona's managed to find herself a family. As I heap another piece of lasagna on my plate, I steal a glance at my best friend.

She's glowing.

And Grant? I didn't know he was capable of smiling so much. His daughter looks exactly like him, and although there's a lingering awkwardness between them, it's nothing like what I'd expect from this situation. The three of them just *get* each other.

"So you're staying in Heart's Cove?" Grant asks me.

I grin. "You sound disappointed. I couldn't leave poor Fiona here all by herself, could I?"

"She's not alone," he says, shifting his gaze to Fiona.

"Okay, okay, we get it," Clancy huffs, rolling her eyes. "You're in love. Don't make me barf up my dinner."

I laugh into my fist as Fiona's back straightens, her eyes darting to Clancy, then to Grant. Her cheeks are red as she returns her gaze to her plate. So she doesn't realize she loves him yet—or doesn't want to admit it. Interesting.

Dinner leads to wine on the veranda, and Clancy disappears to her room. I sit back, inhaling the fresh air, and turn to look at Fiona and Grant. "She's a good kid."

Grant's eyes gleam with fatherly pride. "She is. Got a rebellious streak, though. She's been trying to stay out late with Allie and I'm having a hell of a time getting her to come home."

"She's used to having free rein," Fiona says, sighing. My best friend glances at me. "We're having a party for her birthday. You want to help plan it?"

"Don't have anything else to do, so sure."

"Your enthusiasm is staggering," Fiona deadpans, and I can't help but laugh.

"I've been thinking, Fiona," Grant starts, clearing his throat. "Maybe keeping the party small would be better. You said yourself she doesn't do great in crowds at the café, and if there are too many people here, we won't be able to pay attention to her. Maybe we should just keep it to close friends and let her have time with Allie. Just a nice barbecue or a dinner or something."

Fiona shifts, biting her lip. "I've already organized catering with Jen and sent out invitations. Fifty-two have RSVP'd already."

"*Fifty-two*?" Grant's eyes bug. "I didn't even know I had fifty-two friends."

Fiona shifts uncomfortably, throwing me a glance before turning back to Grant. "You want me to cancel? Tell them we'll just do something small?"

Grant takes a deep breath and finally shakes his head. "If people have RSVP'd already, we can't take it back. I'll just have to make sure Clancy feels okay about it all." He reaches over and puts his hand on Fiona's, lifting her fingers up to his lips.

My best friend's lips melt into a soft smile as my heart grows in my chest. "Good to have you back, Fi," I say. When she tilts her head, I raise my glass of wine toward her. "You weren't yourself these past years."

She shifts her gaze to Grant, a soft smile on her lips—and I know Clancy was right. Fiona's in love.

. . .

IT ONLY TAKES me a week and a half to find a place to live. Turns out Dorothy and Margaret know someone who has an apartment, and I'm able to move in right away. It's small—right on the main drag through Heart's Cove across from the yoga studio and café—and best of all, it's cheap. My finances are still strained and will be until the sale of my house closes, but at least I'm moving on. I can run my copywriting business from here and try to rebuild. Restart.

Worked for Fiona, didn't it?

ASIDE FROM DOING a few freelance jobs, I spend my days helping Fiona plan Clancy's party. It'll be at Grant's house, and we have a thousand and one little jobs to do. Fiona is in full event-planning mode, and I don't remember the last time I saw her with this much energy. I visit her at the café every morning and do some work on my laptop, then spend the afternoons hanging out, doing yoga, and helping her plan. We fall into an easy rhythm together.

A week after I move into my new place, and only four days before the party, I grab a coffee from Fiona and head back to my place across the street. On my way there, though, I spot a very large man standing near my front door, arms crossed, eyes on the café.

"Wesley!" I call out. "Looking pleasant as usual."

He scowls at me. "What are you doing here?"

"Bringing a fresh, hot coffee up to my apartment so I can get the last of my work done for the day. You?" I keep my smile bright, eyes drifting over his muscular chest and all the way up to his eyes. I try not to falter when I see the animosity simmering in his gaze. I squeeze my thighs together as heat whips through my core. Why does his hatred turn me on? Have I lost my mind?

Wait. Don't answer that.

"You live here now?" His voice is a gentle rasp, and the fire in my stomach moves lower. Wesley's eyes are bright as they flick to my lips for just a moment before moving back to my eyes. His scowl deepens, as if he hates the fact that he looked.

"Just one big, happy family." My grin widens, and I'm pretty sure I'm just baring my teeth at this point. I spin around and follow Wesley's gaze toward the café as I sip my drink. "Pretty popular place."

"So was my parents'."

Before I can answer, a delivery van stops on the street right beside me. I turn to see a man in a yellow polo shirt opening the van door and producing a large vase overflowing with flowers. He looks at my building, and when he goes to press the buzzer for my door, I stop him. "That's my place," I say. "Simone McMaster." I point my thumbs to my chest.

The delivery man checks his paper and thrusts the vase into my hands. I sign his clipboard and watch him walk away, then let my eyes dart to Wesley.

"Secret admirer?" he says, the growl in his voice sending shivers coursing through my blood.

"You shouldn't have, Wesley. Hanging around my door and buying me flowers...it's too soon. You'll scare me away. I'm not into the whole stalker vibe." I grin and bat my eyelashes, laughing at the horror on his face as he starts to shake his head.

Then I flip the card on the flowers and see my ex-husband's name. Anger whips through me. "How the *fuck* did he find me? I meet up with him *one time* after eight years, and all of a sudden he's trying to woo me? The man has lost his damn mind. Not that he ever had one to begin with."

Marching over to the garbage can on the corner of the street, I upend the vase and dump the flowers, water and all. When I tuck the vase under my arm and turn back toward Wesley, he's staring at me, brows drawn together. "Remind me to never buy you flowers."

"It's a long story."

"I bet. Didn't want to throw out the vase?" He nods toward my arm.

"I'm broke. I can use all the vases I can get."

Is that a hint of a smile I see on his face?

Lingering by my door, I'm not quite ready to head upstairs. Wesley's eyes have drifted back to the new café across the road, and I find myself leaning against the wall beside him. "Does it bother you that they opened another café?"

"Why would it bother me?" His voice is gruff, low. As if there might be a ball of emotion in his throat he's struggling to speak around. His eyes drift down the street to the boarded-up windows of his parents' old café. As a soft breeze ruffles his golden-brown hair, a muscle feathers in his jaw.

"Fiona told me that their business license runs out at the end of the year. By September they have to decide if they want to renew it or not. She said they were thinking of expanding to a bigger space. Maybe somewhere with a kitchen so they can serve brunch, too."

"Why are you telling me this?"

"Seems to me you have a bigger space." I jerk my head toward the dark coffee shop his parents used to run. "Maybe you and Fiona could work together."

"I'm not interested in running a brunch restaurant." He pushes himself off the wall, turning away from me. My eyes snag on his t-shirt, which is straining hard to stretch over the slabs of muscle that make up his body.

"You wouldn't have to run it," I say softly. "You'd just have to lease them the space."

He grunts, not turning to look at me. I ignore the twinge in my chest as he walks away. Drops of water fall out of the vase and soak my shirt. I groan, shaking out the wet fabric.

An ex who doesn't want to leave me alone, a grumpy asshat who doesn't want to help my friend, a dangerously low bank account, and no new jobs on the horizon. My life is just peachy. Exactly what I expected for my forties. At least I can enjoy the party this weekend. I'll be able to forget about the shitshow of midlife for at least one afternoon.

# TWENTY-EIGHT
# GRANT

THE MORNING of Clancy's birthday party, I find myself staring at the ocean with my daughter by my side. The sun is warm at our backs as we dangle our feet off the end of the pier, and I savor every minute I have with her. Nudging her shoulder, I give my daughter a grin. "You still like it over here?"

She nods once, just a quick dip of her chin. "Allie said her school is really good. She said she'd introduce me to all her friends."

My heart squeezes. "You know we might not be able to do that this year, right? We still need to wait and hear what the lawyers say about custody. Your mom might not want you to stay here."

"I don't care about what she wants."

"The courts do, though." A wry grin tugs at my lips at Clancy's stubbornness. Her fire. How she managed to survive these past fifteen years, I'm not sure. All I know is she's strong—stronger than I was.

Over the past few weeks, we've spent more and more time together. With Fiona there as a buffer between us, I've watched Clancy slowly relax and open up to me. She's sought me out in the evenings, often just to sit quietly near me. I still can't believe she's mine, that she had the courage and determination to make a trek across the country by herself. That she *made* it.

"Was it scary to leave home?" I ask.

Clancy purses her lips, her eyes taking on a faraway look. She nods again—that one quick dip of her chin. "Yeah. But I wanted to meet you at least once. And things at home..." She grimaces, falling silent. In all our talks, in all the time we've talked to each other, she's never told me what her home life is like beyond saying it's bad, and that Sylvie drinks.

Until now.

Clancy takes a deep breath, her fingers curling over the edge of the pier. "Mom's boyfriend is mean when he drinks," she says, and I inhale a breath through my teeth, willing my anger to stay down. Clancy's eyes narrow. "Her last boyfriend was okay. He didn't like me, but he mostly stayed out of the way. But this one..."

"*Did he hurt you.*" Not a question. A demand. My voice is low, cold.

"He tried." Her fingers curl harder around the timber beneath us, knuckles turning white. "He moved in the week before I left. I knew if I stayed there..."

My breath is shallow as I struggle to maintain a semblance of calm.

Clancy lets go of the pier and turns to look at me, no doubt taking in the clench of my jaw, the tension rippling through my body. Slowly, she moves her hand on top of mine and curls her fingers into my palm. She lifts my hand and lays it across her lap, leaning her body against mine. "I don't want to go back."

I squeeze her hand, knowing I can't let her go. I can't let her go back to that place, no matter what the courts say. I need an emergency custody order. Evidence that Sylvie isn't a fit mother. I'll get Fiona to write an affidavit about the state of Clancy's clothes when she first got here. Her hygiene. What Sylvie said to me on the phone.

I won't let her go back. I won't put her in harm's way. I'll move to New York myself if I have to, just to prove to the judge that I'm serious.

"I've never had a birthday party before," Clancy says quietly.

Her words pierce through the veil of anger and protectiveness that had been choking me, and I find myself lifting my arm to lay it across Clancy's shoulders. I pull her into me, her wiry arms wrapping around my waist.

Maybe Fiona was right to plan something big for Clancy. She needs to know we want her here. *I* want her here.

Then, reaching into my pocket, I pull out a small package—barely a scrap of wrapping paper—and hand it to Clancy. "Fiona organized your real birthday presents, but I wanted to give you this."

Clancy tucks a strand of blond hair behind her ear, her throat bobbing as she gulps. She looks up at me, eyes wide, and I'm struck again by the fact that this girl is my kin. Her eyes are my eyes, and I'm so fucking proud of her it hurts. Nodding to the small package, I give her what I hope is an encouraging smile. "Go ahead."

She flips the square of wrapping paper over, feeling the hard metal inside. Sliding her finger under the tiny piece of tape, she opens the package and pulls out a key.

"For the house," I say, jerking my head toward the house behind us. "It's your home as much as it is mine."

Clancy's eyes widen, tears pooling in them. She wraps her arms around my neck and nearly tackles me to the ground, her whole body shaking. When she pulls away, she wipes her tears on the back of her sleeve—an old flannel shirt of mine that she must have stolen at some point—and stares at the key as if it's the most precious gift in the world. She cups it in her palms like a precious baby bird.

The sun rises a bit more behind us, gilding her hair, her skin, her tears. My daughter sniffles, shaking her head, and slides the key into her pocket. "Thank you," she says, lifting her gaze to mine.

I give my daughter another hug and ruffle her hair for good measure, even if she yelps and pulls back, then stand up and extend my hand to her. "Come on. We'd better help Fiona with the preparations for the party."

She hooks her arm through mine, patting her pocket, and my heart feels so full it's about to burst. I find Fiona in the kitchen—her first coffee already drank to chase away the morning grumpiness, thank goodness—and my heart gives another hard thump when she smiles at me.

"Happy birthday, kid," she says to Clancy. "You ready for today?"

"Ready to party," Clancy replies, a mischievous gleam in her eye. "I have to get dressed." Rushing down the hall, she disappears up the stairs, every footstep like thunder over our heads.

I walk behind Fiona and wrap my arms around her, holding her back to my front as I nuzzle her neck and inhale her. The woman who made all this possible. The woman who opened me up enough to allow my daughter in. The woman who welcomed Clancy, who became the sounding board, the neutral ground, the space in which the start of my relationship with my daughter could grow.

"Thank you," I whisper.

Fiona lifts her hand and slides it through my hair, leaning against me as she sighs.

I kiss her neck, her earlobe, her jaw, reveling in every soft noise that comes from her.

"Remember when I said I didn't want anything serious?" Fiona says. Her eyes are closed, lashes fanning over her cheeks as she leans back against my shoulder, lips dangerously close to mine. "That didn't exactly work out as planned, did it?"

I chuckle, wrapping my arms tighter around her. "Not quite."

"This is better." A whisper. Her voice barely more than a breath, but the words clang through my body like a church bell.

Yes, this is better. Life with her is better. Life with Clancy is better. The promise of a future brighter than I ever thought I deserved.

. . .

CLANCY'S PARTY is organized chaos. I'd say most people are just here for the promise of free food and drink, but as Fiona plays the gracious host and the afternoon wears on, I know they're here for her, too. Because she's imprinted herself upon this town in a few short months, just as she branded herself on my heart.

Allie arrives with Candice shortly after the start of the party, and Clancy quickly drags her new friend away. They head to the pier and I watch them disappear over the knoll, my daughter turning back to look over her shoulder, a bright smile across her face. She dips her chin down and lifts her arm in a wave, and I let my lips slip into a smile.

"The hardest part of being a parent is letting go of the reins," Candice says as she steps up beside me, watching her child disappear over the knoll with mine.

"Clancy and Allie seem to get along."

Candice grins at me, shaking her head. "Still remains to be seen whether that's good or bad. Those two girls will get into a world of trouble. Mark my words."

I laugh, then find myself walking inside again to pilfer something tasty from the food table and get myself another drink. This is more than a birthday party, I realize. As Dorothy and Agnes exchange tense glances across the room, and Mr. Cheswick tells a less-than-appropriate joke to his captive audience, and Simone helps Fiona clean up empty bottles and cans, I realize this is a welcome party, too. A welcome to Fiona, Simone, and Clancy, but also welcome to me. After nearly fifteen years in this town, I can finally call it home in my heart and my mind.

We see very little of the girls, but I'm too busy feeling warm and happy to notice. As the sun starts to set and Fiona says something about cake, I volunteer to go wrangle the birthday girl. My steps are light as I make my way across the vast yard, the glimmering surface of the ocean revealing itself to me bit by bit as I crest the small hill on my way to the pier.

A panicked scream reaches my ears first, then the sight of them, two girls looking unsteady on the pier. I frown, eyes darting to a few bottles of alcohol lying on the grass. They must have snatched them when no one was looking.

Anger whips through me, unsure whether to blame Allie or Clancy. Those two girls are as bad as each other.

Clancy's name dies on my lips when I see her stumbling on the pier, clothing drenched, steps unsteady. She trips, half-falling off the pier, then sliding all the way into the water. Her body hits the surface of the ocean, limp.

*Shit, shit, shit.*

I don't realize I'm running or yelling until Allie's head turns toward me. Clancy's face is still down in the water, and I haul her limp body up in one movement, gripping her face with my hand. "Clancy!"

Her eyes blink open, hazy. The reek of alcohol is strong as her head nods to one side, then the other.

I hold her upright, water up to my mid-thigh, saying her name over and over and over again. Panic is like ice in my veins. I can't think, can't breathe, can't do anything except hold my daughter. *Clancy Clancy Clancy.* "Open your eyes, damn it!" I haul her higher, trudging through the thigh-high water and onto the sandy shore.

Finally, she opens her lips to speak, and the only thing that comes out is vomit. It covers my chest, soaking into my shirt and dripping down to the sand below.

"Out, *now,*" I bellow to Allie, who has quieted down completely and is doing her best to look sober as she gathers her things. "*Get in the house.*"

I barely recognize my own voice as I take my daughter in my arms, not caring about the vomit soaking into my shirt, and rush toward the house. Her eyes are closed, as if she can't keep them open. I keep her head off to the side in case she vomits again, but panic nips at my heart as I run. Up the hill, across the grass, all the way to the porch where I've spent every evening with Fiona and Clancy.

I can't think. This *fucking* party. I knew it was a bad idea. I knew we should've kept things small. But no, Fiona wanted something big. She wanted to spoil Clancy, but this wasn't about my daughter. This party turned into something else, something bigger. And now look! My fucking daughter is passed out in my arms. Fear like I've never felt before grips my chest, squeezing so hard I can hardly breathe.

I lay her down, calling my daughter's name as the guests start to filter outside.

"*Allie.*" Candice's voice snaps through us all, and her daughter stiffens beside me. "Get over here right now."

Fiona appears in the doorway, eyes wide. "What happened?"

"Your stupid fucking party happened, that's what," I spit.

Fiona winces, stumbling back.

"Watch your mouth," Simone hisses, stepping in front of

her friend.

An ass—I'm being an ass. But my *daughter*. My daughter that I didn't even know about is unconscious in front of me. She was in the water and—a sob racks through my body as I try to revive Clancy again. Vaguely, I hear Fiona's voice on the phone, calling for an ambulance. The hush of the party that was so lively only minutes ago feels crushing. Too heavy. Too *quiet*.

"Clancy," I beg, and my daughter's eyes flutter open. She groans, and all I can do is say her name again.

"The ambulance will be here soon," Fiona says. "We need to get her in the recovery position."

I snarl when Fiona gets closer, registering the hurt in her eyes but not able to feel anything about it. She takes a step back, and her red-haired friend—what the hell is her name again? I can't fucking think. Can't breathe. *Simone*. Simone snarls right back at me and snaps her fingers in my face, waving me away. I almost lunge at her when she touches Clancy, rolling her onto her side and positioning her head, legs, and arms so she's braced on the floor, not at any risk of choking if she vomits again.

I haven't felt this out of control in over a decade. Not since I came home to find Sylvie gone. Not since I landed in intensive care myself when my heart nearly burst. Putting a hand to my chest, I grab towels that someone hands me and dab at my daughter's face, her body.

This is worse than when Sylvie left. Worse, because it's not me who's hurt. It's this helpless, smart, fiery girl who only came into my life mere weeks ago. She's everything that was missing in my life, and any chance of being able to give her the home she deserves is slipping through my fingers.

Anger sizzles through me, burning any trace of feelings from my heart. My eyes lift, finding Fiona's, and it's pure venom that comes from my mouth when I speak. "This is your fault."

# TWENTY-NINE
## FIONA

"HE DIDN'T MEAN IT." Simone squeezes my hand as the paramedics haul Clancy into the back of the ambulance.

"Could have fooled me." My voice is flat. Emotionless. I watch Grant get in the back of the ambulance, his vomit-crusted shirt balled up on the ground and a clean shirt laid over his lap. In any other situation I'd be laughing at the fact that even in the back of an ambulance, he manages to end up shirtless.

But I'm not joking now. He lifts his gaze for a few long moments, meeting my gaze. There's nothing in his eyes. No warmth. No affection. No love.

Just haunting emptiness.

My heart stutters as the paramedics close the back of the ambulance, cutting Grant and Clancy from my sight. I turn away, mumbling nonsense to party guests who pat me on the shoulder and make their way out of our house—no, *Grant's* house. This isn't mine, no matter how close we've grown over the past few months.

Bottles clank in the kitchen as I pad toward the room. Simone is cleaning empties from the countertops and tables with a big black garbage bag in her hand. Her orange-red hair is piled high on her head, deep lines carved around her mouth. Glancing up, she gives me a sad smile. "Everyone's gone. I can drive you to the hospital."

I shake my head. "I'll drive. Grant will want a car there."

She holds my gaze for a few moments, then turns back to the mess of the party. I make my way down to the pier and see the bottles of alcohol the kids stole, a crushing weight sitting in the center of my chest.

*This is your fault.*

He never wanted this party. Clancy never asked for it. In fact, Grant tried to convince me not to have it.

*This is your fault.*

She wouldn't have drunk this much if I hadn't been busy inside with the rest of the guests. I should have known she needed more attention. Should have known she didn't grow up with a role model, and drinking was something to watch out for. I should have seen this coming.

*This is your fault.*

Grant's words rattle through me, playing on repeat as I pick up the bottles and cups and garbage the kids left strewn on the beach and the pier. My heart squeezes into a tight ball and I take short, shallow breaths just to make it through. With one glance out toward the ocean, I trudge back up the slope and into the house.

Simone has cleaned all the empty cups, cans, and bottles, and she's putting the leftover food in plastic containers. My friend works quietly, efficiently, only looking up to give me a quick nod.

"I'll head to the hospital now," I say.

"You okay? You want me to come?"

I shake my head, another weight pressing down on my chest, my shoulders, my whole body, as if the weight of the world is trying to grind me to dust. "I should go on my own."

"She'll be okay, Fi," Simone says softly, putting her hand on my forearm. "She'll be fine."

"But Grant won't." I pinch my lips and try to smile, but my face won't cooperate. Simone squeezes my arm again and drops her hand, and I head for the front door. Thankfully, I was too busy to drink more than half a glass of wine over an hour ago, so I'm okay to drive. I grab Grant's keys and get behind the wheel of his truck, staring at the big, gorgeous house through the windshield.

No matter what Simone says, I can't get the image of Grant's face out of my mind. The anger simmering in his gaze. The total darkness in his eyes. The lack of anything warm toward me.

Something changed today. I fucked up. This party was a bad idea.

Sighing, I pull myself together and turn the key in the ignition. The hospital is in the next town over, giving me half an hour to drive and let my thoughts overwhelm me. By the time I make it to the hospital, I feel like something has shifted beneath my feet. Nothing will be the same after today.

I find Grant leaning against a vending machine down the hall from a hospital ward, his face lined with worry, his shoulders crumpled inward.

"Hey," I say softly, coming to a stop a few feet from him. "I brought your truck."

He takes the outstretched keys and slowly, slowly lifts his eyes to mine. I resist the urge to stumble back. His gaze is nothing like the Grant I knew. Anger boils just below the surface, capped off by frigid cold. "What were you thinking?" His voice crackles at the edges.

It takes all my strength not to take a step back.

"I told you that party was a bad idea. I told you we should have kept it small." The cold in his eyes deepens. Bottomless.

"Grant, I—"

"But no, you had to go ahead with the stupid party that Clancy didn't even ask for. The doctor said she had severe alcohol poisoning. She had to have her stomach pumped. She'll be here overnight."

"She'll be okay?" I ask, my voice so small I barely recognize it.

I should fight this. I should tell him he has no right to talk to me this way. Yes, I planned the party, but no one could have predicted this would happen. We didn't know how Clancy would react to having a party. We don't even know if she's ever drank before, or who decided to steal those bottles of alcohol. And where was *he*? Why is this only my fault?

This *isn't* my fault. It's no one's fault.

But I should have been watching her. I should have asked her if she wanted this. I should have listened to Grant, Clancy's father. Because who am I in this situation? Not even a girlfriend. Not a partner. Not a mother.

I drop my chin to my chest. "I never meant for this to happen, Grant."

"Well, it did. Now I have to wonder if I'll ever get custody if the judge hears about this. It could fuck everything up, Fiona. Everything."

I lift my gaze to his, horror flooding my blood. It sinks down to my marrow as his words hit me. "You think this will hurt your chances at getting custody?"

Grant snarls, none of the man I know in his expression. "How could it not? I'm trying to argue that her mother has a drinking problem, yet it's under my care that Clancy lands in the hospital with alcohol poisoning." He shakes his head. "I knew that fucking party was a bad idea. I *told you* we shouldn't have anything that big."

*I didn't know.*

*I didn't think.*

*It's not my fault—it's no one's fault. She's just a teenager.*

Any excuse that comes to my mind sounds so small, so insignificant. His words play on repeat in my head as we stand there, the distance between us like a chasm.

*This is your fault.*

And it is! How can I argue against that? His daughter is in the hospital because I wanted to have a party. Because I thought she needed something big—or was it just my own stupid obsession with planning events? I thought because I ran the café project well, I was untouchable?

"I'm sorry, Grant," I whisper.

"Sorry doesn't fix the fact that my little girl is laid up in a hospital bed. It doesn't change the fact that I could lose her because of this." He spits the words at me, and they feel like jabs on my chin, one after another.

There's no affection in his eyes, his voice. Something fundamental has changed between us, and somehow, with all my desire to keep this casual and keep from getting tangled, I'm the one who's out in the cold. I'm the one standing here, wanting to drop down to my knees and beg for forgiveness. I'm the one who feels small, insignificant, alone.

Again.

When Grant snarls at me, saying something else I don't hear, all I see is my ex-husband. I see the way he squares his shoulders and takes a step toward me, using his size to make me feel small. I see the anger brimming in his eyes and the tatters of our relationship flapping between us.

"What are you doing here, Fiona?" His eyes shoot fire. "I didn't ask you to come here."

"I thought you'd want someone beside you."

"All I want is Clancy, and to be left alone." He turns his back to me and starts walking away, every step carrying him down the hall, stretching whatever connection we have until it finally tears.

There's no coming back from this. There's nothing I can say to defend myself. He won't forgive me—I know that as well as I know my own name.

When he ducks around a corner and out of view, I sink into a chair and drop my head in my hands, but tears don't come. Nothing comes. I'm empty. A shell.

I came to the hospital hoping he'd take back his words. Hoping he'd reach a hand out toward me and accept the comfort of my touch. Hoping he'd forgive me for wanting to throw a stupid party.

All I got were a few cold words and the sight of his retreating back.

Dragging myself off the hard plastic chair, I find a taxi and make my way back to Heart's Cove. Simone is gone by the time I get there, the house dark. I take my time cleaning everything, folding Clancy's laundry, making sure the house is in order. I cook some food and leave it in containers in the fridge, knowing they'll be in no mood to cook when they get back.

Then, it only takes a few minutes to pack my own things and throw them in the back of my Mercedes.

That stupid car. Even after all this time, it's the only thing I have of my own. Two broken relationships and all I have to show for it is a heart shredded to ribbons and a car I don't even like. I drive away from the house I thought was home and make my way to the Heart's Cove Hotel.

Dorothy is behind the desk, a deep purple cardigan thrown over her shoulders and her favorite turquoise jewelry adorning her neck. She arches her brows when I walk in, then sweeps around the desk and wraps me in a hug. "It'll work out, Fiona. He'll come around."

I nod, bone-tired. I don't have the energy to tell her that I know it won't work out. I could see it in Grant's eyes. Whatever we had is dead. Our relationship is over.

He doesn't trust me. Doesn't love me. Doesn't want me.

I let Dorothy lead me to one of the cabanas without a word.

I lock myself inside and lie on the bed, staring at the ceiling, seeing nothing.

# THIRTY
# GRANT

I'M FLOATING in a pool of darkness. I can't think of anything except Clancy's soft breathing, her hand soft and warm beneath mine. In a small corner of my mind, I know I was wrong to push Fiona away. I know I was wrong to blame her for this.

But louder in my head is the beating drum that only says one thing: *Your fault, your fault, your fault.*

My daughter stepped into my life only a few weeks ago, and I already feel like I'm losing her. I lost Sylvie, tried to keep her too close and she ran away. She didn't want to tell me about Clancy, didn't want to let me be a part of her life.

I lost all those years with my daughter, and for what? To live in this town by myself? To start a casual-but-not relationship with a woman I barely know?

If I have to choose between Fiona and Clancy, I choose Clancy. I wasn't here for her for the first fourteen and a half years of her life, but I'll be there for her now. I'll fight to stay by her side. I'll be the father I didn't have the chance to be.

As I watch my daughter's chest rise and fall and feel the car keys digging into my ass in my back pocket, I wonder if I have to choose at all. Earlier, when Fiona was here, I could have opened my arms and I know she would've run to me. I know the guilt of throwing the party was eating her up and all she wanted to hear was that I wasn't mad at her.

The truth, though?

I am mad. I'm furious. I *knew* that party was a bad idea, but went ahead with it anyway. I can't let my fucking cock or my heart or my stupid emotions make decisions for me. Not like this. I can't let Fiona swan into my life and change everything I've spent so long building. Why would I care if she's upset or not? She told me she wanted to keep things casual. She told me she didn't want strings.

Well, I'm snipping every one of them. The strings I didn't want and never asked for. The strings that grew despite my best effort. The strings that were based on nothing but loneliness and mutual attraction.

At the end of the day, what's left between Fiona and me?

My heart is black, and I don't have an answer. All that's left to do is wait by my daughter's side and hope she wakes up tomorrow morning.

CLANCY DOES INDEED WAKE up with what I imagine is the mother of all hangovers. I want to shake her and ask her what the hell she was thinking, but instead, I just put my hand on her shoulder and squeeze gently. When she's discharged, I load her up in my truck and let her snooze in the seat as I drive us home.

The house is dark, empty. When I tuck Clancy into bed, shushing her when she mumbles apology after apology, I head to my bedroom to see all of Fiona's things gone.

She left.

I stand in the room as a chasm opens up inside me.

She *left*.

I know I pushed her away. I know I told her to go. I gave her no reason to stay. Still, being alone in the bedroom where I felt whole with Fiona breaks something deep inside me.

Maybe I thought she'd stay. Beg. Grovel.

But she left.

I STAY at the house for three days. Clancy recovers fairly quickly, sleeping lots and eating less than I'd like her to. Clancy looks sheepish when she apologizes for the thousandth time, her finger finding a groove in the butcher's block island as she perches on one of the bar stools. We haven't eaten at the table since Fiona left. "I know it was stupid to drink," she says, eyes not meeting mine.

"It was dangerous," I growl.

"Are you mad at me?"

I take a deep breath. "Yes. And worried. And disappointed."

Clancy flinches. "I'm sorry."

"Did you drink a lot at your mom's house?"

She shakes her head, blond hair shivering by her face. "No. I never... That was the first time I got drunk like that. I don't know why I did, I just felt... I don't know. I felt like I could finally have fun."

My heart freezes over, and part of me wants to wrap my arms around my daughter and call Fiona over to come back. Clancy didn't get drunk because she was nervous or anxious about all the people. She got drunk because she felt *comfortable* here.

I'm an ass.

But I'm still angry. Still scared.

I drop my head, shaking it from side to side. "If you want to stay here, Clancy, there are going to be rules. Drinking won't be tolerated."

Clancy gulps.

"And you'll have to go to counseling."

Her eyes dart to mine. "Counseling? Like therapy?" She crosses her arms.

I nod. I've thought about it a lot ever since she got here, and again when I sat in her hospital room. My daughter needs more help than I can provide. Hell, *I* need help. I'm not too proud to ask for it. "We could go together to start, and individually too."

Clancy's pose softens. "You'd want to go with me?"

I nod.

"You don't think it's dumb?"

"I think it's necessary. Those are the rules if you stay here, Clancy. Counseling, no drinking, no drugs, and you have to maintain good grades in school. You think you can do that?"

Clancy nibbles her bottom lip and finally nods. "Uh-huh." She pauses, hesitating. Then she asks, "Where's Fiona?"

The question sends pain rattling through my chest. "She left."

"Where'd she go?"

"I'm not sure. The hotel, probably."

Clancy's eyebrows arch, worry filling her deep blue eyes. "Because of what I did?" Her voice is so small it breaks my heart all over again.

I shake my head. "Because of me. Our relationship... It wasn't meant to be. It's got nothing to do with you."

Clancy just stares at me, not believing a word I tell her.

ON THE FOURTH DAY, I head into town for groceries. I pass by the café and my heart jumps in my throat when I see Fiona inside, smiling at Agnes as she bags an almond croissant. My heart is lifeless, a block of ice in my chest. My steps slow and Fiona's eyes find mine, as if she can always sense my presence.

I start walking away, only to hear her rushing behind me. "Grant!"

That voice. It's only been a few days, but I've missed it. I've missed her grumpy face in the mornings, her laughter, her kisses, her sex. I've missed her company.

But I turn, my lips curling down. "What?"

"I..." She hesitates, stopping four feet away from me. "How is she?"

"She's fine. I'm going to New York next week to sort out the custody agreement with Sylvie."

"Oh." She wrings her hands, gulping.

I could fix this. I could close the distance between us and tell Fiona it's not her fault. She didn't ruin anything. I have feelings for her that scare the fucking shit out of me, and I panicked. I panicked at the thought of Clancy being hurt, at feeling my heart being held by my daughter and Fiona and control slipping from my fingers.

But I say nothing.

I sink into the loneliness and the familiar waters of isolation. I let the cold grip my limbs and hold me steady, reaching for what I know best. Living alone on the edge of town. Surviving by myself. Not letting myself give in when Fiona breaks down my barriers and exposes me to all this hurt.

I have a daughter to think of. I have to do what's best for Clancy.

"The lawyer said it was best if I said I'd take care of Clancy alone. He said casual relationships are frowned upon."

Fiona startles, her eyes darting to mine. Shoulders dropping, she nods. "I understand."

I turn and start walking away, even though everything inside me is screaming to stay. To turn around and tell her I'm an ass and I know it. That I don't deserve her. That I never meant to hurt her. That all I know is how to survive, and the only way I can do that is on my own.

I want to tell her that what we had meant something to me. She was the first bright light in an ocean of darkness. She made me *feel*. She made me want more. She opened me up so that when Clancy arrived, I was ready to give my little girl my heart.

It's because of Fiona that I'll be able to fly to New York and fight for the right to be a father.

But I say nothing. I walk away.

"Grant," Fiona calls out. "I'm sorry."

I look over my shoulder. She's rooted to the same spot on the pavement, her arms hanging limply by her sides. My heart stutters, trying to break free from the heavy chains and armor I've welded onto it over the past four days.

*Go to her.*

But I can't. I have to choose between Clancy and Fiona, and I choose Clancy. Fiona packed her things and moved out of my house, and there's nothing left for us to say.

It was fun. It's over.

My eyes drift to the café, then back to Fiona. I'm not even sure if she'll be here when I get back. It would be easier if she wasn't. I turn back around and get in my truck. If Fiona still held a piece of my heart, when I turn the key in the ignition and drive away, it crumbles to dust in my chest.

There's only one thing for me to do now—fight for my daughter. Nothing else matters.

Not love. Not Fiona.

# THIRTY-ONE
# FIONA

THE DAY GRANT leaves for New York, I wake up feeling heavy and empty all at once. Every day since the party, I've waited for him to call. I wanted to give him space to sort through his emotions, time to think about what he wants.

I thought he'd want me. Hoped.

But he left. Walked away from me without a word, without forgiveness.

I spent twenty years with a man who made me grovel. Who made me feel small. Been there, done that, got the t-shirt. And by t-shirt, I mean divorce papers and a broken heart. So, when Grant leaves for New York without a word, I know it's over.

Pain pierces my chest, and I'd be lying if I said I didn't cry. I give myself one night to wallow. I lock myself in my room and watch bad reality TV, eat more than I should, and drink a bottle and a half of wine. The hangover is almost unbearable, but I drag myself to the café, unlock the door, flick the lights on, and go on with my life.

I'm too old to pine after a man who doesn't want me. I've been through too much shit to rake myself over the coals for something that wasn't my fault.

Sure, I planned the party, but he could have watched Clancy more closely. Anyone could have checked on the girls at the pier. He could have asked Clancy if she'd ever had alcohol before, especially considering her mother's past. We could have talked to her about it.

Candice disciplines Allie by grounding her and taking her phone away. She's been doing her penance at the café every day. She's quiet, and I often see her staring out the window. I wonder if she's thinking of Clancy. Allie told us it was her idea to drink, that the two of them swiped the alcohol together. I wonder if it's true or if she's covering for her friend. I suppose it doesn't matter.

I never wanted Clancy to end up in the hospital. My heart aches every time I think about it, and all I want to do is be by that girl's side. In a few short weeks, I felt like we were forming a family. It felt like the start of something good.

Just more wishful thinking from me, I guess. More desperation, wanting relationships to turn into something they're not. It happened with John, it happened with Grant, it happened with Clancy.

The days drag on as I work at the café, trying to keep a happy face on. The locals stop asking me questions about Grant and Clancy, word obviously getting around that things haven't worked out between us. Thankfully, they still seem to accept me as one of their own. The café is still bustling, and my life takes on a steady rhythm.

Simone, Jen, Candice, and I spend a lot of time together. We talk about expanding the café, and Simone takes on the responsibility of creating our social media pages and putting together advertising for us. That gets her a few local clients for her copywriting business.

Even though Grant isn't here for me anymore, it doesn't mean my life in Heart's Cove is over. I've built something here, and I won't run away because of a man. This café is the first thing that's felt truly mine in a long time, and I won't give it up.

A week after Grant leaves, Simone walks into the café and leans on the counter. "Hey, girl. You still sulking?"

"I don't sulk." I arch a brow, still not quite able to curl my lips into a smile.

"I beg to differ." Simone plucks a pen from the counter, twirling it between her fingers. She glances around the café, then lets her gaze settle on me. "How are you feeling about everything? You going to stay in Heart's Cove?"

"Damn right I'm going to stay." I straighten up. "Sorry. Didn't mean to snap."

Simone grins. "Snap away. I like the fire. And I'm glad you want to stay, because I happen to like this place."

One lonely patron sits at a table outside, and Sven has gone out the back for a break. It's just Simone and me inside, and I move to the big espresso machine to make us both a coffee. Once I have it in my hands, I shake my head at Simone. "Even if things don't work out between Grant and me, I don't want to walk away from this. For the first time in forever, I feel like I have a purpose. I'm *good* at this, Simone. I can run this café in my sleep, and Candice says she's gotten nothing but positive reviews. It's even boosted her yoga class attendance. I'm going to ask her if she'll let me buy half of it out so I have some skin in the game. I want this place to be mine on paper, too. This is a good thing, and I'm not going to walk away because I'm some jilted woman."

"He still hasn't called, huh?"

"No, and I doubt he will." I put my mug down and stare through the window, shaking my head. "I think I'm done with men. Done with the anger and the toddler-level emotional maturity. If he can't get over himself and see me for who I am, then I'm not going to grovel and beg for his forgiveness."

"You have nothing to beg forgiveness for."

"Exactly!"

"Have you spoken to Clancy?"

I bite my lip. "She texted me yesterday," I admit. "I didn't want Grant to feel like I was going behind his back, but it felt good to talk to her, just to make sure she was okay. She said they were back in New York City; she's staying in an apartment with Grant. He's meeting with a lawyer over there to talk about custody arrangements. I didn't ask too many questions because it's not really my place."

"That kid misses you."

"I miss her, too." I take a deep breath, shaking my head. "I knew when this all started that it would get complicated. The last thing I want is for Clancy to feel like she's lost my support, you know? I told her she'd have a part-time job waiting for her whenever she was back."

Simone smiles at me, nodding. "You're a good person, Fiona. Want to go to the hotel for a drawing class once you close up here? Maybe there will be some other hunky man ready for us to ogle. What about that guy Rudy? Didn't Candice say he was giving you the ol' bedroom eyes?"

I wrinkle my nose. "No men. Not for a while. I was supposed to focus on me, and it finally feels like I'm doing it."

Simone nods.

It's the truth, too. With Grant gone, I've picked myself up off the floor and thrown all my energy into the café. I will *not* let another man make me feel small. There's another reason I won't go out with Rudy. It's just too soon. I still feel Grant's touch whispering across my skin. I go to sleep remembering how it felt to be wrapped up in his arms. I miss his kiss—no one else's.

Going out with Rudy or any other man would only make me miss Grant, so I'll go out with no one.

I force myself to smile, then make it through another day where my heart feels like it's been shredded—but slightly less shredded than it felt yesterday. With every hour that passes, as I stay at the café and busy myself running a business I've helped build, I feel like I can stand with my head held high.

Yes, my chest feels hollow, but I'm so fucking sick of letting men define how I feel. Grant had no right to make me feel small. He had no right to blame me for what happened. If his ego is so inflated that he can't see we had a good thing, then I'm not going to crawl back to him.

I have a life to live. I have friends, a business, a future. I don't need him.

That's what I tell myself, anyway. Usually, in the daytime,

when I'm busy running the café or spending time with the girls, it works. It's only at night, when I'm in the honeymoon cabana at the hotel with nothing to keep me company but the creaking of the walls and the crickets outside—that's when loneliness sets in.

Loneliness won't kill me, though. I made it through fifteen months of hell from the time John told me he wanted a divorce to the time I arrived in this town. I can make it through fifteen more, then fifteen after that. There's strength inside me I didn't realize was there, and I'm not going to let anyone—*anyone*—tear me down.

Not John.

Not Grant.

Not even myself.

Days bleed into each other. Clancy and I talk over text messages every few days, but Grant remains silent. The café is bustling, and we're still talking about expanding. Jen drops hints about coming on full time if we open a brunch restaurant, and something that feels a lot like hope blooms in my chest.

One evening, three weeks after Grant leaves town, the four of us—Jen, Candice, Simone, and me—sit in the café after doing our quarterly accounts. We have three bottles of wine on the table between us and three more waiting on the café counter. Simone's telling us about her disastrous lunch date with her ex-husband that happened when she was in L.A. this summer, and all the ways he's tried to weasel back into her life.

"I knew it was a mistake to meet up with him, but I needed to go out while the house was being viewed. The man thinks he can buy me flowers and it'll make up for eleven years of making me feel small." She rolls her eyes as I giggle, topping up everyone's wine glasses. "He's delusional if he thinks I'm going anywhere near him."

Candice leans back, swirling her wine in her glass. "Maybe he senses you're doing well. You've moved on, and now he feels like he's losing you for real."

"He lost me eight years ago."

"Yeah, but you still lived in the house you bought together. He probably felt like you were always there to fall back on if he needed you. Now you're gone. Men will always try to hang onto a good woman when they realize she's finally come to her senses."

Simone laughs, then flicks her eyes to me.

I shake my head. "Think very carefully about your next words, Simone."

She throws her hands up. "I was just thinking that you might get a few bouquets of roses in the next few weeks. Grant's got to realize he can't bear to let you go."

My heart squeezes, a familiar ache that hasn't quite gone away. Pinching my lips together, I shake my head. "We were only together for a short while. I told him I wanted to keep things casual, and now it's over. It's fine. I'm fine. Everything's fine."

"Fine, huh?" Jen arches a brow.

"Look." I suck in a breath, then take a sip of wine. I glance around the café, at my friends, and finally let myself smile. "It *is* fine. Grant came into my life at a time when I probably needed some—"

"Cock," Simone interjects.

"Distraction." I glare at her, and the three of them giggle. "I'm not going to lie, the way he treated me after Clancy's party hurt. A lot. But...I'm done feeling bad about things I can't control. I'd rather be an old spinster with a business and friends than stuck in a relationship that isn't healthy."

"Hear, hear," Candice says, raising a glass. "I will gladly become the town's crazy cat lady with you."

"We could start a club." I grin. "I spent twenty years with a man who didn't appreciate me. I'm not going to make that mistake again."

A murmur of agreement sounds from everyone, and I lean back in my chair, ignoring the ache in my heart. Yes, it hurts. Yes, I still think about Grant more than I should. Yes, he was the first—maybe the only—man who made me feel like I was special.

But I don't need him to feel that way about myself. I can do it on my own, and I will.

# THIRTY-TWO
## GRANT

LEAVING Heart's Cove is like tearing out a piece of myself. As soon as our plane takes off, I know I've made a decision that won't be easy to take back. Clancy sits in the seat next to mine, staring out the window, and I have to remind myself that I'm doing this for her.

I can't focus on my relationship with Fiona when I need to put my daughter first. For once in her life, she needs to have someone in her corner willing to fight for her.

I know I was an ass to Fiona, but if Fiona doesn't understand that my daughter is the most important thing right now, then she has no right to be in my life.

There's lingering anger smoldering in my veins. The feeling of my heart being wrenched out my chest when I saw Clancy unconscious in the water is something I won't forget. Not ever. I've never known fear like that. Never felt that kind of blind terror.

So, I curl my hand around Clancy's and fly across the country, even if I know I'm leaving a bit of my heart behind.

"I'm still going to talk to Fiona," Clancy announces, pulling her hand out of mine and jutting her jaw out. "You can't stop me." She holds my gaze.

"Okay." It's a lame response, but I can't think of anything else to say.

Clancy nods, then goes back to staring out the window.

I'VE RENTED a short-term two-bedroom apartment not far from Sylvie's house. Clancy claims one of the rooms and shuts herself inside, and I do a slow turn of the tiny apartment. At least it's clean.

I miss the space in Heart's Cove. I miss my four acres, my coastline, my large home. I miss the smell of coffee in the morning and the grumpiness Fiona always greeted me with when she first shuffled into the kitchen.

I miss Fiona. I'm not afraid to admit it—but as I glance toward Clancy's closed door, I know there are more important things to deal with right now.

After I talk to the lawyer tomorrow, I'll call Sylvie and set up a meeting. I don't know how she'll react to me wanting full custody, and I'm not sure if she'll ever agree to me taking Clancy away. We'll have to come to some compromise. Either that or I'll take her to court. I'm not putting Clancy in a bad situation ever again.

That evening, after a simple dinner with a quiet Clancy, I lie on my bed and stare at the ceiling. For the first time since

Clancy's birthday party, I wonder if I truly made a mistake by breaking things off with Fiona. She would have come with me if I'd asked her. She'd be here beside me, making Clancy feel like she had a family.

Instead, Clancy's locked in her room and I'm in mine, and it feels like there's a hole in my chest.

I'll have to deal with the consequences. Maybe when I get back to Heart's Cove, I can try to fix this. By then, I hope the anger in my veins will have died out. I'll be able to tell Fiona how I feel. I'll be able to apologize.

But I'm not there yet.

MY MEETING with the lawyer goes well. She tells me I have a good chance of getting custody, but the easiest way to do it will be with Sylvie's permission.

So, gathering all my courage and once again wishing Fiona's quiet strength was beside me, I head to a diner where Sylvie and I agreed to meet. It's on the outskirts of the city, and taking the train brings back lots of memories of my time here. Work, pain, stress. Memories I'm ready to forget.

I slide into a vinyl booth a few minutes early and order a coffee from the thin, silver-haired woman who comes to take my order. She calls me *sweetheart* and smiles at me, and for a moment I miss Dorothy and Marge, too.

I hadn't realized how much Heart's Cove had become my home until now. How much all those people have become my family.

The diner door opens, and my heart squeezes. Sylvie looks

old beyond her years, with cracked lips and deep wrinkles lining her face. Her blond hair, once golden and shiny, is dull and matted. She has a baseball cap on her head and a thin rain jacket on, with old, ripped jeans and dirty Converse sneakers. Spotting me right away, she shuffles across the restaurant to sit across from me.

"So, you're here," she says. "And you want to take my daughter away."

The anger in my blood flares up, and I do my best to clamp it down. Through clenched teeth, I try to force the words to sound calmer than I feel. "I could say the same to you, Sylvie. You left without even telling me you were pregnant."

"I was helping you." She waves the waitress over, ordering a coffee of her own before swinging her hazel eyes to me. They look...haunted. Nothing like the bright eyes I fell in love with.

My coffee tastes bitter, so I dump another spoonful of sugar into it, but that only reminds me of Fiona and my stomach turns. "How was it supposed to help me to deny me the chance to be a father?"

"You would have stayed with me," Sylvie says. The waitress fills her mug with steaming coffee from a carafe, and I watch as Sylvie tears little cream packets open and dumps them in. Her spoon clinks against the mug as she lifts her eyes to mine. "You didn't want to be with me, Grant, but you would have stayed for Clancy. You would have convinced me to make it work when we both knew I was dragging you down."

"You weren't..." I trail off, not quite able to say the words.

Sylvie lets out a bitter laugh. "See? You know it's true."

"You denied me the chance to be with my daughter."

"I gave you a chance at a better life."

"So, what, I'm supposed to thank you?" I grip my coffee mug to stop my hands from trembling. Everything inside me feels empty. Dead. Only anger remains.

Sylvie shrugs a too-thin shoulder, leveling me with a glare. "I don't care what you do. When I found out I was pregnant, I knew you'd keep trying to save me. You'd fall over yourself to take care of me, and I didn't want that. I just wanted to live my own life without feeling like I was letting you down."

"Letting me down?"

"You thought rehab fixed me, Grant. When I came back and I wasn't drinking, I could see the relief in your face, and you thought it was over. It's never over. I knew I'd go back to the bottle. I knew I'd fail. Maybe not after a month or a year or ten years, but I knew it would be a constant battle. I didn't want to put that on you."

"That doesn't mean you should have taken Clancy away from me. She's my *kid*, Sylvie."

Something a bit like regret flashes across Sylvie's face, and she lets out a long sigh. "I didn't drink for a few years when she was little. I had a job and things were going well. But then I got laid off and I thought one drink wouldn't hurt." She huffs. "And here we are. My daughter hates me and my ex wants to take her away."

Her eyes are faraway, as if she's reliving those years of her life. The years I spent building myself back up, tinkering in Mr. Cheswick's garage with not a care in the world. All that time, Clancy was living with Sylvie, struggling to survive. It kills me. Absolutely kills me.

Sylvie's shoulders round, as if the weight of her life is finally crushing her. "I can't afford a lawyer. I'll never win against you." Her eyes crawl back to mine. "Let me see her a few weeks out of the year, Grant. Don't take her away from me completely."

For a few long heartbeats, there's only silence between us. My throat feels tight, and the only thing keeping my hands from shaking is the grip I still have on my mug. Finally, I gulp and dip my chin down once. "Of course not, Sylvie. We'll come up with something that works. Summers, holidays..." I arch my brows. "You could move closer."

Sylvie shakes her head. "No. I'll only poison whatever good life you've made for yourself." Sylvie takes a deep breath. "Clancy sent me pictures, you know. She texted me photos of her room, of your house, of the café. Your girlfriend is beautiful." A sad smile tugs at her lips. "I knew you'd land on your feet. I can't give Clancy the kind of life you can give her."

Stunned, I lean back in the creaky vinyl booth and stare at the woman who crushed my heart all those years ago. I thought I'd have a fight on my hands. I thought she'd drag me through the courts, fighting every day for visitation with Clancy. But she's just...giving up. As if life has become too much, and this is her final act of sacrifice.

She's doing the same thing she did to me, except now I finally understand. She was trying to help me when she left. Trying to save me from her inevitable self-destruction—and now she's trying to save our daughter, too. I don't know if I'll ever forgive her, but I...I can understand it. I'm grateful, if only for the fact that Clancy will come home with me.

It breaks my heart to see Sylvie like this. It hurts to think of what Clancy went through growing up, of all the things I missed. But I finish my coffee, leave some money on the table, and stand up. "I'll be in touch. School starts in four weeks, so we'll have to be back in Heart's Cove by then."

Sylvie nods but doesn't meet my eye, so I walk away.

WITH THE HELP OF A LAWYER, I get new custody papers written up that give me full custody of Clancy. We spend our free time eating, exploring the city, and getting to know each other. Clancy shows me her old school, her house, her favorite hangouts. We go on walks and bike rides, visit museums (which are soooo boring, apparently) and watch a few movies. Clancy always gets extra butter on her popcorn, eyes darting to me with mischief dancing in her gaze, daring me to say no to her. As if I ever could.

I'm not sure how things would have been if Fiona were here. I think about her all the time, wondering if she'll be in Heart's Cove when I get back. If she'll ever want to speak to me again, or if she'll disappear like Sylvie did. Somehow, I doubt it.

I don't want her to.

A part of me clings onto that idea—that once we get back to Heart's Cove, I'll have time to figure it out. Time to sort through my emotions and see if Fiona and I will ever have a chance. Time is all I need.

As Clancy starts to laugh more and even gives me hugs almost daily, I can't help but feel grateful for this time together, too. Without Fiona here, we have no choice but to talk to each other.

When all the papers are signed, bags are packed, and final goodbyes are said, it's been four weeks since I left Heart's Cove. Four necessary weeks for Clancy and me to learn each other's habits and moods. Time spent cementing the fact that this is what we both want. A life together. A future.

Then my daughter boards the plane with me again, and we fly back home. Nerves tighten around my gut as the flight wears on, and I still don't feel quite ready to face Fiona. What happened between us was fun, but I ended it. It's over.

Even though I've thought about her every day and I know she's spoken to Clancy, she hasn't contacted me. Unlike Sylvie, I know Fiona isn't walking away to do me a favor. She's doing it because I pushed her.

# THIRTY-THREE
# FIONA

CLANCY AND GRANT arrived in town yesterday. I know this, because Clancy texted me as soon as the plane landed. She told me to expect her at the café bright and early for work today, which must be some kind of teenage miracle.

Except when I get to the café myself, I'm not sure I'll have a job for her after all.

My feet splash through a large puddle on the sidewalk twenty feet from the café. Water runs down the gutters and into the stormwater drains, even though the rest of the street is dry. It hasn't rained, so where did this water come from?

Then I see Candice and Simone standing on the far side of the street, right outside Simone's door. Candice has her phone to her ear, and Simone looks like she's about to throw up. My eyes drift back to the café, and I see the source of the water.

It's coming from just outside the building, another crack in the pavement cleaved open by the force of the water. It's not a geyser this time, but the direction of the water flow isn't out toward the street. It's *in*, toward the café. A few more steps, and I see the water line inside the shop, half a foot up the wall. Everything is soaked. The walls look destroyed.

We won't be opening today, or any day soon.

My stomach sinks like a stone, and I stand in the middle of the sidewalk, water flowing over my shoes, horror sinking into my bones.

Our business...is gone.

"Fiona!" Candice waves me over, and I trudge across the street. Simone purses her lips, putting a hand on my arm. Candice shakes her head. "The city workers are on the way. It looks like another water main."

"So this place really does have poor municipal plumbing," I answer, numb. "I was only joking on our first day here."

Simone lets out a sigh. "You got insurance?"

Candice nods. "Yeah, but I don't know if this will be covered. I don't know if we'll be able to open again. There's so much damage. The power short-circuited at some point, and it looks like the water soaked through the floor. If it's been going all night, it could have ruined all our equipment. Everything." Devastation is written all over her face.

The space we created for our community might not be able to survive. We stay huddled on the far side of the street as crews arrive, turn off the water and power, and start investigating.

Candice wipes a few stray tears away, and in that moment I know she's not the only one who found a home in that café. Even Simone is silent, without a joke or snarky comment to share. A few more locals come out to stand next to us and offer words of support, but they fall flat.

Until a bicycle bell rings, and I see a blond-haired teenager cruising down the street. My heart leaps, and for the first time in a long time, I smile. "Clancy!"

She hops off her bike, letting it fall on the asphalt, and runs toward me. I hug her tight, feeling my heart shatter all over again.

"I missed you," I say, pulling away to look at her face. "You look good. Did you have fun with your dad? How's your mom?"

"So many questions," Clancy grumbles, but her lips curl into a smile. "It was good. I start school on Monday." Her eyes drift to the commotion on the other side of the street. "What happened?"

"Burst water main. We're waiting to find out how bad the damage is."

A man with a thick mustache and a belly overhanging his belt waddles over to us. He hooks his thumbs into his pockets and looks at the three of us, then Clancy. "Well, ladies, I have bad news, and I have worse news. Which would you like to hear first?"

"Just spit it out, Frank." Candice sucks in a breath to brace herself.

"There was another fault in the water mains. We're going to have to dig up all of this section of downtown to do the repairs. Because of the slope of the land and the location of the fault, it looks like your building took the brunt of the damage. Water flowed for hours. From what we can tell, at least eight to twelve hours since the main breach. There's an incredible amount of moisture in the soil, which points to the fact that the mains have been leaking underground for a long time. Weeks. Maybe months. The foundation of the building might have been compromised." He pinches his lips, his mustache wiggling slightly. My heart sinks. "The building inspector's on the way, but I don't have much hope for this one, girls. The building will most likely be condemned."

"Please don't call me a girl," I grumble. "It's infantilizing."

Frank swings his gaze to me, surprise lighting his eyes. "Right. Of course. Ladies. Women." He clears his throat. "I hope you have insurance, is what I'm saying." He gives us a tight smile and walks away.

I exchange a glance with Candice, whose shoulders are so rounded she looks like she's about to collapse. "Even if we get insurance money, it'll be weeks before we can find a new space and open up again. I can't even use the yoga studio, because it's above the café. I can't pay you or anyone else, and all our bags of beans were on the floor. They'll be ruined. Insurance money might take a year to pay out." Her voice cracks, tears welling in her eyes. "It's ruined."

"We'll figure it out," I say.

"This might be it, Fiona." Candice shakes her head. "We can start over a year from now, maybe for next year's Fringe Festival, but until then...there's nothing. If that building is condemned and we've lost all our supplies and equipment, we don't have enough money to start over. We don't even have a space or a permit or the capital. I don't see how we can come back from this. Not for a long time."

Hearing the truth in her words, I ignore the sharp pain in

my chest and wrap Candice in a hug. Simone's hand appears on my shoulder, and the three of us lean on each other.

"What are we going to do?" Candice squeaks as she pulls away, clearly trying and failing to keep it together. "Fiona, I can't pay you. There's no job here for you anymore. I want you to stay here, but..."

Pain shatters across my chest. "I don't know what I'll do." I open my mouth again, but nothing comes out.

When I turn around and wipe at my eyes, I find Clancy standing apart from us, sadness marking her features as she looks at the café. She swings her gaze to me. "I got to go." She grabs her bike and pedals back the way she came, and I just stand on the sidewalk and stare at the ruined coffee shop that meant so much to me.

If the café is gone and Grant wants nothing to do with me, what's left for me here? I have friends, sure, but I'll have no job. No business. No purpose.

I'll have to leave.

For the first time since that day at the hospital, I feel like crumbling to the floor. In some corner of my heart, I think I hoped Grant would come back and sweep me off my feet. I'd hoped I could stay in Heart's Cove and maybe have another chance with him. Another chance at love.

*Stupid, stupid, stupid.*

But as I stand here, watching people work on turning the water off and assessing the damage to the one thing that's felt like it's all mine, I finally accept the truth. If Grant wanted to see me, he'd have called. Texted. Knocked on my door last night or this morning.

He would have said *something* to me over the past four weeks. He would have fought for me.

Maybe this flood is a sign I should pack up and leave while I still have part of my heart intact. I can walk away from the home I thought I was creating and start over...again. This time, I won't be wooed by a sexy shirtless man. I won't open myself up to the first man who tells me I'm pretty. I'll harden up once and for all.

The writing is carved into the crumbling foundations of the café I've grown to love. I just have to look down and read it: I need to leave this place. I'm not welcome here.

My lip wobbles. Candice meets my gaze, and I don't have to say anything to know she understands.

Simone straightens up, a light shining in her eyes. "I have an idea. Fi, give me your keys. I need your car."

"For what?"

"To ask for a favor." She wiggles her fingers until I put my car keys in her hands, then takes off at a jog toward my car.

"What's that about?" Candice asks, still sniffling.

"I'm not sure." I watch my best friend get into my car. The engine roars to life and she takes off toward the coast, and I let my eyes drift back toward the ruined building. I don't have the energy to care. Candice leans her head on my shoulder and we watch the men work as I resign myself to the fact that this might be over.

As soon as the building inspector confirms the building is condemned, I'll know my future in Heart's Cove was never meant to be.

# THIRTY-FOUR
## GRANT

"THE CAFÉ FLOODED. They said the building is condemned." Clancy slams the front door as she yells through the house.

Poking my head around the corner, I frown. "What?"

"I said the café flooded. They said the building is condemned."

"I heard you. I mean, what happened?"

Clancy tilts her head, eyebrows inching together. "I'm not sure how else to explain it. Flooded, like water everywhere. Condemned like, damaged."

"Right." I clear my throat, returning to the eggs cooking in the pan. I plate them up as Clancy slides into a stool near the island, already staring at her phone. I sit down beside her. "What are they going to do?"

She doesn't look up. "Who?"

I try to keep the frustration from my voice. "Candice and

the rest of them, Clancy. What are they going to do with the café?"

"Are you afraid to say Fiona's name or something?" She glances at me, popping a brow. "Ever since my birthday party, you've been acting weird."

"It's complicated."

"Doesn't seem complicated to me. Seems like you're being a little wuss."

"Clancy."

If my daughter hears the warning in my tone, she ignores it. Returning to the screen in her hands, she shrugs. "All I'm saying is you used me as an excuse to break up with Fiona. Seems like a dumb reason."

"It's more complicated than that." Discomfort squeezes at my stomach as I shovel a bite of food in my mouth.

"Is it?" Her head swivels toward me again, eyes boring into mine.

"Yes. You wouldn't understand."

"Wouldn't I?"

"Stop doing that."

"Doing what?" Her head tilts, sass incarnate.

"Asking rhetorical questions."

"They're not rhetorical if you answer them."

Inhaling slowly through my nose, I count to five to try to regain control over my quickly spiraling frustration. It isn't Clancy's fault. I'm not mad at her. I don't know what I'm feeling.

My daughter slips off her seat and shrugs. "I heard Candice saying they won't be able to open the café again for a while.

Maybe not until next year's Fringe Festival. Fiona's going to leave."

I freeze, my fork halfway to my mouth. It takes all my effort to get the utensil moving again, but when the eggs hit my tongue, they taste like ash. I swallow the glob of food, hoping it won't get stuck on the way down. "She's leaving?"

Clancy's shoulders round. "There's nothing for her here, now." She turns and starts walking away, and I spin to watch her leave. My daughter doesn't look back at me as she exits through the front door and closes it behind her, leaving me alone.

*Alone.*

The word echoes through me.

*Alone, alone, alone.*

Isn't this what I wanted? When I told Fiona to stay away, wasn't I resigning myself to living with Clancy? Closing myself off from a woman's love, I thought I was doing the right thing. I was giving Clancy what she needed—me.

But now...

Fiona will leave. There's no café to keep her here. No job, no future, no me. She'll walk away, just like I asked her to. I might never see her again.

My eggs are cold. I push them around the plate as my blood slowly turns to ice.

She's leaving.

I slip off my seat and start toward the door, then stop. What am I doing? I should be happy she's leaving. This is what I wanted. I can go back to my quiet life and live the way I meant to. I can turn my back on women and live out my days with Clancy and no one else.

This is what I wanted.

Isn't it?

I stare at the door where Clancy disappeared, horror spreading through my stomach and clawing at my chest. No, I don't want this. I don't want to see my daughter crumple because the one woman who was a mother figure to her is leaving—leaving because *I* asked her to. Because I pushed her away. Because I'm too much of a fucking coward to face the feelings I have for her.

I thought I was being strong on my own. I thought I was saving Fiona from me. Keeping her away from my crushing embrace, from the part of me that wants to smother and protect everything I love.

But Fiona wasn't smothered. She thrived. *We* thrived. She made me feel like I didn't *need* to protect her, because she could do it on her own. She made me want to cherish her without feeling like I needed to be her safety net. She's strong enough to stand on her own, and strong enough to stand up to me when I act like she needs my protection.

She's nothing like Sylvie, and she'll never end up like her.

*I can't let her leave.*

As my heart starts to thump, I realize I never wanted her to walk away. I told her to leave, but I was hoping I'd come back to Heart's Cove to find her here. I told her to leave me alone, but I did it knowing she'd always be at the café. I wanted to come back to her.

I was a fucking coward and a fool. The only reason I was

able to tell her I didn't want to be with her was because I knew she'd be close. But if she leaves Heart's Cove, I might never see her again.

Panic boils in my blood, burning away the cowardice and the fear. My breaths are short as I rush toward the front of the house. Clancy's nowhere to be seen, her bike tipped over in the front yard. I'll tell her to pick it up later. Right now, I need to go —shit, my keys are inside. Spinning on my heels, my feet pound on the pavement, then stomp up the stairs as I make it back inside. I grab the car keys from the bowl near the entrance and turn back around, slamming the door behind me.

I can feel the clock ticking with every heartbeat, like seconds counting down on the end of my life. If I let Fiona walk away from this town, I know I'll end up alone.

Not on my own, puttering around my workshop and doing odd jobs living a quiet, content life. No, I'll be *alone*. Lonely. Miserable.

I've been a *fool*.

My truck roars to life, a cloud of dust puffing behind my back wheels as I accelerate down my long driveway. I grip the steering wheel as if it's the only thing keeping me from drifting away, narrowing my eyes to focus on the road. It's only a few minutes' drive into town, but it feels like an eternity. I pass a few cars on the way in, vaguely realizing the drivers are waving to me. I can't wave back. The only thing I can think of is getting into town before Fiona decides to leave. Before she makes any decisions.

I'll get on my knees and beg. I'll tell her I've been an idiot to push her away. I'll tell her I was afraid of ruining a good thing, and in my infinite idiocy I decided to ruin it before it started. I'll tell her the party wasn't her fault—it was mine. I should have talked to Clancy. Should have checked on her. Should have been a parent.

Me, not Fiona.

Parking my truck crookedly next to the hastily-erected barricades around the café, I jump out and scan the street. There are workers from the city inspecting the damage, a man in a white button-down shirt and a hard hat with a clipboard, but no Fiona. No Candice. No Simone.

Jogging to Simone's apartment, I ring the doorbell.

No answer.

I ring it again.

I pat my pockets for my phone, needing to call Fiona. *Fuck.* Forgot it at home. My panic mounts even as I try to talk myself down. She won't leave right away. Fiona will stay for at least a few days. I'll see her. I'll explain.

But even as logic tries to war with my rioting emotions, I can't shake the feeling that I need to fix this, and do it now. If I wait a second longer, she'll make a decision. I'll lose her.

Frank, a city employee, surveys the work with his arms crossed. I jog over to him. "What's going on, Frank?"

He looks at me, rubbing his fingers down his thick mustache. "Hi there, Grant. Didn't know you were back in town."

"Yeah, got back yesterday. What's going on?" I repeat, waving toward the café.

"Slow leak from the city water mains underground. Compromised the foundation. When the pipe burst last night, it ruined most of their equipment. Sure hope those gir—women have insurance."

"Where are they?"

He looks around, as if surprised Fiona and Candice aren't still here. His casual shrug infuriates me.

I jog away before he can answer. Heart in my throat, I aim for the hotel. That's where they'd go if they weren't at Simone's place. There, or maybe Candice's house. Or Jen's? Why didn't I bring my stupid phone!

...and then I see her. She's walking toward me with a blue folder hooked under her arm, Candice and Simone flanking her. Wearing the same navy wrap dress and strappy sandals as the first day I met her, Fiona looks like a goddess. Her eyes lift to mine, widening slightly, and she stops walking.

I slow, heart thumping, coming to a stop a few feet away from her. Every part of my body screams at me to close the distance, to wrap my arms around her, to beg for her forgiveness—but I know I haven't earned it. I don't deserve her affection.

She tucks a strand of dark hair behind her ear as her forest-green eyes shine, and a thunderbolt cleaves my heart.

I thought I could walk away from her? I thought I could let this go?

"I've been an idiot," I say.

A snort sounds from behind Fiona, and Simone's voice cuts through the fog in my mind. "Ya think?"

Ignoring her, I take a step toward Fiona. Her brows lower, and I pause. "I'm sorry." I spread my hands, gulping. "I'm so sorry, Fiona. I treated you like dirt. I blamed you for Clancy's party when I had no right to treat you that way. I pushed you away when I should have brought you closer. Then every day that went by, it became harder and harder to pick up the phone. I didn't know what to say to fix it."

"So what changed?"

*Weeks*—it's been weeks since I've heard her voice. It rocks through my chest, warming every part of me. It takes all my self-control to stop my lip from trembling.

"I heard about the café. Clancy told me you were going to leave, and I realized what a fool I've been to push you away, Fiona."

Candice snorts. "Didn't I say men will only come to their senses when they think they're going to lose you?"

"Typical," Simone grumbles. "Next thing he'll be stalking her and sending flowers to her new address. Tread carefully, Fi. You could be dealing with this shit for the next decade."

Fiona waves a hand to quiet her friends, her eyes still on me. She lifts her chin, pure confidence and defiance in the motion. "You tried to make me feel small. You pushed me away when I was trying to help. You blamed me for things that weren't my fault. You treated me like I was nothing when I've spent months doing nothing but making your life easier."

Shame hits me in the gut, but I don't drop my gaze. Fiona's eyes blaze as she stares at me, strength rolling off her in waves.

I thought my protective streak would ruin her? I thought pushing her away was for her own good?

Dropping to my knees, I shake my head. "I'm sorry, Fiona. I'm so, so sorry. You came into my life and showed me everything that's been missing. Not just for the past fifteen years, but forever. You showed me what it means to be a strong woman.

What it means to be independent and confident and loving. You broke down every wall I had with quiet strength and you made me laugh more than I have in decades. You make me better, and it scared the absolute shit out of me. You were more of a parent to Clancy than I was, and I punished you for it. If you never want to see me again, I'll understand, but I need to say this first."

My knees dig into the concrete, but I won't get up. I can stand a bit of pain if it makes Fiona understand. I take a deep breath, bracing myself for the words I've wanted to say for months. "I love you, Fiona. I knew it for sure the day Clancy showed up and you were so fucking beautiful and loving and kind. I knew I didn't deserve you. I thought I'd ruin you. I was afraid of how much I cared for you. How much I loved you. You're like a sunset over the ocean, Fi. Shining and brilliant and so beautiful it hurts to stare. This past month without you has been darker than the years I spent on my own. I know I don't deserve your forgiveness, but I'm begging for it."

Silence answers back for a heartbeat, then another. Fiona stares at me, her face unreadable. Then, she takes a step toward me. And another. And another. Her fingers slide over my cheekbone and I close my eyes, inhaling her scent and melting into her touch.

She's everything to me. As her fingers skate over my temple and slide into my hair, I know I'll never be able to live without her. "You're my air, Fiona. I can't breathe without you. Please don't leave. *Please.* I'm not too proud to beg." My eyes are closed, and I feel her other hand rest on my shoulder. Her touch is so sweet, it scares me. If this is the last time I get to be this close to her...

"Stand up, Grant." Her voice is a breath. A whisper.

I look up to see silver lining her eyes. She blinks, a tear sliding down her cheek. Rising up onto my feet, I swipe the pad of my thumb to brush the tear away, then catch another one with my lips. She shudders against me, her hands curling into my shirt.

"I love you, Fiona. You don't need to say it back. I just needed to tell you before you decided to leave."

She reaches for the blue folder tucked under her arm. She opens it up, her lips curling. "I'm not leaving, Grant. We just signed a three-year lease with Wesley Byron. We're moving to his parents' old space and expanding the café. I'm not going anywhere."

My jaw goes slack as my eyes widen.

Fiona laughs, tilting her head. "You still mean what you said?"

"That I love you with everything I have? That I'm sorry for how I treated you? That I can't live with the thought of you leaving?" I gulp. "Yes, Fiona. A million times yes."

"Good." She tilts her head toward me. "Because my next stop after we signed this lease was going to be your house. I wanted to tell you to put your big boy pants on and own up to what you did. And"—she bites her lip—"I wanted to tell you that I think I love you, too. I'm not just staying here for the café, Grant. I'm staying here for you."

Happiness like I've never felt before floods my heart, my soul, my body. I slide my fingers over Fiona's jaw, stare into her eyes, then angle my lips to hers. When we kiss, it's like the final knot of tension in my heart unwinds. My love for her bleeds into every corner of my body, writing this moment of my story in permanent ink. The moment Fiona became mine, and I became hers. The moment we both decided to run to each other, to admit we want this.

"I love you," I say against her lips, feeling her mouth curve into a smile.

"I love you, too."

Those words send another wave of warmth through me as I deepen the kiss, sweeping my tongue over hers and groaning when I taste her. Fiona. My love. The woman of my dreams, who ripped me out of the darkness and showed me what it means to live.

Then, a battle cry.

I pull away to see Agnes hobbling toward us, a bucket of water sloshing by her side. Dorothy's advancing behind, anger in her eyes.

"*You.*" Agnes lifts a finger to point at Dorothy, who snarls. Then things happen in slow motion. Dorothy gets closer, swinging a baseball bat—a freaking *baseball bat*—and her eyes drop to the bucket.

"That better not be what I think it is," she says. "This is my favorite dress."

"That horrible zebra print monstrosity?" Agnes snorts and starts swinging her bucket backward.

I break away from Fiona's embrace, stepping between the two women. I don't know what happened between them this morning, but I know Agnes is in the mood for destruction. It'll end in carnage and another hospital trip unless I manage to stop it.

So I step into the line of fire just as Agnes winds back, the bucket already swinging. Ice water slaps into my chest. I gasp, blinking, as Agnes startles. “Grant.” She doesn’t say anything else—most definitely not an apology.

I look down at myself, totally soaked, blue dye soaking into my shirt, my pants, my skin, face—everywhere. I’ll be blue for weeks if this is permanent.

Blue dye drips onto the sidewalk as everyone stills, and I hear Simone let out an exaggerated sigh. “Well, go ahead. Take your shirt off. We know you want to.”

# EPILOGUE

## FIONA

I DON'T KNOW how Simone convinced Wesley to let us lease the place, and she keeps strangely silent about the whole thing. All I know is I'm staying, and I have a business and a boyfriend—man-friend?—and a new family. I have a home.

Scrounging together all our funds, Candice, Jen, Simone, and I manage to scrape together enough money to get the café started again. We submit the insurance claim right away, but as expected, it takes forever to process. With the four of us pitching in, though, we're able to start over.

Candice's yoga studio moves to the Heart's Cove Hotel, with plans to expand the second floor of the café into a new studio once the insurance money comes through. Under the cover of night, the four of us and Grant smuggle the dozens of boxes full of pink t-shirts from the old yoga studio attic to a storeroom in the new café.

Mr. and Mrs. Byron's former chef, Fallon, agrees to take his old job again. The man is a six-foot-four beast of a man with biceps the size of my head. He glides through the kitchen like a dancer, and for the first time I feel like I'm seeing an artist at work. He moves around a kitchen like he was born to do it, his food so good it draws crowds from miles around.

Jen's face when she first sees him eyeball a hollandaise sauce is something I'll never forget. Her eyes bug out, hands curl into fists, and a strange red tinge sweeps over her cheeks.

Fallon arches a brow at her, watching her line up her kitchen scale and all her baking implements with millimeter precision. "You doing surgery over there?" Fallon asks, his voice deep and rumbly. If I wasn't head over heels for Grant, I'd probably swoon.

Jen just scowls. "You stay on your side and I'll stay on mine. Anyone can poach an egg, big guy. Not everyone can make flaky croissants."

I turn my head back to the front of the house with a grin on my lips as Candice straightens up the chairs and opens the door for our first day. Her smile is blinding, and she comes around the counter to give me a hug. "Couldn't have done it without you," she says. "Or Simone. Or Jen."

"It was meant to be," I reply.

Our first customers are familiar. Grant and Clancy walk through the open door, their eyes luminous. Clancy has a brand-new backpack slung over her shoulder, her thumb hooked into the strap. She smiles at me, swaggering up to the counter like only a teenager can. "One Earl Grey tea, please."

"Good choice." I grin, making her tea as Sven starts on Grant's coffee.

My heart flutters as Grant's fingers wrap around the cup, brushing against mine. He catches my hand with his other one before I can pull away, tugging me across the counter to lay a kiss on my lips. "I'm proud of you, Fiona."

"I'm proud of me, too." I laugh, kissing him once more. "See you this afternoon?"

He nods, light shining in his eyes. Slinging his arm over Clancy's shoulder, the two of them head off toward the truck to drive Clancy to school.

I turn back to my work, feeling light and happy and hopeful.

This is the first day of our new café and restaurant. The first day of my new life. There will be growing pains, there will be challenges, but as Simone ducks through the door with a broad smile, Jen bickers with Fallon in the kitchen, and Candice wipes down the last of the tables, my heart thrums with a steady rhythm.

I'm home.

THAT AFTERNOON, I get home to rose petals strewn over the floor and two flutes of champagne on the console table near the front door. My lips curl as Grant walks up to me, sliding his hands over my hips to pull me close. He brushes his lips against mine, gentle, tender.

I melt into his embrace, eternally grateful that he came to his senses. "I was thinking," I start, "about the day you apologized."

"Mm," he says, lips gliding over my neck, teeth scraping my earlobe.

A shiver tumbles down my spine as my back arches toward him. "I kind of like how you did it. On your knees in front of me. Reminded me of the first time."

He pulls away, brows arching. By the heat in his gaze, I know his thoughts are exactly where mine are, in that rickety outdoor shower where we first came together.

"You like that, huh?" His voice is a rasp.

I nod, moaning as his hands slide lower, pulling my hips toward him. His hardness is there, insistent, pressed up against my stomach. "I like it a lot," I whisper. "You on your knees, begging me, telling me you'd do anything."

A growl rumbles through his chest, and in a flurry of motion I'm thrown over his shoulder. The rose petals are forgotten, champagne is left, and I'm hauled up to the bedroom. Grant kicks the door closed and tosses me on the bed, a laugh bubbling up through my lips.

He tears my clothes off and shows me just how much he loves me with his hands, his mouth, then his cock. I sink into the covers and fall apart in his arms, sighing in contentment when we finally fall away from each other, my hand sliding against his.

With my fingers intertwined between his much larger ones, Grant brings my hand to his lips. His eyes sparkle as he stares at me, a smile spreading over his face. "Congratulations on a good first day at the café," he says. "I knew you'd do great."

"First day of many."

His smile widens. "First day of many," he repeats. The words sound different when he says them. Deeper. I know he's not just talking about the café—he's talking about us. We have things to figure out, of course. How to parent, how to live together, how to make our new lives work together.

It'll be complicated and I'm sure there will be issues, but nothing we can't overcome. Because we've committed to each other. Committed to Clancy. Committed to this life together.

"I love you, Fiona," Grant says, pulling me closer. "It doesn't feel like enough to say that, but there are no more words. You make my life worth living."

I smile, laying my head on his shoulder. "I love you too, Grant."

The door slams downstairs, and a groan sounds from the entryway. "I'm home!" Clancy calls out, probably louder than she needed to. She probably saw the rose petals and champagne. A teen in the house will take some getting used to.

With a grin, I lay one more kiss on Grant's lips and extricate myself from his arms. "Let's go downstairs before Clancy swipes that champagne."

"Too soon," Grant grumbles, but his smile gives him away.

We pull our clothes on and walk down together to find Clancy with her head in the refrigerator, her schoolbag thrown on the floor. Yes, all of this will take some getting used to, but it's worth it.

With my new friends, my partner, and my almost-daughter, I think I could get used to anything.

# SIMONE

A MONTH after the grand opening of the new café, I find myself outside a little log cabin not far from Grant's place. Knocking on the rough, timber door, I take a step back and clasp my hands in front of me.

Heavy footsteps approach, and I brace myself for the sight of Wesley. The lock slides right before the door swings open.

*Nope, still wasn't ready.*

His broad frame fills the whole doorway. Fabric clings to every hard plane, and the image of his shirtless, sweaty chest flashes into my mind. My eyes drop to his hands to check for an axe, just in case. He's not holding anything, but my gaze snags on his palms, then his forearms corded with muscle, then his biceps. My mouth goes dry.

What was I thinking? I shouldn't have committed to anything, but Fiona needed this. *I* needed this. I needed to convince Wesley to let us use his parents' old coffee shop.

Wesley's hair looks more brown than blond in the low light of his house, and his pine-green eyes sweep over my body. Heat blooms across my cheeks as I shift my weight from foot to foot.

I cross my arms. "I'm here to get this over with."

"You were the one who told me you'd do anything to help Fiona get a space for the café." He arches a brow, eyes gleaming. "*Anything*, you said. Now you're coming here with a bad attitude making it sound like I forced you into this."

"Look, the lease is signed. I could walk away and forget I promised you anything. I'm here out of sheer goodwill."

He snorts, then opens the door wider.

My heart stutters as I cross the threshold, inhaling the scent of fresh-hewn wood and the spicy, citrus male scent that has made my head spin from the first time I slid into Wesley's car.

Looking over my shoulder, I watch Wesley close the door and turn toward me, his body towering over mine. Heat tears through my core, leaving me raw and nearly gasping.

Yep, no doubt about it. This was a terrible idea.

*Simone and Wes's story continues in*
*Book Two: DIRTY LITTLE MIDLIFE MESS*

# EXTENDED EPILOGUE

# FIONA

I WIPE the sweat off my brow with the towel slung over my shoulders, staring around Candice's yoga studio tucked in one of the old cabanas of the Heart's Cove Hotel. Candice blows out a candle and smiles at a student who comes to talk to her, and I heave myself up to my feet.

I'm getting a bit more flexible, I guess. A bit stronger. I've been coming to Candice's classes three times a week for months, now, and I can almost make it through the whole thing without feeling like my heart's going to explode.

It's good, though. Something I'm doing for *me*—and aren't there a million more things that I'm doing for myself these days? After years spent putting myself last, I finally have the space and opportunity to take care of myself, too.

Grant gives me that opportunity. He's independent and thoughtful, and I no longer have to spend my days making sure all the housework is done because I know he won't lift a finger to do it himself. I don't have to remind Grant to call his family for their birthdays or organize presents that he won't bother to buy himself. I don't need to remind him about doctor's appointments or ask him nicely to please, please put his own plate in the dishwasher.

I'm dating an adult man for the first time in my life, and it's amazing.

"Hey, Fiona!" Candice pads toward me in her bare feet, her floral yoga pants hugging every muscular curve of her short, strong body. "Have you spoken to Fallon? He wanted to add some lunch items to the menu."

I roll my yoga mat and nod. "He gave me a sample of the sandwich he wanted to serve next week. It's incredible."

Candice smiles at me as I gather my things, and the two of us walk back toward the front of the hotel. We need to pass through the lobby to get to the exit, a walk I'm now used to making multiple times a week. I'll have to get Dorothy and Margaret a nice bottle of wine to thank them for letting us use their space.

"Did you hear about Agnes and Mr. Cheswick?" Candice's eyes sparkle. "Apparently they're going on a cruise together."

"Scandalous." I laugh, nudging her shoulder. "There must be something in the water in this town."

"Hopefully, she doesn't rip his head off."

"She seems to have a soft spot for him." I smile, pushing open the door to the hotel lobby. My eyes drift over the familiar furniture as I inhale the comforting scent of the hotel—a mix of lavender and jasmine that the twins somehow imbue in every room of this place.

Then I freeze.

Candice keeps walking a few steps, then pauses, glancing over her shoulder at me as she frowns. "Fiona?"

I can't move. Can't speak. Can't think.

My ex-husband is leaning over the reception desk, dangling a black credit card between his fingers. I've seen the look on his face many, many times before. It's a look that says, *Do my bidding, minion, because I'm better than you.*

The minion in this case being Dorothy, who has storm clouds gathering across her brow. Uh-oh.

John's head swivels toward me, the superiority in his eyes slowly morphing into recognition, then surprise, then...attraction?

I haven't seen that in his eyes for a long time.

"Fiona." He straightens up, his fancy credit card still dangling from his fingertips. "What are you doing here?"

My ex-husband's eyes drop down my body, which, admittedly, has become a lot firmer now that I've been more active and eating healthier for a few months.

I clear my throat. "I live here."

"At the hotel?" He frowns.

*No, you idiot, I don't live at a hotel. Just because you divorced me doesn't mean I'm homeless.* I paint a smile on my lips. "No, I've got a place on the edge of town. Are you here for...work?"

When we were together, John only ever traveled for work. But my eyes flick to his companion, a woman in her late twenties or early thirties wrapped in a tight body-con dress that looks nearly impossible to walk in. Her hair falls in loose, styled waves down to her thin waist, and perfectly-applied makeup makes her already-beautiful features look even more stunning.

A year ago, seeing them together would have caused me to spiral. I would've felt frumpy and lumpy in my yoga clothes, cursing the fact that my face turns beet-red with any bit of exercise.

Now, though?

I kind of feel sorry for her. I see the way she stands a bit apart from him, how insecurity flashes across her face as her eyes dart from me to John and back again.

*Keep him, honey.* I sure as hell don't want him back.

"We're here for the weekend," John says. "Needed to get away from work. Talia and I have been working on a tough case and it just finished, so we thought we'd take some time off."

*Talia.* I remember that name. He hired her as a junior partner nearly five years ago, mentioned her in passing a few times, but never introduced me to her. Now I know why.

I let my lips tug into a smile and to my surprise, it's not forced. Seeing him with another woman doesn't cause my heart to pang. I feel...nothing. "Enjoy your stay."

Here it is. My opportunity to make a graceful exit, to walk away with my head held high and show him that his presence does nothing to me. I win this breakup, because I'm happy. He didn't ruin me.

But I've only taken one step when the lobby door opens, and Grant stalks through. His eyes find mine in an instant, and his face splits into a smile. "Hello, gorgeous."

His long legs eat up the space between us, and I don't have the time to protest about my sweatiness or our audience before he wraps his arms around me, tangles his fingers through my hair, and kisses me like we're never going to see each other again.

It's not a chaste kiss. It's not a peck.

This is a *kiss*. Open-mouthed, tongue lashing, heat blazing.

Oh my.

When we fall apart, John's face is so red I think steam might start billowing out of his ears. My ex-husband's eyes dart from me to Grant, pausing on Grant's sizeable biceps, broad chest, and trim waist, then back to me. He clears his throat. "I don't think we've met."

Grant tears his eyes away from me for a moment and arches a brow, looking at John for the first time. He says nothing.

John, forever challenged by his own inability to read a room, valiantly takes a step forward and extends a hand. "I'm John. Fiona's husband."

Talia bristles.

I freeze.

Grant smiles.

*Oh, no.*

It's not a bright smile. It's not the kind of smile that makes my knees weak, or the kind of smile that makes every part of my body tingle. No, the smile on Grant's lips sends chills skittering down my spine.

He draws himself up to his full height, topping John by at least six inches. "*Ex*-husband," Grant corrects.

The redness on John's face somehow deepens. "Are you...?"

No one speaks.

I take a step forward, throwing Grant a look that I hope

screams, *I love you but please don't make a scene and also if you could just make my ex-husband feel really small and insignificant and show him what he threw away when he divorced me, that would be great.*

I might look unhinged.

"Am I what?" Grant slides his arm around my waist, pulling me close. Candice looks like she's doing her best not to laugh. Dorothy isn't even trying to hide her grin from behind the desk.

"Are you dating my—Fiona?" John's shoulders straighten, his normally infallible confidence and arrogance obviously wobbling when faced with someone like Grant.

Just because I can, I lean my head against Grant's shoulder and give him a sweet smile.

Grant freezes, his eyes taking on a steely glint. "*Your* Fiona? Last I checked, you divorced her a few days before Christmas."

Dorothy lets out a squeak, outrage flashing across her face. Then, the lobby door opens again, swinging so hard it hits the wall and bounces back. Agnes stands silhouetted in the doorway, face a mask of fury.

*Oh for crying out loud. Not now. Please, not now.*

But Agnes's anger only lands on Dorothy for a moment before shifting to the little alpha-male standoff occurring between Grant and John. Her brows arch ever so slightly, and she takes a step inside.

I'd be lying if I said this didn't tickle a certain hidden part of me. Seeing Grant puff his chest out, watching John's face turn nearly purple... This may or may not have featured in a few of my non-sexual fantasies.

"Who the hell are you?" Agnes says. Each word is a dagger aimed at John's back.

He turns slowly, shifting his body so he can keep Grant in his line of sight. I resist the urge to roll my eyes. As if Grant would ever deign to fight John.

"Me?" John frowns at Agnes.

"Yes, you dingleberry. Why the hell does it feel like the Wild West in here? The only person that gets to come in here and make a scene is me. You hear me?" She plants her hands on her hips, marching toward John. She barely reaches his armpits, but somehow manages to look down her nose at him. "So tell me, who the hell are you?"

"I'm a tourist. A guest."

"Oh, look," Dorothy says, brows drawing together as she stares at the computer screen in front of her. "Looks like we're full."

"What? You just said my room would be ready!" John splutters, whirling on Dorothy.

She gives him an exaggerated apologetic glance. "Looks like I made a mistake."

"This is ridiculous. Do you have any idea who I am?"

I resist the urge to roll my eyes. John hasn't changed a bit.

Dorothy leans a hip against the desk. "Enlighten me."

John whirls again, pointing at me. "This is your fault. I had a room here, but now they're trying to kick me out. Why? Because I divorced you? You were the worst wife I could have asked for, Fiona. Your whining and complaining and constant need for fucking attention—"

"Choose your next words very carefully, boy." Grant's voice

is full of thunder. He takes a step in front of me, shielding me with his big body.

My heart thumps. Adrenaline dumps into my veins, but a kind of giddy excitement floods me.

John's words didn't hurt. They bounced off my skin and clattered to the floor, and I'm still standing.

He didn't hurt me. He tried, and it didn't work.

I'm free.

A smile stretches across my lips, and Agnes chooses that moment to tug a bundle of decorative sticks from a vase in the corner and brandish them at John. "Say that again, you weak little man. Spread your little lies and make yourself feel good by putting other people down, and you'll see how far that gets you in this town."

I never thought I'd say that Agnes's violence warms my heart, but here we are.

John spins around again, his hands balling into fists, his precious credit card still clasped in one of them. "I'm not. I don't—"

"Let's go, John." Talia reaches for him, putting a manicured hand on my ex-husband's forearm. Her eyes look sad, and all I want to do is run to her and tell her to get out before it's too late.

But that's not my fight. I've moved on from my life with my ex-husband, and I've found something better.

Grant's arm slides across my shoulders. John pauses by the doorway and glances over his shoulder. Grant chooses that moment to slide his fingers over my jaw, tilt my chin up to his, and brush a delicate kiss on my lips. The lobby door slams as John leaves, and Grant's lips curl into a smile against my mouth.

I pull away, arching a brow. "You're pleased with yourself, aren't you?"

"If he ever tries to come back here and make you feel small, I'll show him exactly how much it bothers me that he hurt you. One punch at a time."

"No violence, please." I brush my fingers over his cheek, letting a smile tease over my lips. I wouldn't want Grant to beat up my ex-husband, of course, but something about the promise and the fire in Grant's eyes makes my core clench with delicious heat.

"If Grant won't beat up that prick, I will." Agnes harumphs.

Dorothy grunts in acknowledgement. "Not if I can get to him first. He's officially blacklisted."

Agnes nods at Dorothy, spins on her heels, and marches outside. I watch her wave a closed fist in the direction of John's car and a giggle bursts out of me. "I love you guys."

"You're one of us now." Candice winks. "We defend our own."

"He's an asshole and he never deserved you." Grant's arm squeezes my waist. He dips his lips to mine, brushing a kiss over the corner of my mouth.

"Divorcing John led me to you. In a weird way, I'm more grateful to him for being a jerk than anything good he ever did."

A rumble sounds in Grant's chest, and he doesn't take his arm off me as we say goodbye to our friends and make our way home together.

*Home.* With Grant. Exactly where I belong.

## ABOUT THE AUTHOR

Lilian Monroe adores writing swoonworthy heroes and the women who bring them to their knees. She loves making people laugh and is eternally grateful to have found people who share her sense of humor.

When she's not writing, she's reading (or rereading) a book, walking, lifting weights, or attempting to play the guitar with very limited success.

She grew up in Canada but now lives in Australia with her Irish husband. He frequently asks to be used as a cover model for her books, and she's not quite sure whether or not he's joking.

## ALSO BY LILIAN MONROE

For a complete book list, visit:

www.lilianmonroe.com

**The Four Groomsmen of the Wedpocalypse**

Conquest

Craving

Combat

Calamity

**Manhattan Billionaires**

Big Bossy Mistake

Big Bossy Trouble

Big Bossy Problem

Big Bossy Surprise

**Later in Life Romance**

Dirty Little Midlife Crisis

Dirty Little Midlife Mess

Dirty Little Midlife Mistake

Dirty Little Midlife Disaster

Dirty Little Midlife Debacle

Dirty Little Midlife Secret

Dirty Little Midlife Dilemma

Dirty Little Midlife Drama

Dirty Little Midlife (fake) Date

**Brother's Best Friend Romance**

Shouldn't Want You

Can't Have You

Don't Need You

Won't Miss You

**Protector Romance**

His Vow

His Oath

His Word

**Enemies to Lovers/Workplace Romance**

Hate at First Sight

Loathe at First Sight

Despise at First Sight

**Secret Baby/Accidental Pregnancy Romance**

Knocked Up by the CEO

Knocked Up by the Single Dad

Knocked Up...Again!

Knocked Up by the Billionaire's Son

Yours for Christmas

Bad Prince

Heartless Prince

Cruel Prince

Broken Prince

Wicked Prince

Wrong Prince

Lone Prince

Ice Queen

Rogue Prince

**Fake Engagement Romance**

Engaged to Mr. Right

Engaged to Mr. Wrong

Engaged to Mr. Perfect

**Mountain Man Romance**

Lie to Me

Swear to Me

Run to Me

**Doctor's Orders**

Doctor O

Doctor D

Doctor L

Printed in Great Britain
by Amazon